How to
Seduce
a Texan

How to Seduce a Texan

KAREN KELLEY

BRAVA

KENSINGTON PUBLISHING CORP.
www.kensingtonbooks.com

BRAVA BOOKS are published by

Kensington Publishing Corp.
119 West 40th Street
New York, NY 10018

All Kensington titles, imprints, and distributed lines are available at special quantity discounts for bulk purchases for sales promotion, premiums, fund-raising, educational, or institutional use.

Special book excerpts or customized printings can also be created to fit specific needs. For details, write or phone the office of the Kensington Special Sales Manager: Attn.: Special Sales Department. Kensington Publishing Corp., 119 West 40th Street, New York, NY 10018. Phone: 1-800-221-2647.

Brava and the B logo are Reg. U.S. Pat. & TM Off.

ISBN-13: 978-0-7582-2574-0
ISBN-10: 0-7582-2574-1

First Kensington Trade Paperback Printing: June 2009
10 9 8 7 6 5 4 3 2 1

Printed in the United States of America

Checklist:

1. *Must love our son, even though he doesn't pick up his dirty clothes*
2. *Can tolerate our son's (loud) snoring*
3. *Enjoy large, noisy family gatherings*
4. *Love shopping, shopping, shopping . . .*
5. *Love sappy movies*
6. *Can bake yummy Holly Berry cookies*
7. *Must have a pulse*

Number one, yep. Number two, yep. Amazing! Number three, four, five, six, and seven: yes! yes! yes! yes! yes!
   Welcome to the family Ms. Jodie Kelley!!!

Chapter 1

If Cal Braxton had to explain one more time the workings of a dude ranch, he'd rip out the phone, throw it against the wall, and say to hell with everything.

What? People couldn't figure it out for themselves? A ranch was a ranch. Horses and cows equaled ranch.

He sighed deeply. Damn, was this what his life had become? When had his temper gotten so short?

Yeah, right, as if he didn't already know the answer to that. About a week after he'd dropped in at his little brother Brian's ranch, which had been turned into a . . . a resort, of all things. Cal could take fresh air only in small doses, no matter what kind of label his brother had put on it.

The country was starting to get to him. It always did. That was the reason he'd left in the first place. He might've been raised on this ranch, but country life wasn't for him, unlike Brian, who seemed to thrive on living out in the middle of nowhere.

Cal wasn't a phone person, either. Never had been, never would be. But baby brother had stuck him with the chore when Shelley called in sick with a cold.

Ringggggg!

He glared at the phone. It was possessed—taunting him.

He took a deep breath and jerked it up to his ear. "Crystal Creek Dude Ranch, Cal speaking."

"I'd like to make a reservation," a very sexy, throaty voice drawled.

Her words wrapped around him, caressed him. His gut clenched. He suddenly realized something else he'd been missing while on his self-imposed hiatus from city life—a hot sexy woman.

A spark of interest swept over him. So maybe his day wasn't going to hell after all. "What exactly are you looking for?" He leaned back in his chair, propping his feet on the desk.

"What do you have?" she flirted.

She *was* flirting, wasn't she? Did it matter? Well, yeah, sort of. Damn, he liked the sound of her voice, though. He switched the phone to his other ear. "Will you be alone . . . or with someone?"

"I'm definitely single, and I don't plan to change that fact anytime soon."

Oh, yeah, he really liked this lady a lot. He wanted to stay as far away from serious relationships as he could get. The female with the hot voice was exactly what he needed.

He pictured her sunning herself beside the pool wearing only a thong bikini, tanned curves stretched out on a lounge chair for his lengthy perusal.

"Let me see what's available." His boots slapped the floor as he opened the registration book. Fanning the pages, he came to the current month.

Oh, man, this wasn't right. Not right at all. They were full. The first opening wasn't for two months. He probably wouldn't be around by then. He had no choice except to tell her she'd have to continue looking for a vacation spot somewhere else—unless . . .

Hope sprang inside him. The old homestead was empty. Not surprising. That place was nearly always open. Just as quickly as the spark of hope ignited, it died. Nah, he wouldn't foist that place on anyone, no matter how horny he got. It wouldn't be fair.

Man, it was a damn shame, too. The country had finally started looking better. He took a deep breath to tell her they were full up but stopped at the last second.

Then again . . .

"Just how rough do you like it?" he asked.

Her chuckle rippled across the line and down his spine. "I like it real rough."

He immediately lost himself in a fantasy of a sexy lady wearing black leather and stilettos walking slowly toward him. Lips painted red, blond hair flowing down her back in soft waves.

A door slammed. He looked up. A young couple strolled toward one of the cabins, their two redheaded sons in tow. The mother looked tired and worn.

Those were the type of people who visited a dude ranch. Families. Not sex-starved playgirls. The woman on the phone probably wanted to get back to basics: roughing it in the backwoods, seeing how pioneer women lived. He wouldn't doubt she was a dumpy, middle-aged history teacher . . . but with a really sexy voice. He might be desperate, but he wasn't that desperate.

He cleared his throat. "I have one secluded cabin that's open."

"Book me for the next two weeks. My name is Nicole Scott."

He had to admire her guts. Two weeks in the old homestead would certainly be roughing it. No electricity, no running water—just a pump in the kitchen . . . outside toilet facilities, as in the outhouse from hell, complete with a half-moon cutout. A shiver of revulsion swept over him. Yeah, the woman had a lot of guts.

But maybe he should explain it a little better just so she would understood. "This cabin doesn't come with a lot of amenities. . . ."

"I'm sure I'll manage."

Yep, definitely a spinster schoolteacher or maybe she was

an older widowed woman and wanted to relive the Depression. She'd get her wish. The cabin would depress just about anyone.

He pictured his eighth-grade history teacher. Miss Horton had never married, and he could understand why. She wore her hair short, no make-up, and dark green heavy shoes.

The way the story went, her parents had died and left her the farm when she was sixteen. She'd had to work like a man to keep it going, and then once she was able to make it profitable, she sold it and went to college to get her teaching degree, but she never lost her mannishness.

Except she'd had a really nice voice.

Before he could push it back, a vision formed of Miss Horton wearing a black leather dominatrix outfit and combat boots. The image did as much good to bring his thoughts back to the present as if he'd jumped into the river during the middle of winter.

Back to business. He finished making the necessary arrangements with Ms. Scott and hung up. A shame.

Dumpy history teacher or not, she had a voice that warmed him all over. It would be interesting to see exactly what she looked like. Since she was arriving tomorrow, he wouldn't have long to wait.

Nicole Scott. Hell, he even liked the sound of her name when it rolled off his tongue. What if she was young and attractive? For just a few seconds, he closed his eyes and imagined her walking toward him, peeling off each layer of clothing she wore.

Just when it was starting to get good, he heard the mother of the wild little boys screech at one of them. For some reason, she sounded like Cynthia, his ex fiancée. That was enough to kill his amorous mood.

He almost hoped Nicole was matronly. He didn't need to start another relationship. Just look what happened with the last one. He'd glanced away and found himself engaged to Cynthia—the witch from hell who'd decided she wanted him on a leash, another toy to add to her collection, then discard when she was tired of her plaything.

He hated manipulative women. No, make that rich, spoiled, manipulative women. Women who didn't know or care about the meaning of survival. They ranked on the top of his list of people to avoid—right along with reporters, who'd dogged his football career right from the start and made his life a living hell.

But like his grandpa had always told him, what goes around, comes around. He had no doubt that someday the people he wanted to avoid would realize the errors of their way, and if he ever got the chance to help them see the light, he planned to take it.

Nikki cringed when she hit another pothole. She expected her little black sports car to plunge into one any minute and she and the convertible would never be seen again.

The Bermuda Pothole.

Lord, she should've at least put the top up. The dust was choking her to death. It wasn't doing a whole hell of a lot for her white blouse, either.

And she was going through this why?

As though she didn't know the answer to that one. Because she'd gotten the hots for a face on a glossy eight by ten. Well, that and her editor could talk her into doing just about anything, and Marge really wanted the scoop on Cal Braxton.

A fluff piece! How could Marge do this to her?

She must be losing her touch. Cal Braxton was a football player, for Pete's sake. When he grinned it would probably be like looking into the Grand Canyon: no teeth whatsoever. He was just another big dumb jock and she didn't even like sports.

A flash of heat suddenly swept over her and it wasn't from the heat of the sun.

Ahh, but with his mouth shut, he looked pretty yummy: thick black hair, deep green eyes that seemed to look right back at her. Hell, if he could flirt that good in a picture what would the real thing be like?

Then there was his voice. Goose bumps popped up on her arms when she remembered his soft Texas drawl. When they'd talked on the phone, his voice had practically curled her toes.

So what if this was a fluff story? The fairy-tale prince falls in love with the princess, one Ms. Cynthia Cole, and they get engaged. Except something goes wrong and there's no happily ever after ending. The kind of story most women devoured.

Maybe it wouldn't shake up the political arena, but she needed a break—she needed something . . . something different. Besides, how bad could the country be?

The right wheel dipped deep, then the car righted only to dip again when the back tire hit the same hole. She bounced against the door then quickly took a firmer grip on the steering wheel.

Damned bad!

Jeez! Did no one pay county taxes out here? A little asphalt would be nice right about now.

How much farther was it? Her teeth had been rattled for at least twenty miles. The old man at the gas station had said "a fair piece." Whatever the hell that meant.

And it was so isolated. She hadn't seen a barn or house for miles. It was more than a little creepy. Surely it wasn't that far now. She was hungry, hot, and tired—in that order. All she'd had to eat today was Texas dust, and a lot of it.

Her hands choked the steering wheel. This story had better be worth it. Hell, Cal Braxton had better be worth it. But then, if he looked anything like his picture, he would be.

A smile curved her lips. She'd get her story and her man. She never lost. The word wasn't even in her dictionary, not that she planned on losing.

She hit another pothole.

Dammit! They came out of nowhere. As soon as she got

home, she'd need to take her car in for realignment. And she'd send Marge the bill.

She topped a rise and slammed on the brakes, the car fishtailed, spewing a thick cloud of dust behind her. Her heart felt as if it had taken residence in her throat. She skidded to a stop, barely missing the cow that languidly stood in the middle of the road looking unconcerned that it had almost been splattered across her windshield.

Nikki's heart pounded inside her chest and her hands shook. She closed her eyes and took a deep breath. When she opened them again, the black and white cow looked at her with total unconcern. This was so not how she wanted to start her vacation slash investigative reporting.

"I almost wrecked because of you." She glared at the cow. Her cold-eyed, steely glare that she'd perfected over the years. If it had been a person rather than a dumb animal, it would've been frozen to the spot.

The cow opened its mouth and bellowed a low, meandering, I-was-here-first moo.

She didn't think the cow cared one little bit that it had almost become hamburger. Damned country. She'd take city life and dirty politicians any day.

"Move!" She clapped her hands.

The cow didn't get in any hurry as it lumbered to the side of the narrow road and lowered its head. The four-legged beast chomped down on a bunch of grass, then slowly began to chew.

She shifted into park, then waved her arms. "Shoo!"

Nothing.

She honked the horn.

Nothing.

The hot sun beat down on her. A bead of sweat slid uncomfortably between her breasts. She judged the narrow road, wondering if she could maneuver around the cow without going into the ditch.

Before she decided to attempt it, another sound drew her

attention. She glanced down the dirt road, shielding her eyes from the glare of the sun as a cloud of dust came toward her. The cloud of dust became a man on a horse.

Correction. A cowboy on a horse.

Hi-ho, Silver, the Lone Ranger, she thought sarcastically.

But the closer he got, the more her sarcasm faded. The Lone Ranger had nothing on this cowboy. Broad shoulders, black hat pulled low on his forehead . . .

Black hat. Bad guys wore black hats. Right? Things were looking up.

At least until he brought the horse to a grinding halt and dust swirled around her—again. She coughed and waved her hands in front of her face.

"Bessie, how the hell do you keep getting out?" he asked.

His slow, southern drawl drizzled over her like warmed honey, and she knew from experience warmed honey drizzling over her naked body could be very good. Sticky, but oh so sexy.

Did he look as good as he sounded?

She shaded her eyes again at the same time he pushed his hat higher on his forehead with one finger. Cal Braxton's tanned face stared down at her. His cool, deep-green eyes only made her body grow warmer with each passing second.

So this was the infamous playboy star football player. The man who had a pretty woman on his arm almost every night of the week—at least until Cynthia Cole had come into his life.

"I almost hit your cow," she told him as she slipped off one of her high heels and rubbed the insole with her other foot. It didn't stop the tingle of pleasure that was running up and down her legs. He could park his boots by her bed any day.

"Sorry about that. Bessie thinks the grass is greener on the other side of the fence."

He pulled a rolled-up rope off the saddle horn and swatted

the end of it against Bessie's rump. The cow gave him a disgruntled look before ambling down the road.

His gaze returned to her . . . roaming over her . . . seducing her. "Are you lost?"

"On vacation."

He easily controlled the prancing horse beneath him. "Staying nearby?"

"At the Crystal Creek Dude Ranch."

His grin was slow. So, he did have all his teeth, and they were pearly white. She ran her tongue over her dry lips.

"My brother owns it," he said. "I'm helping him out. It looks like we might be seeing a lot of each other. Name's Cal—Cal Braxton."

His thumb idly stroked the rope. For a moment, she was mesmerized as she watched the hypnotic movement.

"You know, you shouldn't drive with the top down in this heat," he said.

She almost laughed. It wasn't the heat from the sun that had momentarily stolen her wits. Cal was good. Ah, yes, he knew all the moves that made a woman yearn for him to caress her naked skin. And he made those moves very well.

She drew in a deep breath. "I'm Nicole Scott. You can call me Nikki—most people do."

He leaned forward, resting his arms against the saddle horn. "The one who likes it rough."

He'd remembered. Her pulse sped up a fraction.

He glanced down the road. The cow was trotting off completely unconcerned that she wasn't supposed to be out of her own pasture. Before he decided to chase after the cow, Nikki spoke.

"You have something against liking it rough?" She certainly hoped not.

He straightened, reining in his prancing horse. "No, but I never would've expected it from someone like you."

Now what did he mean by that?

"Bessie, damn it, not that way!" He glanced at Nikki once more and smiled. "The ranch is just up the road on the left." He pointed toward an intersection. "Watch for the signs.

"I should be up there before you get signed in and I'll show you where you'll be staying." He whirled the horse around and took off after the cow.

She smiled to herself, liking the idea that he'd remembered she liked it rough. Maybe she should've told him she didn't like to give up control, either. She preferred being the one in charge, no matter what she did.

But then, why scare him off?

She laughed and shifted gears. Tonight should prove interesting. But first, she wanted to soak in a hot tub of bubbles and wash off the layer of dust it felt like she wore.

Did they have spa treatments at the ranch? She could certainly use a massage and a facial. Maybe she'd splurge and have a pedicure, too. After all, Marge was paying for it. She might as well get her money's worth.

This was going to be the easiest assignment she'd ever had. A little rest and relaxation, and from the way Cal had looked at her, a whole lot of hot sex.

Yum . . . this was too, too sweet.

Man, this was sweet. Cal wondered how he'd gotten so lucky. Nicole Scott had left the top button of her white blouse undone. But had she left it unbuttoned to let the wind cool her skin or because she knew it would stir a man's blood to the boiling point?

Sex appeal had oozed from her. From her long, lingering looks to her full, pouty lips. His gut told him Nicole was the kind of woman who didn't play for keeps. And that was just the kind of relationship he wanted—the kind he was used to. No strings attached. He'd learned his lesson about getting even a little serious. He'd dated Cynthia for a couple of weeks and he still hadn't shaken her loose. The woman didn't know the meaning of the word no.

His cell phone rang as he herded Bessie back into the pasture. He pulled it out of his pocket and flipped it open. Jeff? What did he want?

"Yeah?"

"You're about to have a visitor, buddy."

Cal's eyes narrowed. He and Jeff went back a long way. They'd roomed together in college and been friends ever since. Jeff was one of the few sports reporters who actually cut him a little slack.

Cal scanned the open pasture, not liking the sound of Jeff's dire prediction, then shook his head. Paranoia didn't sit well with him.

"Who?"

"A reporter."

A sour taste formed in his mouth. The press had labeled Cal the bad boy of football. Maybe he hadn't been a saint, but they'd painted the picture blacker than it was. That, and Cynthia, were the reasons he was at his brother's ranch. He'd needed a change of scenery so he could get his head screwed on straight.

But it seemed they'd found him.

"Who is he?"

"Not a he. A she, and they call her The Barracuda."

"Great." This was all he needed. "Talk to me."

"Nicole Scott. She goes by Nikki."

His eyebrows rose. That hot little number in the black sports car? He shook his head. Nah. Sexy, yes. Hot, yes. But a hard-edged reporter? Not likely.

"I've met her. She doesn't look like a sports reporter." Jeff had to be pulling his leg. And his brother was probably in on the joke.

"She's a looker, isn't she?" Jeff asked. "I've had a few daydreams about her myself, but the one time I asked her out she gave me a cold stare that practically froze me to the spot. Then she informed me that she made it a policy to never date coworkers. But she's definitely hot looking."

"That's an understatement."

Jeff's cynical laugh came through the phone. "Don't make the same mistake I did and let her sexy looks fool you. She didn't get the tag Barracuda for nothing. Her parents are two hotshot lawyers. Remember the Snyder case from a few years back?"

"Isn't that the one where they had the corporate lawyers crying when they left the courtroom? It was all over the papers."

"Her mother and father are the ones who got all that money for the families. Believe me, Nikki Scott takes after her parents. She might have grown up with a silver spoon in her mouth but when she goes after a story, she's like a starving dog after a meaty bone. She's the one who went head-to-head with the man running for senator. James Rutledge, remember him?"

Before Cal could say anything, Jeff continued.

"She exposed the family that he'd dumped. Hell, he didn't even pay child support. Let his kid grow up practically in the gutter. She became a bounty hunter or something. It was in all the papers."

"If this reporter is so tough, then why is she here? I'd think my story would be the last thing she'd want to cover. Are you sure she's not here to just relax and take a nice vacation?"

"I don't think she would have agreed to do the story if the boss hadn't talked her into taking it. I bet that's exactly what happened, too, because Marge came to me first and asked about you, and believe me, there were dollar signs flashing in her eyes. I told her I didn't have any idea where you were, but apparently, she did some research. And as long as I've been at the paper, Nikki Scott has never taken a vacation. If I were you, I'd hightail it to an island far, far away."

Cal looked at the cloud of dust Nikki's car had made. It was just settling back down to the road.

Nikki had set him up, and what was worse, he'd fallen for it. She was probably laughing her ass off at his gullibility.

His jaw began to twitch. "No, I won't be running away."

"I don't like the sound of your voice."

Cal chuckled, but his laughter held little humor. "Maybe I'm tired of being crucified by the press—present company excluded. It's time I gave a little back."

"I almost feel sorry for her."

"You should." Cal said good-bye and closed the phone before slipping it back inside his pocket.

He'd had his fill of people who lied through their pretty, white teeth. Finally, he had the upper hand. He'd give Nikki her story, but she'd damn well earn every word she wrote about him.

He was going to enjoy this.

Chapter 2

Just follow him, that's what Cal had told Nikki. But where the hell was he taking her? She was starting to get a little nervous. Really, what did she know about this guy, except what she'd researched? Not a whole hell of a lot. He could be a serial killer or something.

She could see the headlines now: *THE DUDE RANCH MURDERER STRIKES AGAIN!*

Now she was being ridiculous. She had a good instinct when it came to people. Not one alarm had gone off when she met Cal earlier today. Nor when he'd joined her at the ranch. Nikki thought she'd caught a subtle difference, not quite as friendly, but shrugged off the feeling. It had been a long drive and she was tired.

She hit a pothole that almost swallowed her car, effectively drawing her back to the present. That would teach her to pay attention to where she was going and not where she'd been.

The road they were on was worse than the dirt road she'd traveled to get to the ranch. This wasn't much more than a path. Her car would definitely need an alignment job when she returned to the city, and detailed from end to end. It looked more gray than black. And it was starting to smell like the country. Her nose wrinkled. And country air was a little too aromatic for her.

Cal rounded a corner and pulled in front of a dilapidated shack straight out of *Deliverance*. All it needed to complete the picture was a couple of men on the porch playing banjos and a floppy-eared hound dog dozing between them. Her brain began sending warning signals. This wasn't good, not good at all.

She stopped behind Cal and cut the engine before getting out. Dread filled her.

"Why did we stop here?" she asked.

"This is the old homestead," he proudly proclaimed as he walked toward the porch.

"And your point is?" She eyed the shack with more than a little trepidation. The exterior needed painting—or maybe glue would be better, because it looked as though there wasn't much holding it together. She had a bad feeling about why he'd stopped in front of it.

"You said you liked it rough." He smiled at her, but his smile didn't quite reach his eyes.

Boy, did they have their wires crossed. "You expect me to stay here?" No story was worth living in this run-down hovel. She wanted a resort, massages, pedicures—hot oil sliding over her, a man's hands massaging it into her body.

"It's the only thing available."

Her thoughts came to a screeching halt. This was it—the only thing they had vacant?

She glanced around. Her opinion of the place didn't get any better. There was a small barn and pen just off to the right that looked as though it was in better shape than the cabin, a few trees, and that was it. She'd be stuck out here by herself—at least a half mile from the main ranch. Hell, it could've been ten miles and it wouldn't have made a difference. If she screamed, no one would hear her. A cold chill of foreboding ran down her spine.

This was so wrong. Visions of how she would kill Marge filled her thoughts. If she got an all-city jury, she'd get off, hands down.

She hugged her middle. "I'm surprised anyone would stay here."

He shrugged. "This was my grandparents' first home. They seemed to manage okay. Some people like returning to the old ways. Did you know there's a pueblo in Taos, New Mexico, and some of the buildings are over a thousand years old? No utilities, none of the luxuries we take for granted, but there's a tribe of Indians who live there because they respect the ways of their ancestors."

Well, it wasn't her style. And she wasn't about to . . .

"But then, some people don't have what it takes." He casually leaned against the post that held up a slightly warped roof.

One eyebrow shot upward. Was that a challenge? It had sounded like one. At the very least, he questioned if she could stand up to the rigors of a life without amenities. She'd faced Fort Worth's mean streets. Even covered a gang war once. She could certainly handle staying in a place that had seen better days and having . . . what? No microwave?

"Of course I'm staying. This is exactly what I was looking for. I just questioned whether the cabin would hold up if a strong wind should blow through. I'd hate for it to fall down around me."

He studied her. Was that a smidgin of respect she noted in his eyes? If it was, it was gone in the next second.

"I'm glad you're happy," he told her. "Because this is about as rough as it gets."

His gaze lingered long enough for her to start feeling a buzz of anticipation. The cabin had thrown her for a loop, but as her body came to life under his mesmerizing eyes, she thought about the fantastic benefits that went along with this assignment.

"You did say you liked it rough." His gaze caressed her, sending a flash of heat coursing through her body.

She nodded, afraid that speaking would be too difficult. Her mouth had gone completely dry as images of entwined naked limbs flashed across her mind. She inhaled a ragged breath. She really needed to get laid more often.

When he turned and started up the two lopsided steps, the spell was broken. Oh, yeah, he'd definitely earned his reputation as a lady's man. Her panties had come close to the melting point.

He nodded toward a triangle of rusted metal that hung from the porch. "If you do get in a bind, just ring that. But don't forget about the boy who cried wolf. It's only for emergencies."

"I have a cell phone." She made her way up the steps.

"It doesn't always work at the cabin. Unless you want to crawl up on the roof. You might get better reception there, but I don't suggest it. I'd hate for you to fall off and break something."

Okay, what was going on? Her gut told her something had changed since their first meeting. When he'd ridden up on his horse to get the cow back on the other side of the fence, Cal had flirted with her—hadn't he? He was still flirting with her, and the look in his eyes when he glanced her way was more than heated. Hell, it scorched her skin.

But he also acted as though he expected her to run screaming back to her car. It was almost as though he hoped she *would* run screaming back to her car. The mixed messages didn't make sense.

Maybe the sun pounding down on her during the drive here had fuddled her brain. Right now, Cal acted as if he was happy she'd picked up the gauntlet—but not in a good way.

Nonsense of course. She was overly tired. She'd been putting in long hours at work. When was the last time she'd even taken a vacation?

Her parents had once told her to put in the hours while she was young. There would be time to enjoy the fruits of her labor once she'd established herself. Except for the occasional long weekend, she didn't take vacations. It was probably time she did.

She pushed her hair behind her ear. No, she was only imagining his changed attitude toward her. There was no way Cal could know the real reason she was here. Marge was too crafty to let the cat out of the bag, and as far as anyone at the office knew, she was on vacation—completely plausible.

The drive to the Texas hill country had taken her longer than she'd expected because she'd gotten lost—twice. She was tired. Nothing was going on. When she returned home, she was getting a GPS.

Cal stepped inside the cabin, then held the door open for her.

She brought her attention back to the present and walked past him. The interior was even worse. A layer of grime and dust covered the probably once white sheets that draped over the furniture. She was so going to kill Marge for this.

"The maid's day off?"

"Most people who stay here want to do everything—including cleaning the place." He let his gaze slowly roam over her. "You don't look the type. I wouldn't blame you if you left."

She waltzed past him. "I don't mind a little hardship if I get what I'm after."

He crossed his arms in front of him. "And what are you after?"

You. A juicy story.

No, better not mention that. She didn't want to scare him off. She had a tendency to be a little too blunt at times. Most men were intimidated by her aggressiveness. She glanced over her shoulder and eyed the football player turned cowboy. He didn't look like the type who would easily scare.

"I'm researching a book." She shrugged. "I'm writing about how the early settlers lived." That sounded good, but did he buy her lie? She didn't even blink as his gaze met hers.

"The best way to write about it is to live it." She held her breath to see if he'd buy her story.

"You'll certainly be able to do that here," he finally said before looking away.

Hook, line, and sinker. She was so good that sometimes she amazed herself. But that's why they called her the barracuda. Oh, yeah, she knew the tag they'd given her and she was damned proud of it.

She glanced inside the bedroom. A sheet covered the mattress on the black iron bed to protect it from the dust. Her gaze quickly scanned the room. One window. No curtain.

Lovely.

She backed out of the bedroom and went into the kitchen. A mammoth black stove graced one wall. She'd been afraid of this: no microwave.

Near the stove was a sink with a pump. How archaic. At least she wouldn't need to haul water. A scarred wooden table sat in the center of the room along with two rope-bottomed, ladder-back chairs.

Home sweet home. She checked her shudder of revulsion and smiled at him. "This will do just fine."

"Then you're staying?"

"Of course. I'm a little surprised it's this rustic, but I'll manage. I'm tougher than I look." That should make him think twice about what she was made of. Ha! Nothing scared her, especially living conditions that weren't up to her standards.

She sauntered over and opened one of the cabinets. Black, beady eyes stared back at her. She couldn't move. Her heart thumped loudly inside her chest, and blood drummed inside her ears.

Except for wild animals. Wild animals scared the hell out of her.

Run! her brain screamed as the fight-or-flight response triggered. The electrical warning charges zipped across her brain, quickly catching up with her nonmoving limbs. She slammed the cabinet closed and whirled around, throwing herself at Cal.

He wrapped his arms around her. "Easy now."

"Easy?" she squeaked. "There's a wild animal in the cabinet." She clung to him.

After a few seconds, she realized how nice it felt to be this close, especially when she inhaled his spicy aftershave. Not bad, not bad at all. At least, until his chest rumbled. She moved away and glared up at him. He dared to laugh? No one had ever laughed at her.

"There's a wild animal in the cabinet," she repeated. How could he be so unconcerned? She wasn't good around animals. Hell, she'd never even been to the zoo.

"That's just Bandit," he said.

His attempt to keep a straight face wasn't working. It wasn't funny! She planted her hands on her hips. "What the hell is Bandit?"

He put his hands on her arms, but before she could savor his touch, he set her to the side and ambled over to the cabinet.

She took a step back. "You aren't going to open the door, are you? Shouldn't you call an exterminator or something?"

"No need."

When he opened the cabinet door, she saw that the animal was a fat raccoon, complete with black mask, just like in the pictures she'd seen. Pictures were fine, but up close she could do without a wild animal—or any animal, for that matter.

"This is Bandit."

"Well, make him go away."

"How'd you get inside?" Cal asked as the animal waddled backward out of the cabinet, landing with a thump on the counter.

"Is it tame?" She wasn't taking any chances and kept her distance.

He shrugged. "As tame as any wild animal can get. I was staying at the cabin when a pack of wild dogs killed Bandit's mother and her other babies. I rescued Bandit and he sort of hung around." He went to the screen door and opened it. Bandit waddled out quite unconcerned he'd nearly scared the living daylights out of her.

Nikki hugged her middle. "But he doesn't actually live here. I mean, in the cabin. Right?"

His grin was slow, warming her blood. "Why? He doesn't eat much."

Okay, this story didn't look quite so easy. People, she could handle, but she knew nothing about animals. She'd never even had a dog or cat when she was growing up. Her parents had said they didn't have the time to devote to a house pet, and they couldn't very well ask the maid to clean up after one. They were right, of course.

"Bandit usually hangs around the barn. I'll find out how he got inside and make sure he doesn't bother you again."

She breathed a sigh of relief.

"Of course, there's one houseguest I can't get rid of."

Great. If there was a pet snake or mouse, that was it. Marge could get her own story.

"What?" She warily eyed the corners of the kitchen.

"The ghost."

She laughed.

He didn't join in.

"You're serious."

"Dead serious. No pun intended."

She smiled. "I don't believe in ghosts."

Maybe this was part of staying here. Ghost enthusiasts would love this place. She had never believed in anything she couldn't see, taste, or touch.

Ghost stories never terrified her when she was growing up. Her parents always explained how the special effects created the ghostly images in the movies. "I'm not afraid of things that go bump in the night."

"Good, then you won't mind the one here." He tugged his

hat down a little farther on his forehead. "I'll just go see if I can find where Bandit got in while you look around."

There was one pressing matter she needed to take care of, and it couldn't wait. "Where exactly is the bathroom." She hadn't seen a door that might lead to it.

He gave her a look that said he'd thought she'd never ask. "Out back."

She raised her eyebrows in question. What did he mean, "out back"? The bathroom wasn't attached to the cabin? Now that would be damned inconvenient.

He motioned toward the back door. She hesitantly walked to the screen and glanced out. Oh, good Lord. "That's an outhouse."

"A two-holer. State of the art. Complete with a Sears catalog." He looked at her, his expression serious. "I might be able to scare up a JCPenney if you'd prefer."

He was trying his hand at being funny, and he seemed to relish the discomforts she would be going through. His fiancée must've really done a number on him because he seemed to have decided to take his angst out on Nikki.

She'd read that Cynthia Cole was an only child of business tycoon Milburn Cole. Her investigation before she'd left Fort Worth had given her enough information that told her Milburn Cole didn't do anything illegal, but he was so close to committing a crime that you could almost see the prison stripes on his Armani suit.

On the other hand, his daughter was the darling of society. Elite boarding schools, a private college, the best sorority— and lots of wild parties. She made Paris Hilton look like a choir girl. Cynthia had been in rehab so many times that they'd dedicated a wing to her.

So, was Cal pining for his love and decided to take his frustrations out on Nikki? Which one had broken the relationship off? Cynthia? Or him?

A week. That's all it would take before she had her answers. She'd bet her next paycheck on it.

But for now, she had to deal with the outhouse. How hard could it be?

She smiled up at Cal. "No problem." She opened the door and stepped out, then cautiously looked around. The raccoon wasn't anywhere that she could see, thank goodness.

She followed the well-worn path to the little wooden structure. Packed earth from years of use made it a little easier to walk in her heels.

She kept her eyes focused on the small building. It looked rather quaint.

Whatever she had to tell herself, right?

Just before she opened the rickety door, she looked over her shoulder. Cal watched her. Did he think she wouldn't go inside?

She'd show him, although the prospect of stepping inside the building held no appeal whatsoever. But she really had to go bad, and if she stood outside much longer, she'd be squirming and that wouldn't look at all good.

She kicked the door a couple of times, to scare any creepy-crawly bugs or spiders out of the way; opened the door; and stepped inside.

The door bumped closed behind her.

Her eyes began to burn. She stumbled back against the door, her arms waving in front of her as she fought for air that wasn't rancid from years of waste products. Oh, God, this must be what hell was like. No wonder someone had invented the toilet!

Her mind screamed hurry as she tried to focus in the dim light that came from the half-moon cutout. Thankfully, not enough that she could fully appreciate her surroundings. She saw the two holes. Where were the toilet seats? There were no toilet seats!

Don't panic. She took a deep, calming breath . . . and gagged. *Just do it*. Yeah, right. Try filming a commercial in here, *Nike!*

She jerked her skirt up and her panty hose down. Had no

one ever heard of air freshener? Stickups? Candles? Okay, maybe lighting a flame wouldn't be good unless it was someone's intention to blow the place up. Which right now sounded like a good idea to her.

She finished in record time. He'd lied; there *was* toilet paper. She jerked her panty hose up only to snag them on a sliver of wood that was sticking out, sending a three-inch run from thigh to ankle.

At this point in time, she didn't care that she'd paid twenty frigging dollars for the hose. Marge would replace them. Boy, would she replace them.

She yanked the panty hose off and tossed them in the hole before pulling her skirt down, then opened the door. Blessed fresh air from a welcome breeze hit her in the face when she stepped out. She let the door slam behind her. As she walked up the path, her legs wobbled and she was light-headed from holding her breath.

How the hell was she going to manage to stay here until she got her stupid story? The homestead was deplorable. She couldn't live here under these conditions. No one would expect her to.

Was she throwing in the towel?

No, damn it!

At least she'd been saved from Cal laughing at her. He wasn't at the back door. He hadn't seen her humiliation, and she'd make sure he never did. If she had to face outhouses and raccoons every day until she got her story, she would. Giving up was not an option.

A shadow moved across one window. He'd said the homestead was haunted. A cold chill of foreboding swept over her.

Of course the place wasn't haunted! Now she was being utterly ridiculous and she knew better than this. Her parents hadn't raised a fool.

Now, the stupid raccoon was a different matter. She could see it, touch it, and had even smelled it—which hadn't been pleasant. The raccoon made her nervous and she was never, well, hardly ever, nervous.

She would not let a dumb animal defeat her, nor an imaginary ghost or even a smelly outhouse. She was Nikki Scott and no one got the best of her.

Chapter 3

Cal moved from the bedroom window just in case Nikki decided to look his way. She didn't seem quite as confident as she had right before she went inside the outhouse.

Big city had just met country and it hadn't been pretty.

Not that he could blame her for looking a little shaken. You couldn't pay him to go inside an outhouse. In fact, he didn't know why anyone, other than Nikki, would want to stay at the old homestead, but there were actually people who did. If they felt that compelled to know how it was done in the early days, they could read a book.

But Cal knew her reason, and he had her number. She hated it here. He grinned. That was pretty much a gimme and had been from the moment she'd laid eyes on the place. This wasn't part of whatever bargain she'd cut with her editor. He expected Nikki to walk straight through the house, out to her car, and never look back.

Good-bye reporter.

Damned shame, though. If the circumstances were different, he'd have liked to get to know her better. She was a looker, with her short, dark hair and those pouty lips that were made for kissing.

If that wasn't enough, her breasts were full. The kind that were made for cupping, massaging. He closed his eyes for a moment and imagined how they would feel.

And she had great legs. Long and sexy. He bit back a groan as he imagined them wrapping around him and pulling him in closer, deeper. Images filled his mind. Her naked. Him naked. Together. On the bed.

He could barely draw in a steady breath when he heard the back door slam. Man, if his fantasies about her were this good, what would the real thing be like? Not that he'd ever find out. The outhouse was enough to scare anyone away.

He waited for the front door to slam.

It didn't.

He frowned.

Why wasn't she leaving? Any normal woman would've already run screaming from the cabin. But then, Jeff had told him they called her the barracuda.

Maybe she was. The cabin hadn't scared her off. Bandit was an unplanned bonus. The raccoon should've had her running out the front door, but she'd only made it as far as his arms. Damn, she'd felt nice pressed against him, her body trembling. And she'd smelled nice, like exotic flowers.

But he hadn't been able to contain his laughter. Barracuda? Nah, she'd been more like a little harmless goldfish. Well, at least until she'd realized he thought the situation was funny. She hadn't liked that very much. Her eyes had flashed their annoyance.

He kind of liked her annoyed. Sexy as hell. He wouldn't mind spending time getting to know her a little better. Except for the fact she still wanted to fry his ass and he wasn't about to let that happen. So maybe it was time to bring out the big guns, or in this case the broom. Cynthia had turned up her nose at doing any kind of manual labor. Heaven forbid she break a fingernail.

What would Nikki's reaction be?

He went into the living room. He could hear her mumbling to herself in the kitchen. He couldn't make out the words, though. On the other hand, he might not want to know.

"Having trouble?" he asked.

She jumped and whirled around. "This thing is out of water." She waved her hand at the pump.

"Did you lift the handle up, then push it down?"

She squared her shoulders and crossed her arms in front of her. "Yes, but it didn't do anything."

Cal had to at least give her credit for sticking around this long—reporter or not. He'd give her until the end of the day. By the time he finished with her, she'd be glad to give up trying to get a story and run back to the city.

He raised the handle and pushed it down several times before water began to flow. Without so much as a thank-you, she washed her hands, then shook them dry.

He should've known she wouldn't lower herself to his level. Jeff had said her parents were lawyers. That meant money. Maybe not as rich as Cynthia, but he'd bet his last dollar she'd never had to suffer any kind of hardship.

Man, he needed to get away to clear his head. "I'm going back to the ranch to get something to cover the hole where Bandit got inside the house," he said. "There's a broom and a mop on the back porch. You might want to get started on the cleaning before it gets dark.

"Cleaning?"

"That's part of the experience of staying in the old homestead." He smiled and tugged on the brim of his hat before turning to leave.

"Uh . . ."

He looked back. Her expression showed uncertainty. He almost felt sorry for her. Until he remembered why she was there. She wanted to use him just like Cynthia had tried to use him, just like all the reporters who hounded him for a picture or a story. His heart quickly hardened. At least it was his heart this time and not another part of his anatomy.

"You wanted something else?" he asked.

"There isn't really a ghost, is there?"

Not exactly what he thought she was going to ask. Maybe he could cut her a little slack. "I've never seen one, but my little brother swears the cabin is haunted. My grandmother once told me a young woman died here. That's how my grandmother's parents were able to buy this property so cheap. People were scared to live here."

Her forehead wrinkled. "But no one has ever been hurt or anything?"

He could lie, tell her the ghost was evil, when in truth he thought his brother had made the whole thing up. That would have her running to her car.

The last few weeks had been boring as hell, though. Nikki was damned easy on the eyes. He didn't like reporters and he damned sure didn't like manipulating females. It was time he got a little back. If nothing else, for the entertainment factor. He had a feeling Nikki would be very entertaining.

"No one has ever been hurt." He turned and went to the door. Her heels clicked right behind him. When he stepped outside, he started having second thoughts. She was a city girl. What if she hurt herself—even though she was trying to hurt him?

"You don't have to stay here, you know. There'd be no shame in changing your mind." He removed his worn Stetson, scraped his fingers through his hair before replacing his hat.

She jutted her chin out. "Do you think I can't? That I'm too soft?"

His gaze roamed over her. Oh, yeah, she looked as though she'd be real soft. "Sometimes it's better to cut your losses than get in way over your head and take a chance of getting hurt."

"And will I get hurt?"

For a moment, he found himself lost in her eyes. Right now, the way the light and shadows played with them, they reminded him of the color of maple syrup: a soft golden brown.

He cleared his throat. Yeah, she was real good. "You might if you stay. The country can hold all kinds of dangers you'd never even think about."

She stepped closer. Close enough he smelled her fragrance again, like a whispered caress.

"And what about you?" she said in that throaty voice again. "Are you dangerous?"

For a moment he couldn't move, could only stare at her as she sucked him in. She brought her hand up and brushed her dark hair behind her ear. The only thing going through his mind was that he'd like to kiss her neck, nibble on her earlobe.

Now he knew why they called her The Barracuda. It wouldn't take much for him to tell her everything she wanted to know. It was a good thing Jeff had warned him.

He leaned his hand against the wall above her head and moved in a little closer. Close enough that he saw her pupils dilate, saw the gold flecks in her eyes. "I'm only dangerous when someone crosses me," he drawled.

She visibly swallowed.

"But then, you don't have to worry about that," he continued. "You're only here to do a little research for your book."

Nikki wet her lips. A hell of a turn-on. It was all Cal could do to push away from the wall, away from the heat emanating from her body, when all he wanted to do was press closer and feel her breasts pushing against his chest. But he managed to move away—just barely.

He walked down the steps to his pickup feeling as though he'd escaped with his life—at least the parts he wanted to keep private.

As he drove off, he glanced toward the cabin. She was going back inside. It was a damned shame he was about to make her regret ever thinking he was an easy target. Hell, he ate reporters for breakfast every morning, then spit them out.

Nikki turned back and glanced out the screen as Cal drove off. What had just happened? She'd used the ghost as an excuse to get him to linger—and it had worked. But not the way she'd planned. One minute she'd been the seducer, and in the next, Cal was making her forget the reason she was out here. She shook her head to clear it. Then she looked around the front room.

She was alone, and she hated this place. It was all she could do to keep from running back to the porch and out to her car. In a few hours, she could be in Fort Worth soaking in a hot tub in her apartment. All this would be a distant nightmare.

No, not all of it was a nightmare. Cal Braxton was a walking, talking, breathing fantasy come true.

She raised her chin. And he apparently thought she'd run at the first sign of trouble; she'd seen it in his eyes.

Okay, so maybe she had tried to run when she'd opened the cabinet and Bandit had stared back at her. Anyone would've done the same thing, so that didn't really count.

But there was more to it. He didn't seem to buy her act that she wanted to stay at the cabin. What was up with his attitude? It was almost as if he knew the real reason she was here.

She reached in her pocket and brought out her cell phone, but when she flipped it open, she read "no service."

This wouldn't do. Not at all. She didn't like being disconnected from the outside world. Peace and quiet drove her insane. It was the hustle and bustle of the city all the way for her.

She stepped to the front porch and held the phone up. Still nothing. She went through the house to the back. The phone never wavered from its "no service" message. She stepped off the porch. The message blinked. She walked farther away from the house.

Service! Ha! She had service.

Her nose wrinkled. Ugh! She was standing beside the out-house. She grimaced. This was not funny.

Thank God for speed dial. She held the phone to her ear after she punched in the number two and tried not to think how appropriate it was. Marge answered on the second ring.

"Hello?"

"He knows."

"Nikki? You made it to the ranch okay. Good. I was start-ing to worry."

"He knows I'm a reporter."

"Did he tell you he knows?"

She frowned. "No, but he's too happy I've chosen to stay in the cabin away from everyone else."

"Don't sell yourself short. You're a sexy woman. Maybe he thinks he'll get lucky."

"But you should see this place." A shiver ran down her spine. "It's so isolated."

"I'm confused. Won't that make it easier to get the scoop on him? You won't have a lot of pesky vacationers hanging about."

Her eyes narrowed. "The cabin is a relic from the distant past," she said between gritted teeth. "The toilet facilities consist of an outhouse, complete with a half-moon cutout, and I don't even want to talk about how the odor could be used in bioterrorism. The only water is from a pump in the kitchen, and I'm pretty sure it doesn't have hot water. There's not one microwave in sight, either."

"So why did you choose to stay in the cabin? It sounds dreadful."

Nikki drew in a deep breath. Ugh! Her eyes began to water. She rapidly blinked. She had a feeling her phone calls would be a lot shorter from now on.

"The cabin was the only thing available."

"Well, you can't stay there. I wouldn't expect any of my reporters to live in those conditions, let alone a female."

Her back stiffened. "What do you mean by that? I've worked the streets, stayed in some real dumps to get the story, and did a damned good job reporting the truth, too."

"But you haven't had to work the rough parts of the city in a long time. You're out of practice, and really, what do you know about the country?"

"Damn it, Marge, you know I can do this. I won't let a silly fluff story beat me."

"If you think you can, then, by all means, stay. And Cal Braxton doesn't know you're a reporter. How could he? I haven't told anyone—have you?"

Her forehead wrinkled. "Of course I haven't."

"Then he doesn't know. I have to rush out, Nikki. I have an important meeting I can't miss. If it gets too awful, just turn around and come right back to the city. I won't think badly of you for giving up."

There was a distinctive click.

Give up? Give up! She didn't think so. She never gave up.

She snapped her phone closed before it dawned on her that she'd been played. Marge had known she would never walk away from a challenge.

Great, just great. She looked up in time to see Bandit waddle out of the barn and toward a tree.

Maybe Marge *had* played her. It didn't matter. She still wasn't going to quit. She stomped back to the cabin.

Marge was right about one thing: Cal couldn't possibly know she was a reporter. He wasn't on the rebound, either, or he'd be flirting outrageously with her. There had been subtle nuances but nothing blatant. That Cynthia chick must've really done a number on him. At the moment, Cal didn't seem too pleased with the female population. Damn, there went her wild nights of hot sex.

She paused halfway up the path from the outhouse. Was she giving up on the sex?

Cal was a hottie with all those bulging muscles. When

she'd lunged herself at him after going eyeball to eyeball with the raccoon, she'd had the chance to get up close and personal with all those muscles, and they'd felt as good as they'd looked.

And damned if he hadn't caused her pulse to race when he'd leaned close to her right before he'd walked to his pickup and left.

Had he been flirting then? She wasn't sure. Her hormones had been raging so hot they'd fogged her brain. Whatever he'd been doing, it had been nice.

No, she wasn't giving up on sex, either—only regrouping. Cynthia might have done a number on his head, and possibly his heart, but Nikki was there to kiss and make it all better, *and* she'd get her story, too.

The Barracuda never lost.

She grabbed the broom off the hook before she went back inside. He didn't think she'd last.

"Cal hasn't seen nothin' yet. I might not be country, but that doesn't mean I'm soft. I'll show him just what this city girl is made of."

A cloud drifted in front of the sun and the room darkened. Cold washed over her as though . . . as though what? A ghost had reached out and touched her?

Okay, the room was just a little too dark and dismal. She really hated the dark. And that's all this was. Some illumination and she'd be fine.

She reached toward where a light switch should be. It wasn't there. Nor was there one in any of the other rooms. Well, crap. She should've guessed there wasn't any electricity, either.

This wasn't at all funny.

She began to furiously sweep the wooden floor. Cal Braxton would not run her off, even if he was doing it because Cynthia had jilted him!

Nope, she was here to stay. She chuckled. He'd be in for a

big surprise if he knew how she really felt about the cabin. But he didn't, and she wouldn't let him find out, either.

By the time she'd swept the last of the dirt out of the house, Cal was pulling up in front of the cabin.

She stepped to the front porch and leaned the broom against the side of the house. She pushed her hair out of her face as she watched him get out of his pickup, a hammer and tacks in one hand and a square sheet of shiny metal in the other.

"There's no electricity," she told him.

His grin sent tingles down her spine, and for a moment she could only stare, lost in a fantasy of them naked and in bed having hot, wild sex.

"And your point is?"

What was her point? Hell, she'd forgotten what she'd just said. Oh, yeah, electricity. Now he was smirking. She jutted her chin, refusing to back down.

"I'll need a flashlight or kerosene lamp before it gets dark. That's my point." Wasn't that what they were called? Kerosene lamps? The thought of having something so flammable in a weathered and worn cabin did not appeal to her. But she would have it, if it provided light, and even if it killed her.

Oh, not a good thought.

He looked surprised. "You're staying then?"

"Why wouldn't I? This is exactly what I was looking for. Rustic, just like the early days."

"There's a kerosene lamp in the kitchen and I have a flashlight in my pickup I'll loan you."

Her stomach growled, which reminded her of something else. "I'll need food and somewhere to store it. Unless it's delivered." She tried to keep the hopeful note out of her voice. Meals brought to her door would be nice, and it would make it a lot easier to stay in this dump.

He laughed. "Now that wouldn't be roughing it, would it? You'd only be defeating the purpose, and we want you to experience the country to its fullest."

Don't do me any favors. What she wouldn't give for a big, juicy fast-food burger and an order of fries right now.

"I brought some things from the ranch that I thought you might need."

She glanced past him and could see the boxes in the back of his pickup. Not one McDonald's bag poked above the rest. She'd been afraid of that. So what did pioneer women eat? She had a feeling she would be expected to cook. Not good, since she always managed to burn toast.

He went inside and into the bedroom. It took him only a few seconds to tack the metal over the hole where Bandit had gotten inside.

When he stood, she noticed just how tall he was. She was five seven and a half, yet he towered over her. He had to be at least six four or five.

"Come on. I'll help you carry your stuff inside." He didn't wait for her to respond but headed out the door, going straight to his pickup and hefting a box out of the back.

"Don't do me any favors," she mumbled but made sure she hadn't spoken loud enough for him to hear. She didn't relish this much physical labor. An air-conditioned gym was one thing; actually carrying in boxes was another.

She liked the way he hefted, though, but Nikki didn't think he would let her get away with standing on the front porch and ogling his muscles as he carried in the boxes. She was, after all, roughing it.

Whoopie.

"This should give you plenty of research for your book," he said as he paused with his foot on the bottom step.

They were almost eye to eye. He really was very delicious looking.

"You did say you were writing a book, right?"

She stepped around him and down the steps. "Research. Yes, a book. I'm a writer." When she thought about it, she hadn't really lied. Except about it being a book rather than an article. She had a feeling if she was here very long, she could write volumes about Cal.

"Then I'll have to make sure you don't go away empty-handed."

She reached over the side of his pickup and grabbed a box. She could've told him that she was certain she would leave with plenty of information.

But she didn't.

Chapter 4

She'd better get her story soon, Nikki thought to herself as she lugged in another box from the back of Cal's pickup and plopped it down on the kitchen table.

And Marge was paying how much so she could vacation in this dump? Getting back to nature really sucked, and as soon as she had her scoop, she was off to a vacation spot with glitz and glamour—and a massage therapist!

She dug around in the first box and pulled out a cookbook. Oh, goody. "I don't cook," she muttered.

"This will be a great time to learn, then. You should be able to write a fantastic . . . book with all the experiences you'll have while staying at the cabin. I bet it'll be a bestseller," Cal said as he began emptying the boxes.

"I can't wait."

"Enthusiasm, that's good."

She had a feeling he was being sarcastic. Again, she wondered if he knew the real reason why she was here. She mentally shook her head. He couldn't know she only wanted to do a story on him and not a book about how pioneer women had struggled through the Depression. At least now she knew why they were so damned depressed.

She pushed her hair behind her ears. God, she was getting paranoid. Marge was right: there was no way Cal could

know why she was really here. If he did, he'd have run her
out of town by now.

Her stomach rumbled. Food, she needed food. She eyed
the stove. Starvation or blowing herself up. Hmm . . . Which
was the lesser of two evils?

"How do I operate this?" She warily walked over to the
black beast.

"The wood is outside the back door. You'll want to use
kindling to get it started."

He stepped outside to the porch and grabbed a handful of
sticks and a small log, then dumped everything in front of the
stove—on her clean floor. Well, sort of clean.

"You might check first to make sure there's not a critter inside."

"Critter?" She took a step back. What the hell was a critter? She took a wild guess and assumed he must be talking
about a small animal. The thought of another wild animal
did not sit well with her.

Was *she* nervous? The Barracuda? She was a tough city reporter and she never cowered. She squared her shoulders and
lifted her chin as he opened the oven door. But she couldn't
stop the sigh of relief when nothing slithered out.

"All clear except for a few cobwebs."

She grimaced. "I'd just as soon not eat cobweb-seasoned
food."

There were cloths in one of the boxes. She grabbed one
and a small empty tub. At least he'd brought dish soap rather
than lye soap—she'd rather not leave here with chapped, red
hands.

After filling the tub with water, she added a squirt of soap.
She was adapting a little too quickly, she thought wryly. Better to adapt than to run back to the city with her tail between
her legs.

Cal didn't say a word as she began to clean. He also didn't
offer to help. She had a feeling he was having fun at her ex-

pense. Maybe it was time to give a little back. She accidentally sloshed some water over the side of the tub. He moved fast enough then.

"Oops, sorry." But she wasn't.

That had been very juvenile of her. She bit back her smile. It had felt damned good, though.

"No problem." He moved out of her way, then leaned against the table.

Cal was almost certain Nikki had done that on purpose. She was probably getting really pissed at him by now. It wasn't hard to see she didn't like the cabin or anything that went along with it. And she was taking her anger out on the mammoth beast as she scrubbed away the dirt and grime.

It was all he could do to keep from grinning. He casually crossed his arms in front of him. Nope, she wouldn't last a day.

But then guilt began to set in. She was really going to town cleaning that stove. His natural inclination would be to pitch in and help.

He should help. What if she broke a fingernail or something?

Was he losing his friggin' mind? Going soft? Yeah, right, help a reporter who wanted to scoop everyone else with her story on him, and he'd bet there wouldn't be a word of it in his favor.

His gaze moved downward. Besides, he liked the way she moved. When she wiped across the top of the stove, her ass wiggled back and forth nicely. Sweet temptation.

"Now what?" she asked.

He continued to stare at her as if she hadn't spoken. There was a streak of dirt across her cheek, and suddenly she didn't look like city to him. She must really want this story bad.

"You're going to show me how this thing works, right?" she asked.

He glanced at the stove. It almost sparkled. "Yeah, I'll show you," he said as he reined in his thoughts. "We wouldn't want you to blow yourself up or anything." He pushed away from the table and went to the oven.

"This is where you start the fire." He opened a door and stuck the small pieces of wood inside, then crumpled some paper and stuffed it inside as well.

She nodded.

"Wait for the kindling to begin to burn, then add the bigger piece of wood and shut the door." He noticed she watched everything he did. Okay, he'd give her credit for paying attention.

"Then what?"

"You really don't know how to cook?" He thought she'd been joking. She looked serious.

"I microwave dinners or I go to restaurants."

"I don't suppose you've ever gone hunting, either."

She paled. "I have to hunt my food . . . and murder some poor animal?"

This was the time to lie and tell her that not only did she have to hunt it, but she had to skin it as well. She'd be out the front door faster than he could say newspaper article.

But where would the fun be in that? He wanted to teach her a lesson. Let her know she couldn't play with other people's lives.

"No, you don't have to hunt or skin it. I'll bring meat from the freezer at the ranch."

She breathed a sigh of relief and looked around the room. Her gaze landed on the wooden box. "And is that the refrigerator?"

"Icebox. I didn't think to bring a block of ice. I'll bring it on my next trip." He'd thought she'd be gone by now and all that would be left would be a trail of dust as she headed back to Fort Worth. The woman had stamina, he'd give her that much.

"A block of ice?" she asked.

He opened the icebox. "It goes in here. As the ice melts, the water drains through the tube and into a pan." He squatted in front of the icebox and raised a slat, then showed her the metal pan that was behind the slat. "You'll need to keep it emptied or you'll be doing a lot of mopping. Do you think you can handle that?" He straightened.

When her spine stiffened, it was all he could do to keep from laughing. He liked seeing the fire flash in her eyes.

"I'm sure I'll manage."

"I just bet you will."

Their gazes met and held. After only a few seconds, she looked away. It was a small victory, but he savored the moment. He planned to savor quite a few more before she threw in the towel.

"I stuck a jar of peanut butter and one of jelly in the box until you get the hang of it. There's a loaf of bread in there somewhere, too. You'll find silverware and dishes in the cabinets, but you might want to wash them before you use them. No one has rented the place in a few months."

"I can't understand why," she said, then smiled, but it didn't even come close to reaching her eyes. "I mean, I expect to have a wonderful time while I'm here. I'm sure I'll discover a lot more than I'd planned."

"I'll get your block of ice," he said.

Nikki thought she was going to get a story while she was here but that wasn't going to happen. She might be a pretty good reporter but she'd met her match with him. She was in for a big surprise.

He strode toward the front door, letting the screen slam behind him as he left. He didn't look back as he climbed into the pickup and started it up. But before he was out of sight of the cabin, he couldn't stop his gaze from going to the rearview mirror. She hadn't come outside to watch him drive away this time. Had he hoped for one last glimpse?

Yeah, he'd been at his brother's ranch way too long.

Actually, it wasn't so bad. This was where he'd grown up. He and Brian had covered nearly every inch of the place. There wasn't a lot of extra money back then, but they hadn't needed video games or even cable television. They'd had something even better: their imaginations.

Trees had become forts, and hills had been made for capturing and laying claim to. They'd fought battles and conquered marauding Indians and even a pirate captain or two.

Then they'd grown up. At least he had. Sometimes he wasn't so sure about Brian.

He pulled to a stop beside the barn and turned off the engine before getting out. The sprawling ranch house brought back a lot of good memories. It was bigger than when they were kids. Brian had added a wing for guests and put in a swimming pool. It looked exactly like in the brochures, complete with spa packages.

He shook his head. Spa packages.

Not that it mattered to him. And he was still proud of his little brother. Brian had done all he'd set out to do. Cal started toward the house.

"Hey, Cal," Brian called from behind him.

Cal turned around. His brother stood just inside the barn. "I thought you weren't going to be home until tomorrow." He headed back toward the barn.

Brian had gone out of town to look at some horses. Why, Cal had no idea. He had more than enough, if you asked him. Sometimes he wondered how they could be so much alike but so far apart at the same time.

"They weren't what I was looking for. Besides, I have to find a new massage therapist since Amy quit. With Shelley sick, I'm needed more here."

Cal noticed for the first time how tired his little brother looked. Maybe what he had to tell him would lift some of the weight he seemed to be carrying on his shoulders.

"One called asking about the ad that was in one of the papers. Good idea advertising in some of the bigger newspapers, but then, I doubt you would've found one around here."

"That fast? Great. When is she coming in for an interview?"

Brian reached into the cooler that was just inside the barn and pulled out a beer, tossed it to Cal. Cal caught it, twisted off the cap as Brian grabbed one for himself, then joined him at the back of the pickup.

"Tomorrow." At least, he was pretty sure it was tomorrow. Yeah, he was certain she'd said tomorrow. She'd sounded nice. Cal thought he'd detected a bit of desperation in her voice, as though she really needed the job.

What the hell was he supposed to do? Brian needed to fill the position fast and the woman said she had experience. He grimaced, knowing exactly what he'd done. He might have implied that she was already hired.

He'd let Brian sort it out. His little brother was good at fixing stuff. Besides, Brian needed a new therapist. She needed a job. Two problems solved.

"Andy said you put a woman up at the homestead. A young, pretty woman." Brian tilted the bottle against his lips and took a long drink.

"Nikki Scott." The therapist was quickly forgotten as he lost himself in a mental vision of Nikki.

Brian half sat on the open tailgate. "Do you think that was a smart move? No one has stayed there in months."

"It was the only thing available."

"Still, I'd hate for her to tell anyone what it's like out there. That's not what this ranch is about unless someone really wants to see how things used to be. This Nikki Scott doesn't sound as though she fits the bill. What does she do for a living?"

"She's a reporter."

Brian choked on his beer.

Cal pounded his brother on the back. "You going to live?"

He took a deep breath. "Not if she writes about her stay at the homestead. I know you hate reporters, but don't take it out on this woman, especially not on my ranch. Why the hell didn't you just tell her we were full?"

He grinned as he remembered the way Nikki had sounded

on the phone. "She had a voice that made me think of long nights of hot sex."

Brian grimaced. "I would think Cynthia had cured you of those kinds of thoughts—at least for a while."

Cal frowned. "You really know how to kill a moment, little brother."

"If she writes a bad review I'll do more than kill the moment. I've worked hard to make a go of this place. I'd hate to think it was all a waste."

"Yeah, well, maybe you've put too much into it. There's something to the old saying that all work and no play makes a person hard to be around."

Or something like that. It was the truth, though. Brian had forgotten how to play. When little brother frowned, he continued.

"Don't worry, she's not here to write a review about the ranch. Jeff called to warn me about her."

"Jeff? From college?"

"Yeah. Nikki's here to dig up what dirt she can get about me and Cynthia."

"All the more reason to get rid of her," Brian said. "You don't need more reporters hounding you. That's why you came here in the first place."

Cal laughed. "Yeah, I thought Nikki would turn her car around and leave when she saw the place. Man, it looks rougher every time I set eyes on it. Nikki must've thought so, too, but she tried to hide her expression. Not that it did any good. Shock was written all over her face."

"But she didn't leave."

He shook his head. "Not even when she opened the cabinet and came face-to-face with Bandit."

Brian chuckled. "I'd like to have seen that. I can't believe that old coon is still alive. He must be at least twelve years old by now."

Cal realized that was the first time he'd heard his brother

laugh in a long time. It was nice. "No, the best was when I told her about the outhouse. That was sweet."

"I doubt it was to her." He shook his head. "Damn, I should've bulldozed it a long time ago, but I didn't want to get that close." He took a swig of beer and swallowed. "But she's still there?"

"She's tenacious, I'll give her that. Jeff said they call her The Barracuda. I think I'm finding out how she got the name."

"If she sees the ghost, she'll be out of there quick enough."

Cal rolled his eyes. "Don't tell me you still believe the place is haunted."

"I know it is. Saw the spirit myself."

"You saw it?"

Brian shrugged. "Well, yeah—sort of. It was more like shadows and light. Once, I thought I heard a voice call my name. I'm telling you, the place is haunted."

Cal snorted. "Whatever."

"So she has a nice voice, but what does she look like?" Brian suddenly changed the subject.

Cal glanced at his brother, really looking at him. He wasn't all that little anymore—six two, at least—and he was tanned from days spent in the sun. His dark good looks had caused more than one girl to go into a fit of giggles when they were in school. Nikki wouldn't be any more immune than most women. Brian would crook his finger and she'd tremble with anticipation. For some odd reason, that bothered Cal.

"What does she look like?" he repeated Brian's question, then cleared his throat. "Butt ugly. Remember that old nag Grandpa used to have?"

"The gray one with buckteeth?"

"That's the one. If you had a picture of both of them, you wouldn't be able to tell which one was the horse and which one was the woman." He didn't look at his brother but tilted the bottle of beer to his lips.

"But Andy said she was pretty."

Cal snorted. "Yeah, well, look at some of the women Andy has dated."

Brian nodded. "Yeah, he really needs to get his eyes checked." He straightened, drained his bottle of beer, and tossed it toward a large trash can that was near the barn. It clanked as it hit inside. "You can be the one who makes sure she doesn't kill herself while she's at the cabin, then. She's your problem."

That's what he'd hoped Brian would say. He didn't need his brother getting gaga over a pretty skirt and tell things he shouldn't be telling. That wasn't the only reason he'd lied, but it was the only one he wanted to admit to right now.

"Besides," Brian continued. "The old homestead *is* haunted. Don't you remember the stories Grandma used to tell us? I'm not going near the place. It wouldn't matter if Nikki Scott was the hottest woman on earth."

"You're full of it." Cal laughed. His brother would never convince him the homestead had a ghost. "I think you made the whole thing up when we were in high school and you were sneaking up there with Wanda Jo. You didn't want anyone following the two of you to find out what y'all were doing."

Brian's face turned a deep shade of red. "Well, that, too, but there really was a ghost. Why do you think I quit sneaking up there?"

"You're saying I should confirm your story with Wanda Jo?" Cal raised his eyebrows.

Brian shook his head. "No way. She married Wayne Harris and I don't want to cross paths with him."

"Ape Man Harris?" He tried to visualize Wanda Jo with Ape Man. Nope, it just wasn't coming to him.

"Yeah, a couple of years ago. I thought I told you about it."

Cal tossed his empty beer bottle into the trash can and they started walking toward the ranch.

"No, you didn't mention it. I don't blame you for wanting to keep your distance. Is Ape Man still as ugly as he used to be?"

"Uglier."

"Why the hell did Wanda Jo marry him?"

Brian paused for a moment, looking thoughtful. "He has big hands?"

Cal's forehead wrinkled; then he started to laugh. He didn't stop until they were near the back door of the ranch.

"Yeah, Wanda Jo liked . . . big hands, didn't she? Is that why she dumped you?"

Brian grinned. "Compared to Ape Man? No one's hands even come close."

There were some good things about being back on the ranch, too. For just a few minutes, it had seemed as though the years between them were gone. When Cal looked up, he could almost see Grandma at the door holding a plate of cookies and smiling like she always did.

"You boys wash your hands and you can have some of the cookies I just took out of the oven." She wiped her hands on her apron.

And then she faded away.

Some things you couldn't bring back—all you had were the precious memories—but maybe some things could grow stronger. Like his relationship with Brian. It had felt good to cut up with him. They'd each gone their own ways after college.

Before he stepped inside the house, he glanced toward the cabin that was hidden from view by tall pecan and oak trees. Yeah, it wasn't so bad to come back home.

Chapter 5

Nikki didn't like washing down a PB&J with water, but that's all she had. What she wouldn't give to have an ice-cold glass of milk.

At least her stomach wasn't growling anymore. Not exactly five-star cuisine. This was definitely roughing it.

After brushing the crumbs off her hands, she went to her car and retrieved her suitcases from the trunk. She wanted to have most of her things inside before it got too dark.

A shiver of dread ran down her spine. Staying in the middle of nowhere by herself at night didn't hold a bit of appeal. At least in the city, she knew what to expect. This country quiet was more than a little unnerving.

She carried her cases inside and set them down in front of the bedroom door. Hadn't she left it open? Apparently not, or it would still be open. Her short laugh was supposed to reassure her, but it came off sounding a little cracked. There were no such things as ghosts. Cal had probably shut the door when he left and she hadn't noticed.

But after she opened it, she stood there for a moment looking around before she picked up her cases and went inside. Of course the room was empty. Really, what had she expected? A ghost to jump out and scream, "Boo!"?

But it still didn't stop the cold inside the room from washing over her—a damp, muggy feeling.

"I'm really losing it," she muttered.

She carried the cases over to the bed and set them down, then sniffed.

What was that smell? She sniffed again. It smelled like apple pie. She closed her eyes and inhaled a little deeper. Nice. Just as quickly she opened them, realizing just how ridiculous she was being.

This was what happened when she didn't take off time from work. The next time she spoke to Marge, Nikki was going to tell her she wanted a real vacation and she didn't care what her parents thought. She was a big girl.

The bedroom didn't look too bad. She'd removed the two sheets that had protected the mattress from dust. There was bedding in one of the boxes. It took her only a few minutes to make the antique iron bed. It looked comfortable, almost cozy.

Whatever she had to tell herself.

She glanced at her watch. Almost seven. The evening stretched before her. Boredom had never been a problem. She always had an invitation to go to a party or something. Friends, good wine, good food—her nights would stretch into the wee hours of the morning.

She glanced at her watch again. Three and a half minutes had passed.

So now what did she do? Unpack?

There was an armoire, and when she cautiously looked inside, she found hangers. No critters. But when she opened her suitcases, she realized she'd brought all the wrong clothes. She had two pair of slacks that would work, but she was afraid the dresses and her loungewear wouldn't do at all. She certainly didn't want to ruin the expensive clothes she'd worked hard to buy. Maybe the last town she'd driven through would have something more suitable.

She sat on the side of the bed, the energy suddenly draining from her. What was she doing out here? Really. Was she chasing after a story or a man—or something more? Sometimes she felt as though her life wasn't complete. Which was crazy. She'd traveled all over the world; she had an exciting job; she dated, went to lots of parties.

It was because she was almost thirty. That had to be it. She was getting old.

Enough! She wasn't getting old; her biological clock could tick all it wanted because she wasn't keen on having kids or getting married anytime soon, if ever. She stood and quickly went back to unpacking.

Why the hell was she even thinking like this? Hormones? No, that was over last week. Allergies? Maybe she was allergic to all this country air. That had to be it. Once she was back in the city, she wouldn't have time to be morose.

She closed the suitcases after unpacking what she thought she could use, then stuck them under the bed before wandering to the front porch. The rocker looked safe enough. She dusted it off, then gingerly sat in it and gave a gentle push with her foot. At least it didn't collapse beneath her.

Silence.

No, there was another sound. The rumble of a pickup. She stayed where she was as the sound grew closer. Then the pickup came around the corner, headlights glaring at her.

Excitement made her heart beat faster, but she kept her seat. Outwardly, she knew she looked calm. She watched as the pickup came to a stop.

Cal.

He killed the engine and got out, then reached in the back. Her gaze moved south. She liked the way his jeans stretched taut over his backside.

Nice. Very nice.

He turned, grasping an ice chest by the end handles. "Your block of ice. I brought some perishables, too. They're in the back."

She had a feeling that meant she was supposed to carry them inside. His gallantry took her breath away.

Not that it made that much difference. Her parents had always taught her to carry her own weight. Even though they had plenty of money, she had her own chores when she was growing up. It didn't bother her a bit to carry in the other box. She was not a frail female—well, unless there were wild critters around.

She grabbed the open box, glancing at the contents as she carried it inside the cabin. Butcher paper. Meat? Probably. Catsup, mustard, and mayo. No butter. No eggs. She frowned. Eggs would've been nice. Butter, too. Surely it couldn't be that hard to cook an egg.

Cal was just putting the block of ice in the box when she walked inside the kitchen.

"If there's nothing else, I'll see you in the morning." He started back through the cabin.

"You're leaving?" She set her box on the table. "Right now?"

He stopped on the porch and studied her. She could feel her nipples tightening as his gaze slowly caressed her.

"Was there something else you wanted?" he drawled.

Maybe it was the way he'd said the words, all soft and lazy. It made her think he would stay if he had the right incentive. But what else did she want?

Cal in her bed, that was what else she wanted, but she didn't tell him that. He looked a little too smug. She wasn't sure what his game was, but she wasn't playing, at least not this time.

"Is it always this quiet?" she asked instead.

"Quiet?"

She thought for a moment he'd leave, but instead, he half sat on the wooden rail that ran the length of the porch. "It's not quiet at all. Listen."

She did but still didn't hear anything. She shook her head. "What am I listening for?"

"A sparrow is angry. Another bird is probably trying to steal her nest. Can you hear her?"

She cocked her head to the side. The bird was raising a big

fuss. "Yes, I can." Strange that she hadn't heard any birds earlier. "She does sound put out, doesn't she?"

"And look over there in that pile of leaves and sticks. There's a squirrel foraging for nuts."

She followed where he pointed and stared for a few minutes. It was getting dark enough that she could barely see. But sure enough, a squirrel popped its head up.

"The chickens have already bedded down for the night," he told her. "But you'll see and hear them in the morning when you gather the eggs."

"Gather the eggs?"

"They have nesting boxes. It's not that hard. You just reach beneath them and take the eggs."

Eggs didn't sound nearly as good as she had thought they would. "Don't they bite . . . or something?"

He grinned as though she'd said something funny. How the hell was she supposed to know what chickens did?

"They might peck, but most of them don't mind if you get their eggs."

She was stealing their eggs, then eating them. Murdering their offspring. Of course, they probably wouldn't mind. Uh-huh, sure.

"See you in the morning." He straightened and went to his pickup.

She couldn't think of another excuse for him to stay and keep her company. Unless she wanted to rip off her clothes and throw herself at him. She wasn't quite that desperate— yet.

Nikki could only watch him drive away. At least it wasn't quiet anymore. No, now she heard all kinds of animals making noise, rustling in leaves. Critters. She missed the quiet.

She went inside and walked to the back door, then stared at the shadowed outhouse. She'd have to use the flashlight so she could see the path.

How much water would she need to take in to ward off

dehydration but keep her from having to go to the outhouse as often?

Procrastination didn't sit well with her.

With determination, she grabbed the flashlight and went out onto the back porch. She gritted her teeth and stepped off, then marched down the path. She could do this. It wasn't as though she was made of glass. Anything Cal said she had to do, she would do. She was made of sterner stuff than he could even imagine.

She swung the door open and stepped inside.

Oh, Lord, it was worse than she'd remembered. Her eyes crossed as a shiver of revulsion made her tremble from head to foot. She clamped her lips together.

All she had to do was hold her breath. She swam at the gym pool all the time and she could hold her breath a long time. She jerked her skirt up and her panties down, then gingerly sat over the hole, careful not to get a splinter. That's all she needed—an infected ass. Try explaining that one.

Oh, God, she needed to breathe.

Why the hell had she drunk so much water?

She hurried to finish, then yanked her panties up and her skirt down, opened the door, and was halfway down the path before she inhaled. Fresh air.

She stumbled to the back porch, falling across it as she inhaled mouthfuls of sweet air. She finally had her oxygen levels back up to normal and pushed to a sitting position, frowning.

This really sucked.

Bzzzzzz.

She waved her hand in front of her face.

Bzzzzzz.

A mosquito as big as a fly landed on her arm. Nikki swatted it, but his brother attacked her other arm. Great, she'd probably end up with West Nile virus on top of an infected ass!

She jumped to her feet and hurried inside the cabin, closed

the door, and reached for the lock. Not that she thought the mosquitoes could open the door, but she wasn't too keen on burglars or whatever they had in the country. Cattle rustlers, maybe.

No lock. It figured. Not that anyone would have trouble getting inside. Hell, sneeze and the place would probably collapse into a pile of toothpicks.

Marge had told her to come home if things got too bad. Maybe she would take her up on it. She collapsed in the chair, resting her head on the table. Who was she kidding? To leave would be running away and that wasn't in her character.

So, she'd stay. At least for a while longer.

A bath would help. She felt as though she wore at least one layer of dirt. She leaned sideways and eyed the stove.

Hot bath?

Okay, she'd settle for a cold wash. How bad could it be? Especially if she hurried.

Real bad, she found out a few minutes later. The water was freezing. More so than city water. But she did the best she could, then quickly crawled beneath the quilt on the bed to get warm again.

She was physically and mentally exhausted. She only wanted to sleep. Tomorrow would be a better day.

It damned sure couldn't be any worse!

She yawned, closing her eyes, then smiled as she immediately visualized Cal sauntering toward her. She snuggled deeper beneath the cover. Umm, nice dream.

"Cock-a-doodle-do!"

Nikki came straight up in bed. She was being robbed! Someone had broken inside her apartment and in the next minute, the robber would be in her room to do all kinds of bodily harm. Her gaze flew around the semi-dark room.

This wasn't her apartment.

She'd been kidnapped. Drugged and brought to this . . . this dump.

Escape! She stumbled out of bed, dragging the quilt with her, and rushed outside, almost falling off the porch.

She caught her balance and whipped first to the right, then left. Okay, she hadn't been kidnapped. She was at the cabin on the dude ranch. But someone had still screamed out . . . or something.

She had to get out of there. Where were her car keys? Where . . .

"Cock-a-doodle-do!"

She spun around, almost tripping herself as the quilt tangled with her legs. She kicked it out of the way and shoved her hair out of her eyes.

"Cock-a-doodle-do!"

This was her thief? Her intruder? A friggin' rooster?

She looked at the sun, which was just barely peeking over the horizon, then back at the blasted bird. He thrust his chest out and pranced back and forth along the top rail of the wooden fence. Several chickens stood on the ground below as if adoring this wonderful spectacle of arrogant feathers.

She jerked the quilt around her shoulders more securely and glared at the feathered Romeo. He drew in a deep breath and let loose with another screeching yodel. The chickens cackled, apparently thinking he'd performed some grand feat.

Enough was enough. She usually slept until at least eight. Her gaze fell to the ground. She smiled, picked up a rock, and when the bird inhaled again, let it fly.

The rooster squawked, fell off the fence, kicked twice, and lay silent.

Oh, crap!

Her hand flew to her mouth. She hadn't meant to kill the blasted bird, only scare it. In all her life, she'd never murdered anything.

She let the quilt fall and rushed over to the fence. The chickens glared at her. She squatted next to the rooster.

Could you do CPR on a bird? She didn't think she wanted to try. She'd have to live with her guilt.

How proud he'd been prancing along the fence rail, and with good reason. Up close, Nikki could see how magnificent he was. Feathers as bright as a brand-new copper penny, dark red, brilliant orange, emerald green. Sniffing, she gently touched him.

In a flurry of feathers, the rooster leapt up ushering loud noises and flapping his wings. Nikki screamed and jumped to her feet. The rooster turned toward her.

She stepped back.

The bird advanced, no longer prancing but with a slightly off-balance, drunken gait.

Nikki turned and fled back inside the cabin, grabbing the quilt as she went. She scrambled back in bed and pulled the covers over her head.

No utilities. The toilet was outside and smelled horrible. Taking a bath meant she had to risk her life and light the black beast of an oven or wash in ice water. The rooster from hell. Maybe even a ghost—not that she believed in them. She hated it here. She wanted to go back to the city, where toilets flushed and they had real burglars, not some crazy-ass bird!

Was she ready to admit defeat?

She sniffed. Damn it, she wasn't. Not this early in the game. No, she refused to give up. She only needed a few more hours of sleep.

Life sucked right now, but she would get her story. Scrunching down farther in the bed, she pulled the blanket even higher. Her eyes drifted closed as she yawned.

She didn't want to think about any of it right now. She wanted to sleep and dream about ivory towers and palaces. Vacationing where they had room service. She snuggled deeper into the feather mattress. Sunning on pristine beaches. Her eyelids drifted downward. She yawned.

And sex.

How long had it been since she'd had sex? Too long. Immediately a dark-haired cowboy with smoldering green eyes filled her mind.

He walked toward her wearing only a hat, cowboy boots and twirling a rope. There he was in all his naked glory. She snuggled the quilt closer to her. Oh, yeah. This was what she wanted to dream about. It was even better than her last dream—more X-rated.

Cal would jerk the quilt away from her and pull her against him. She would caress each and every one of his delicious muscles as her hands roamed over his body.

She moaned, then stifled a yawn. God, she was so tired. Her whole body ached from being jostled when she'd driven down that damned dirt road.

Cal began to fade as she drifted further asleep.

"Don't go," she mumbled, but it was already too late. She sighed just before sleep overcame her.

Chapter 6

Mooooooooo! Nikki flew out of bed, ran into the wall, bounced around, and stared into the eyes of a big brown beast that had a string of drool dripping from its mouth to the floor.

She screamed.

Cal stuck his head through the open window, shoving the animal back. "Move over, Bessie." Then he turned his attention to her. "Mornin'. Good, I'm glad you're up. I don't suppose you have any coffee made."

"Coffee?"

"No, I didn't think so, but I sure could use another cup. Well, get dressed. I'll get Bessie settled in the barn. Better hurry, though, it's already past milking time and she's getting anxious."

"Milk?"

"Didn't I tell you that's part of the experience? Darn, I can't believe I left that little detail out." His eyes twinkled. "You'll love it."

He moved away from the window, but just as she started to relax, he popped his head inside once more. His gaze wandered very slowly from her head to her feet, then back up. "By the way, I like your pj's." He whistled a jaunty tune as he ambled away.

She glanced down. Her thin red silk teddy left little to the imagination. It was cut all the way down to her navel and the only thing holding it together was one strip of sheer lace.

Not only did it show a considerable amount of cleavage, but the morning air was cool and her nipples were pebble hard.

A wave of heat washed over her. She grabbed the quilt and pulled it in front of her but not for modesty's sake. She felt the need to hold on to something—anything.

No gentleman would've mentioned her nightclothes since they barely covered her. And a gentleman wouldn't have stared so blatantly, either, making her body grow hot, then cold, and then very, very hot.

A slow smile curved her lips. It was nice to know Cal wasn't that much of a gentleman.

Naughty, naughty.

Her mood quickly changed when she thought about the cow. She might have the hots for Cal but she was certain she'd hate Bessie.

Her forehead wrinkled in thought. Hadn't Bessie been black and white yesterday? Not that it mattered one way or the other at this point in time. And did Cal really expect her to milk a cow? She had a feeling he did. Then what would she do? Her job description didn't include milking cows.

She closed her eyes. She would stay calm. None of this mattered as long as she got her story. Breathe in, breathe out. Okay, she was ready—maybe.

She grabbed her clothes and began dressing. She was just tying her hair back when she heard the screen door slam.

"Hey, have you noticed anything strange about the rooster?" Cal called from the other room.

Her hands stilled and her heart began to pound. She pictured the damned bird stiff from rigor mortis, skinny legs straight up in the air.

She took a deep breath and tried to sound innocent. "Rooster?"

"Yeah. He's acting kind of weird and walking funny."

"No, but then, I wouldn't know whether he was acting normal or not," she lied, swallowing past the lump in her throat. At least the rooster was still alive.

"I guess not. Maybe he ate some bad grain or something."

She breathed a sigh of relief. She was off the hook.

But then she looked in the mirror. Blue short-shorts and a yellow and blue top. The cute little outfit was made for walks along the beach or lazing around poolside with a tall frosted drink, not for roughing it. This was all she had that was appropriate, though.

Oh, well.

She glanced toward the door, then unbuttoned the last two buttons of the top and tied the ends beneath her bra. That was better. Slap a piece of straw in her mouth and call her Elly May Clampett. She rolled her eyes and left the bedroom.

She aimed toward the kitchen in desperate need of a strong cup of coffee and a bagel. Not that she remembered seeing any bagels in the boxes she'd carried inside.

"I don't suppose you made coffee while I was getting dressed?" she asked as she joined him, but she didn't smell the tantalizing aroma of a freshly brewed pot. She glanced toward the black beast of a stove and wondered how far it was to the closest Starbucks.

Cal didn't say anything. Just stared. When he continued staring without saying a word, she cocked an eyebrow. "Do I meet with your approval?"

"That's not exactly the kind of clothes made for roughing it."

But that was only his opinion. Her interpretation had a whole other meaning. "I'll need to go into town today and buy some . . ." Her gaze trailed over him. "Something a little more . . . appropriate." She kept her voice soft and sultry as she blatantly flirted with him. "Will this be okay for now?"

He dragged his gaze up to meet hers. "You'll do." His words were gruff. Without waiting for her, he pushed the door open and went outside.

Oh, yeah, he was definitely interested. She grinned. Score one for the city team. She'd have her article by the end of the day.

Just as quickly, her smile faded. There was still the cow to deal with and, apparently, she'd have to wait on coffee. He could've brought her a cup. A cinnamon mocha latte. She really missed the city, where there was a coffeehouse on practically every corner.

She went out the back door and trudged after Cal. "You know, I don't really like milk. It wouldn't bother me at all not to have any." She hurried to keep up with his long strides.

"You'll need the milk to make the butter." He stepped inside the dark interior of the small building.

"Butter? I thought—oomph!" Nikki thudded against his back. "Why'd you stop?" she complained but hesitated before moving away. She liked the feel of his hard, sinewy muscles against her. And he smelled nice, like soap and spicy aftershave. A thrill of pleasure ran down her spine. Now this was more like it.

"Always let your eyes adjust before you walk into a dark building," he informed her, his words interrupting her delicious thoughts.

"Why?"

"You never know what's crawling around."

A shiver ran over her. She had to ask.

"Well, next time tell me before you put the brakes on."

Her gaze moved around the interior, her eyes becoming accustomed to the dimness. To her left, hoes and shovels leaned against the wall. On the opposite side, bales of hay were stacked. The musty, not quite unpleasant scent rose to tickle her nose. She peered around Cal. More light came from the back of the barn. Instead of a wall, it opened into a pen.

Bessie glanced up when they approached and meandered over to the fence. "I thought Bessie was black and white."

"That was the other Bessie."

"Of course, how stupid of me not to have guessed you have two cows with the same name," she muttered.

Cal tipped the lid off a barrel and reached inside. "This is her feed. Give her two heaping scoops twice a day, but not until you're ready to start milking."

"I don't know how to milk a cow." And the other verse was she didn't want to learn.

"I wouldn't blame you if you threw in the towel. This is probably more than you ever expected."

She glared at him, grabbed the scoop, and tossed the feed over the fence into the wooden feed box. Bessie went directly to her breakfast. "Now what do I do?"

With a very snarky grin, he handed her a stool and a bucket. "You milk the cow."

Smart-ass. From his expression, she knew he was just waiting for her to run screaming from the barn. Well, she'd show him a thing or two. She jerked the stool and bucket away from him. Opening the gate, she tromped through to the other side.

When she stood next to the cow, her bluster disappeared. The animal was huge. Her back was almost shoulder high.

But her brown coat looked like the softest suede she'd ever seen. And the cow had big doe eyes with long black lashes. A big, brown Bambi. She was beautiful. She was . . .

Bessie's huge, saliva-dripping tongue emerged and partially disappeared up the cow's nose.

"Gross!" Ugh! Nikki almost gagged.

"What?"

She glanced at Cal, who seemed quite unaware that anything out of the ordinary had happened. "Nothing." She swallowed past the lump in her throat.

Cal opened and closed the gate, joining her in the small enclosure. He calmly waited for her to start. She gritted her teeth and set the stool beside the animal.

How hard could it be? Obviously, quite a few people milked cows because there always seemed to be a plentiful supply in the stores. She'd never heard of a death associated with milking a cow. Not that there couldn't be a first time.

Gingerly, she squatted on the stool and stared at the cow's bag. Four appendages, like fat fingers, pointed downward. Now what should she do?

As if he'd read her mind, Cal took the bucket from her. He walked to the trough and dipped some water. "The weather is warm enough so the water isn't too cool. Don't ever wash a cow's bag with cold water, though."

"How will I know if it's too cold?"

"Oh, she'll tell you. If it's cold to you, then it'll probably be cold to her." He handed her the bucket.

Nikki looked at it, then at the cow's bag. "Uh, do you have a washcloth?"

Cal grinned. "You don't need one. Just reach in the bucket, scoop some water up, splash it on her bag, and wipe with your hand."

"Oh." The instructions didn't sound difficult. Then why did she hesitate? She could answer that easily enough. She didn't want to touch the damned cow!

"At this rate Bessie will never get milked." Cal squatted beside her, took the bucket, and began to wash the cow's bag. "Bessie won't hurt you. A jersey is usually pretty docile." He quickly finished and tossed the unused water. "There, that wasn't hard." He turned to look at her.

Nikki forgot all about Bessie. His face was so close that his warm breath fanned her cheek. Shivers of excitement ran over her body.

He leaned closer. His lips brushed hers, like butterfly wings. Shock waves erupted inside her. He tasted like peppermint toothpaste and heat. Sweet and sexy. Spasms of pleasure stole over her as he deepened the kiss, his tongue caressing hers while his hand slipped around to the back of her neck and lightly massaged. Swirls of heat coiled inside her, then erupted, fire licking her in all the right places.

Cal pulled away all too soon.

She almost fell off the stool. Okay, take a deep breath, girl. She was the one in control.

Her flirting had worked. He'd fallen beneath her spell. It still took her a few seconds to regain her senses. He was a fantastic kisser.

"You kissed me." She leaned a little closer to him. One more and she'd have him completely bewitched.

"You wanted me to." He shrugged nonchalantly as he straightened. "Can't get your research done if all you're thinking about is kissing me."

Her thinking about kissing *him!* The *only* thing she'd been thinking about was seducing a story out of him. Of all the self-centered. . . . Before she could do more than sputter and spit, Cal grabbed her hand and wrapped it around one of Bessie's teats. Then he grabbed her other hand and did the same thing.

"Now, squeeze and pull, alternating hands," he told her.

Ugh! It was worse than she could've imagined. "I can't." Because she didn't want to!

"Pretend you have your fingers around someone's neck that you don't like. I'm sure there has to be someone in your life who pisses you off."

She scowled at him. She was looking right at the person who was currently raising her ire. It wouldn't be his neck she'd pretend she had her fingers wrapped around, though! Nikki squeezed and tugged on the teat, then another.

At first, nothing happened. On the fourth pull a stream of milk squirted out, pinging against the side of the bucket. She jerked her hands away.

"I did it!" She nearly fell off the stool in her excitement. She'd actually milked the cow. "Did you see that? And I hit the bucket, too."

"Yeah, I saw."

"Cal . . ."

"Don't get too excited about a little drop of milk. You still need to fill the bucket."

She pursed her lips as he turned away.

"I'll be back to check on your progress," he tossed over his shoulder as he walked away.

And she'd milk the damned cow even if it killed her. She'd show him! Fill the bucket, indeed! Not that she thought he was telling her the truth about that. It would take her all day to fill the bucket.

Cal drew in a deep breath as he stepped from the barn. Why had he kissed her? That was easy to answer. When Nikki turned to look at him all he saw were those luscious lips tempting him. How the hell was he supposed to resist?

He wasn't immune to her even knowing she was a reporter and was here only to get a story. Damn it! He still shouldn't have kissed her. If he didn't watch out, he'd get himself into trouble because Nikki sure hadn't seemed to mind his touch. But one thing had kept him from seeing just how far she'd let him go.

He didn't trust her as far as he could throw her.

Not when he knew the story was all that mattered to her. He had the upper hand and planned to keep it. He didn't care how she dressed or how much she flirted—he wouldn't fall for her tricks.

If she'd done her research, Nikki would know that she wouldn't get her story that easily. He was a hell of a lot tougher than that.

He strolled to the pickup, grabbed a sack of feed, and slung it over his shoulder before carrying it toward the barn. By the time he got there, he was back in complete control. As he set the sack just inside the door, he could hear Nikki mumbling.

"Well, that's just great!" Nikki jumped from the stool, taking her milk bucket with her.

He leaned against a bail of hay and listened.

"You couldn't wait to go to the bathroom? It's not as though you had all the time in the world before I sat down. I saw you and you were just standing at the fence doing nothing."

A slow grin spread across his face. She didn't really sound angry, just put out. Damn, she was cute.

"In the future, I'd appreciate it if you'd see to your bodily functions prior to being milked. Just because you're a cow doesn't mean you can't have any manners."

Cal barely contained his laughter. She'd call it quits now. She might be The Barracuda, but this ranch didn't have an ocean for her to swim in and it didn't look like it would be that long before she'd go looking for bluer waters.

But she didn't leave.

He quickly sobered when she repositioned the stool and sat back down. She had mettle, he'd give her that. There was no way she'd last, but yeah, she did have mettle. Odd, but his grandfather always told Cal that you could judge a person by how much spirit the person had.

Well, she may have spirit but it was for all the wrong reasons.

"Ugh! You stink."

Bessie turned her head and looked at Nikki, mooing an apology.

"Those big eyes won't get you anywhere, and I'm not going to forgive you—at least not for a while. You should be down here inhaling this obnoxious odor."

Cal grinned as he went back to his pickup for the other sack of feed. It was already proving to be an interesting day. And he had to admit, she was kind of fun to have around. He hadn't minded kissing her, either. No, he hadn't minded that at all.

Chapter 7

"At this rate, you won't finish in time to start the evening milking," Cal said as he came up behind Nikki.

She jumped, almost knocking over the milk bucket, and she'd worked hard for that cup of milk.

She stopped long enough to look over her shoulder and give Cal her freeze-you-in-your-tracks glare. He had the nerve to grin. A lesser man would've turned and run away as fast as he could. Now that she thought about it, that might explain why she hadn't had sex in a while.

Then his words sank into her brain. "What do you mean, *evening* milking?" she asked. Surely, he was joking. She looked at the cow's bag. No, it wasn't possible that it would fill up again that fast.

"Bessie needs to be milked twice a day," Cal said, confirming her worst fear.

Well, hell.

She glanced inside the bucket. "I thought I was doing pretty good," she grumbled. She had enough for a tall latte, except now she thought she might start drinking her coffee minus the milk. It was a lot different when you actually saw where the milk was coming from.

He motioned for her to get up. "Let me show you how a pro does it."

Gladly, and she didn't even care that he was apparently

better at it than her. Not that she thought he would get much more milk out of the cow.

She stood, flexing her fingers, and moved out of his way. She would think on the bright side. If she had to milk the cow twice a day, she would probably drop a ring size by the time she had her story and was out of here.

She eyed the three-legged wooden stool. On the other hand, her butt might get broader from all the sitting. Not a good trade-off. But when Cal pulled the stool under him, she noticed his butt looked pretty darn good from this angle. Not bad at all.

"Sah, Bessie," Cal spoke softly when Bessie turned to look at the newcomer. The cow quickly settled down as Cal began to milk her.

Milk immediately pinged against the sides of the bucket. Okay, so he was better at milking than she'd been. She frowned. But that wasn't all. Bessie seemed more content that Cal was the one doing the milking. It would seem he was good with animals, and women.

Well, except Cynthia. Which reminded her that she was here to get a story.

"You're a lot faster," she told him.

"Years of practice."

"Are you partners with your brother?" she asked, keeping her words casual. For a moment, she wondered if he was going to answer or if he had even heard her. He seemed pretty intent on finishing the milking.

"No, I'm just visiting a few weeks," he finally spoke.

Had the pinging of the milk against the side of the bucket gotten a little faster? Maybe he'd been asked so many questions in the past that he was leery of answering more. But then, she was good at making people feel at ease. It usually didn't take long for them to open up to her.

"It's good that you can visit him." She casually leaned against the fence. "Do you live in Texas?"

"All my life."

That told her absolutely zip. Again, something still didn't feel quite right. It was as though he was evading her questions. She wondered again if he knew her real reason for being here.

"I play football," he said.

She breathed a sigh of relief. Of course he didn't know she was trying to get a story. She really had to stop being so paranoid. Being out of her element was really doing a number on her, and she was so out of her element here in the country.

"Football?" she asked.

"Professional. Do you watch the games?"

"No, sorry. Do you enjoy tossing a ball around?"

"It's a living."

Her ears perked up. "You don't like it?"

"I still enjoy the thrill of competition, but the hard knocks I can do without." He stood, bucket in hand. "That and the nosey reporters. They have a way of taking things out of context. They look at one part of my life and blow it out of proportion."

Yeah, she felt much more confident about prying a story out of him. He needed to look at it from her angle. She was reporting what people needed to know: the dirty politicians, corporations skimming from their shareholders, corruption and fraud in the government.

Except that wasn't exactly the case this time. Not even close, and guilt didn't sit well with her.

"But then, I don't have to worry about reporters out here," he said, drawing her attention back to him.

She couldn't meet his gaze. Instead, she glanced inside the bucket. Her eyes widened. Okay, now he'd impressed her. Frothy white milk came up to the rim of the bucket. "How did you fill it so fast?"

"It just takes practice. I was raised on this ranch and I grew up milking cows."

This was much safer than talking about reporters and she could get a little background on him. "Your parents owned it?"

"No, they were killed in a car wreck when my brother, Brian, was just a baby."

"I'm sorry." And she meant it. She couldn't imagine growing up without her parents. They were great, even though time with them had been at a premium, but the moments they'd shared together had been quality time.

Even now, they made a point of meeting once every two months on the second Saturday. They always went out to eat at her favorite restaurant and caught up with each other's lives. It worked out well all around.

"It was a long time ago," he continued. "Our grandparents more than made up for the fact we were orphaned. They kept the memory of our parents alive while giving us all the love we could ever need. They were very special."

"They're gone?"

He nodded. "But what they taught us lives on. They had a strong code of ethics." He opened the gate, then waited for her to pass. "Like truth, being fair, causing no harm to others, and giving more than you get."

Nikki had a feeling liars would rate low with him. Well, she wasn't a reporter because she was trying to win a popularity contest. People wanted the news and she gave them what they asked for.

She chewed on her lower lip. Except she usually didn't do fluff pieces. She would much rather go after crooked politicians.

They walked out of the barn and up to the house. The air was still cool and crisp as it caressed her skin.

"Did you like growing up here on the ranch?" she asked.

"There was a lot of stuff to do."

"Like what?"

He shrugged. "Chores: milking, feeding the animals, fixing fence. We hauled a little hay. The usual things that people do on a ranch."

"It sounds like hard work."

"Some of it was." He stopped at the porch and looked

around. There was a faraway expression on his face. "But we had good times, too."

She wondered what he saw that she didn't. As she looked around, she thought it might have been nice knowing the young Cal as he galloped across the pasture with his brother.

Damn, now she was starting to sound maudlin. Was this what the country air did to a person? She needed a shot of the city to take her back to reality! Maybe she'd call Marge later and see what was happening. Nikki was already starting to feel disconnected.

Once inside the kitchen, Cal set the milk on the wooden counter; no fancy granite here.

"There was a strainer in one of the boxes," he told her. "Do you remember where you put it?"

She went to one of the drawers she'd cleaned out and got it. She'd wondered why he'd brought it. Made her wonder about some of the other things she'd put away.

He slid a large glass jar closer and put the strainer on top. "Hold it in place and I'll pour the milk."

She did as he asked, her nose wrinkling when she caught the scent of warm, fresh milk.

"It doesn't smell like store-bought. It's a lot richer, too." Cal set the empty bucket in the sink and covered the milk with a cloth.

"I noticed. Shouldn't we put it in the icebox?"

"Not until the cream rises to the top. Then you skim it off so you can make butter."

"I don't really need butter."

"How can you write a story if you can't describe making butter?"

He was right—dammit. "I didn't mean I didn't want to make it, only that I won't need much," she quickly backtracked. "I can't wait to get started making butter."

"Of course." He leaned his hip against the counter and crossed his arms in front of him. "Exactly what kind of book are you writing, anyway? You never really said. Just that it was about how pioneers lived. Is it a straight history piece or what?"

"I'm covering from the statehood forward. It'll be like a textbook. I'm up to the nineteen twenties." That sounded good, believable. She looked him right in the eye, never wavering her gaze even though her body tensed.

"I'd like to read it."

"Now?" Her pulse sped up.

"When you get it finished."

Nikki breathed a sigh of relief. "Good. I don't like anyone to see my work until it's completed. Stifles the creativity and all."

How many lies could she tell in one day? Apparently, quite a few. But he looked as though he bought every word. And why shouldn't he. She was damned good at what she did.

Cal watched for a sign that Nikki might feel an ounce of remorse for lying through those pretty white teeth. He didn't see even one spark of guilt.

It was time to bring out more artillery. No, he wasn't even close to finished with her yet. "You ready to gather eggs?"

She paled just a little. "Will the rooster be there?" She ran her hands up and down her arms as if there were a sudden chill in the air.

What was it with the rooster? He had a feeling it might have something to do with why the bird was acting funny. "I'm sure he'll be around somewhere. He usually watches over the hens."

She drew in a deep breath and nodded as though she were about to face a firing squad and knew she deserved to be shot. Yeah, it was a strange reaction.

And she didn't look any better once they were standing in front of the chicken coop. He was starting to feel a little sorry for her. Especially when the rooster came lurching around the corner. The bird took one look at her and began to flap its wings and squawk.

"Damnedest thing I've ever seen," he said as the rooster

flapped and squawked back around the side of the barn and out of sight like a bat out of hell.

"It won't return, will it?" She hugged her middle and eyed the direction the bird had gone.

He couldn't blame her for being nervous. The rooster acted as though it were possessed or something. "I don't know. I wonder if a rattler might have gotten him."

Her face paled. "Rattler, as in rattlesnake?" Her gaze darted to the ground.

"We have them sometimes. They'll let you know when they're around. The sound of a snake's rattle is like nothing you've ever heard before."

"Oh, that makes me feel a lot better."

"Just stop in your tracks and look around. Most of the time, they're only warning you to keep your distance."

"And what about the other times? Do snakes have really pissy days and strike for no reason whatsoever?"

"I'm sure women who lived on the range had to put up with a lot more than rattlesnakes and a goofy rooster."

Her shoulders squared. "And that's exactly why I'm writing this book."

Cal bit back the words he wanted to say, but it took a lot of effort on his part. Nikki wasn't nearly as good as she thought she was. Even if Jeff hadn't told him she was a reporter, Cal had a feeling he'd see through her act. She might be good with sleazy politicians, but his granddad didn't raise any fools.

But he'd play her game a little longer and see what happened. Maybe because she was so damned easy on the eyes. "Then you'd better gather the eggs."

For all her bravado, she timidly stepped forward, stopping in front of the wooden bins where the hens nested. He had a feeling she didn't back down from much. Not and have a nickname like The Barracuda. She was out of her element and in way over her head at the ranch.

But that didn't make her any less sexy. He caught a whiff

of her perfume, savoring the heady scent as it wrapped around him, tempting him to step a little closer, to do more than kiss her this time.

"Now what do I do," she asked, breaking the spell.

It was probably a good thing she had, too. "Just stick your hand inside and get the eggs. This first one is easy since the chicken is out roaming around."

"She's not going to come back and see me stealing her eggs, is she? I don't want to be on her hit list or anything."

"I doubt it. Didn't you ever hunt Easter eggs?"

"No, my parents didn't want to fill my head with a lot of nonsense."

"Nonsense?" He readjusted his hat and stared at her. "What about Christmas and other holidays?"

"We each exchanged one gift, but they made sure I knew there was no such thing as a fat, jolly man in a red suit." She glanced his way and apparently noted his stunned expression. "You think it's better to lie to a child? Let the child believe in something that doesn't truly exist?"

"I think it's better to let children have fantasies and dreams—let them be children and not force them to grow up, to become little adults."

"Apparently it didn't hurt me."

He begged to differ, but for now, he kept his thoughts to himself. One of his best memories was waking up on Christmas morning to the aroma of fresh-baked pumpkin bread, the Christmas lights twinkling on the tree, and scratchy Christmas songs playing on the old record player.

His grandmother would have the table set with the china that had been passed down from her grandmother. There were a few chips and dings, and it hadn't been a complete set of dishes in years, but the set was priceless to her. His grandmother said each plate had a story, and every year she would tell them one.

He and Brian had discussed her stories once and come to the conclusion that she more often than not made them up, but she was really good at telling them, and they enjoyed listening to them, so they never said anything.

Cal couldn't imagine the kind of holidays Nikki had celebrated. They sounded cold. Maybe that was why people called her The Barracuda.

Nikki reached into the bin and grabbed the egg, then put it in the basket he'd brought with them. She cocked an eyebrow as if to say gathering eggs wasn't all that hard. Then she stepped to the next bin and saw the hen still sitting inside. She stared it down for a few seconds before looking at Cal.

"I don't think she wants to move."

"Probably not."

"And?"

"You reach under her and get the eggs."

"Won't she . . ."

"Peck you? No."

Nikki took a deep breath. He really liked the way she inhaled. He also liked the expanse of skin she showed. When he'd first seen that she'd tied the ends of her shirt under her breasts, he'd wondered if she was trying to seduce a story out of him. Not that he minded that much. He kind of liked the fact she put so much into her job.

"Ow!" She jerked her hand back, then glared at him. "You lied."

"You were too slow. She sensed your fear and took advantage of you. You need to get the eggs faster." He reached under the hen and got the egg the chicken was sitting on. The hen didn't do a thing to him. "Easy as pie."

"I wasn't afraid of her." She jutted her chin.

The chicken rose slightly, puffing out her chest. "Block, block, block."

"I think she's taunting me, though."

He laughed. It was hard to stay angry with Nikki, especially now that he knew a little more about her. So what if she was trying to get a story. It didn't mean he had to give her one.

And she'd definitely chased away his boredom. He liked

watching her as she faced challenge after challenge and didn't back down. Kind of reminded Cal of when he played football. He never let anyone stand in his way.

Of course, she'd probably kill him when she found out he knew she was a reporter after a story on him and Cynthia. He kind of figured turnabout was fair play, though.

She reached under the next bird and brought out two eggs, then placed them in the basket. She tried to bite back a smile, but it still formed on her face.

"I did it," she said and didn't have to add, "I told you so" because it was written all over her face. When he didn't say anything, she continued, "Unless I have to do something else with the egg? I don't, do I?"

"No, just fry it and eat it."

She sighed with relief.

A soft morning breeze blew a strand of hair across her face. He automatically reached over and brushed it back. His hand stilled, liking the silky-smooth texture of her cheek. Yeah, his life was definitely not boring with her around.

"Are you going to kiss me again?" Her lips pouted in open invitation and she leaned a little closer.

It would be damned easy to fall into her trap. "I don't think so." He turned away and quickly gathered the rest of the eggs.

She squared her shoulders. A frown wrinkled her forehead. "Why not?"

"Why not what?" He pretended not to know what she was talking about as he walked back toward the house.

"Why don't you want to kiss me? We both enjoyed the first one."

He didn't answer until he had gone inside and set the basket on the counter. "Because you look like you want it too much." He could've added, "because I want it too much," but he decided that much knowledge could be dangerous in her hands.

"And there's something wrong with that?"

He made the mistake of looking at her. She leaned back, elbows resting on the counter, which thrust her breasts forward. Damn, his hands began to itch with the need to touch them, massage them.

Before Cal could stop himself, he let his gaze move over her. From her sultry half-closed eyes, to her full lips, down to the expanse of bare skin below where her shirt was tied. Past her tiny waist and over her gently rounded hips and down her long, long legs.

He slowly made the trek back to her face and the knowing look in her eyes. Yeah, she knew exactly what she was doing to him, and what's more, she was doing it very well.

Swallowing was difficult. Hell, it was even hard for him to breathe when all he could think about was kissing her, stripping off her clothes, and making love to her.

Dammit, she was taunting him.

He sauntered closer. So close there were only inches between them. Nikki tilted her head and looked up at him, then slowly licked her lips. It was all he could do to stifle the groan that threatened to escape.

"Sweetheart, I more than enjoyed the kiss. It made me think of other things that I'd like to do." He brushed her hair behind her ear, enjoying the feel once again of her soft skin.

She probably used the finest creams to keep her skin soft. He remembered what Jeff had told him about her parents: wealthy lawyers. Maybe she hadn't celebrated holidays the way he had, but she'd led a life of privilege, never knowing any kind of hardship. Just like Cynthia.

He planned to teach Nikki a lesson she wouldn't soon forget. Before she left the ranch, she'd have a whole new outlook on life.

"Other things?" She visibly swallowed.

His gaze dropped down to her breasts. Her bra must be thin. Silk? Her nipples were pushed tight against the fabric of her top. He lightly circled one before he ran his finger over the pebbled hardness. She whimpered. He watched her face. Her eyes had closed and she nibbled on her bottom lip.

His body began to throb. He hadn't meant to go any further than this, but what he shouldn't do was pushed to the back of his mind as the need inside him grew stronger. How far would she go?

He leaned closer, testing the waters. "I want to see you naked. I want to suck on your breasts, caress your skin."

He slipped his hand between her legs and rubbed it against her sex. She nudged her crotch against his hand, silently begging for more.

"Are you hot? Are you damp with need? Do you want me inside you?" he whispered.

Chapter 8

Nikki couldn't swallow. Hell, she could barely breathe. Only one thing ran across her mind: she wanted Cal Braxton, had wanted him from the moment she saw his picture.

Now he was touching her, whispering words in her ears that made her burn with desire. The story didn't matter as she lived out the fantasies she'd been having about the rugged football player.

Oh, yeah, she could care less about the damned story. At least, at this moment in time. She'd think about it later. But the man? That was a whole different matter and she most certainly wanted him.

"Make love to me," she moaned.

"Are you sure?" he muttered as he nuzzled her neck, his hot breath teasing her neck.

"Yes," she said, barely holding back a moan of desire. She tugged his shirt out of his pants and quickly unbuttoned it, then could only stare at his male beauty. *God, look at all those delicious muscles!* And they were all hers to caress while she had her way with Cal.

He pulled at the knot in her shirt until it came loose, then fumbled with the buttons, not having much luck.

"You're too slow." She brushed his hands away and unbuttoned her top, then yanked it off. Her bra quickly followed.

Cal stood in front of her, mouth open.

She arched an eyebrow. "Don't tell me you've never seen a naked woman, because I won't believe you."

He came out of his daze and practically ripped off his shirt the rest of the way. "No, I've seen lots of naked women, but they're not quite this brazen about it."

"Does it bother you?"

"Not in the least."

She popped the button on her shorts through the hole and slid the zipper down. "Good, because when I see something I want, I usually go after it. Why should I deny myself?"

He grinned. "You want me?"

Oh, Lord, now he was going on an ego trip. She slid off her shorts, then her panties. "I'm naked and I'm standing in front of you. What do you think?" she asked as he kicked out of his jeans and briefs.

She'd known there was a reason she wanted him. Nice, very nice and she couldn't resist not touching a second longer. She stepped closer, running a fingernail over the hard ridges of his chest, the six-pack abs, all that deliciously tanned skin.

"No tan lines," she said.

"There's a pond on the ranch that I like to go swimming in when I'm here."

"And you don't own a suit?"

"Don't need one since no one goes there but me. I don't wear one when I go swimming in my pool at home, either."

"I bet your female neighbors just love that." She stepped closer, licking across first one nipple and then the other. He tasted salty, nice.

Before Nikki could do more exploring, he ran his hands through her hair, then grasped her neck and rubbed lightly. She closed her eyes, then leaned back. He took the opportunity to massage a breast, tweaking the nipple.

"Oh, yes, that feels good." She opened her eyes, saw the passion in his. She liked knowing he wanted her as much as she wanted him.

"It seems like forever since I've been with a woman."

She had to bite her tongue to keep from asking about Cynthia. His ex-fiancée didn't matter. Not right now. Nikki only wanted Cal buried deep inside her.

But curiosity got the better of her. "You haven't been with anyone in a while, either?" she asked, liking that he hadn't been with Cynthia recently. If he wasn't lying, that is. Men seemed to know what they should say to a woman, and she'd heard it all before in other relationships.

He stilled. "Do you really want to talk about past affairs?"

She shook her head. "No."

He relaxed. "Good."

Cal scooped her into his arms. She grabbed him around his neck as he headed toward the bedroom. Naked skin against naked skin. She'd never been carried to the bedroom before. It was something she could get used to.

But when he set her on her feet, she took charge again. It was a role she didn't give up easily and she wasn't about to start now.

She pushed on his shoulders until he was sitting on the bed. Her plan was to be the one on top, but he caught her unaware again.

"Nice view," he drawled.

His breath blew lightly across the curls that covered her sex. Cal didn't just look but clasped her bottom and brought her body closer to his face, his mouth.

"I'm supposed to be on top," she gasped, grabbing hold of his shoulders for support. "I wanted you to lie back on the bed."

His chuckle vibrated against her, sending trembles of delight over her. She bit her bottom lip. God, that had felt good.

"So, you were going to have your way with me." He began to place soft kisses against the folds of her sex.

"Yes," she gasped as she clung to him. "Right there. Yes." She pressed her body closer. So what if she'd let him take control. As long as he didn't stop what he was doing, she didn't care. His tongue was making her wild. When he told her to spread her legs, she obeyed without question.

He inserted a finger inside her and began a slow in-out motion while his mouth continued its heated assault. He licked up her clit, then back down before sucking on the fleshy skin. She couldn't stop the moan as it escaped past her dry lips.

The blood rushed through her body. She could feel her heart beating faster and faster. A deep, throbbing began to build inside her. Her body clenched, then unclenched. She couldn't take a deep breath. All she could manage to draw inside her oxygen-deprived lungs were little puffs of air.

Her body began to tremble as his mouth continued to suck, his tongue scraping across the fleshy part, drawing it into his mouth. She cried out as intense pleasure washed over her, wave after wave of incredible gratification.

She vaguely knew when Cal picked her up and laid her on the bed. She curled on her side, her legs clasped together. He covered her with the quilt.

A condom, of course. He would be slipping back into the kitchen to get one out of his pants. She should've told him there was one in the bedside drawer. Too late now.

When he returned, they would finish what they'd started. She would just rest for a moment. Damn, he was good, damned good, but as soon as he came back, she would be in charge and she had a few tricks of her own.

Cal walked into the kitchen and grabbed his briefs off the floor, pulling them on. When his hand bumped his dick, he groaned. Ah, damn, the ache inside him was almost too much to bear.

This was the craziest thing he'd ever done and he was afraid it was only going to get worse. He planned on leaving. That would piss her off. Show her that he had no invested interest in her. She was just a woman who'd needed gratification and he'd given her that. This would really teach her a lesson.

Had he lost his freakin' mind?

What the hell was he doing?

He closed his eyes, but all he saw was Nikki—naked and waiting for him. He could be plunging into her wet heat right now.

Involuntarily, his hips thrust forward but there was nothing there to sink into. He grabbed the edge of the counter and held on for a moment, taking deep, steadying breaths.

His body throbbed with need. He could almost taste her again, could almost feel the softness of her skin, could almost see her legs parting for him.

Lesson be damned. Leaving now was a crazy idea.

He grabbed a condom out of his pocket and jerked off his briefs before heading back into the bedroom. She lay curled on her side, but she'd tugged the quilt under her chin until her backside was exposed. He reached out and lightly stroked the cheek of her ass.

Nikki stretched and turned. As she did, she pushed the covers off and spread her legs in invitation. He swallowed hard and gazed down on that sweet clit he'd sucked on only a moment ago. Heat spread through him like a fire out of control.

He lay down beside her, and she turned and wrapped her arms around him. As his mouth lowered to hers, he cupped her ass and brought her against his dick. Man, just the contact with her sex against his almost made him come.

She teased him with her tongue, stroking his. He relaxed, enjoying what she was doing. When she shoved him to his back, he was caught off guard, not that he wouldn't have gone willingly at this point in time.

"I don't know how long I can last," he told her. "Two seconds might be an accurate assumption."

"Are you in pain?"

Her innocence didn't fool him for a second. There wasn't anything innocent about her. "You know damn well I am, and I think I dropped the condom."

She scooted to her knees and stared down at him as he lay

naked in front of her. "Then let me remedy that." She leaned over him, her breasts brushing across his face as she reached inside the drawer of the bedside table.

He couldn't resist. He sucked a nipple into his mouth. She gasped with pleasure.

"I'm supposed to be relieving you of your pain," she told him, her words raspy, but he noticed she didn't seem to be in any hurry to move away.

He swirled his tongue around her nipple one last time before releasing it. "I thought you were offering up your delights for me to savor."

She grabbed a condom and tore it open, but when he reached for it, she moved it away.

"I'll do it." She slowly rolled it down his length.

He only thought he was in pain before. He gripped the sheet in his hands. When she licked her lips, he lost it. He flipped her onto her back and drove into her hot, slick body. She dug her fingernails into his back and gasped.

"Damn, I'm sorry. I didn't mean to be so brutal."

"Brutal? I don't think so." She laughed as she wrapped her legs around him so that he sank deeper inside her body. "I told you, I like it rough and I like it hard. There's nothing soft about me, baby."

With a growl, he pulled out, then plunged back inside. The heat of her body wrapped around him. He plunged in again and again.

"Oh, yes, harder, faster."

He looked at her face and saw the passion building. She bit her bottom lip, her breathing ragged. His body burned with the need for release, but he still held back.

"Oh, God, yes. This is what I want. Now, now!" she cried out. She arched toward him as she came.

He might have cried out, but he wasn't sure. Lights exploded around him, plunging him forward into a haze of brilliant color. His body trembled and the burning ache inside him began to relax its hold.

This was good, damned good. He'd never been with a woman who enjoyed sex as much as Nikki did. He sank down to the bed, careful to roll to his side. She opened her eyes and looked at him—then laughed.

He frowned and she laughed even more. "I can say with one hundred percent certainty that no woman has ever laughed after I've made love to her."

"I laughed because I've never had sex this good. I've dreamed about it, came close to experiencing it, but it's never been like this." Her grin was wicked. "Was it good for you?"

For a moment, he let what had happened wash over him.

He'd made love before. The first time had been in the back of Jenny Bradley's Mustang. She'd been a senior in high school and he a lowly freshman. Cal had thought he'd died and gone to heaven that night. Some part of him had known he'd never feel the same kind of intensity that only the first time brings with it.

Until now.

This was some lesson he was teaching Nikki. At least, if she wrote about making love with him, it would be a great series of articles.

Chapter 9

"Hey, Shelley, feeling better?" Brian asked his secretary as he started toward his office. Her nose was a little red and she still talked funny. He wondered if she should've stayed at home another day or so.

"I feel better." She grabbed a tissue out of the box and sneezed. "I hate getting a cold at the end of summer. People should only get colds during the winter—when it's cold. This is so not fair."

He frowned. "You don't look like you feel better. Maybe you should take another day or two off."

She handed him the morning mail. "All I do at home is sleep."

"Did you ever think your body might be trying to tell you something?"

"I'm fine, really."

He still didn't like the way she sounded or looked. "If you're still fine by lunch I want you to go home."

"Funny," she muttered.

He glanced at the stack of letters. Shelley would've already gone through the mail and discarded the junk. Brian didn't know how he'd ever managed without her.

"I'm glad you came in today, though," he told her.

She gave a very unladylike snort. "That's because your brother was screwing everything up."

He paused, hand on the door, then nodded thoughtfully. "Yeah, that pretty much sums it up. Great football player but lousy secretary."

"You should see the sticky notes he left all over my desk. It's a good thing I came in early to sort through them. I'm still not finished."

"Then I'm doubly glad you're back." He smiled. "But I still want you out of here by lunch. And remind me to give you a bonus."

"You already give me a very nice one at Christmas, thank you very much." She sneezed again.

"Then remind me to make it bigger this year."

Her chuckle turned into a cough.

Brian started to go inside his office but paused at the last second when he remembered something else. "Do you know what time the woman I'm interviewing for the massage therapist position is supposed to be here?"

Shelley held up a small pile of sticky notes. "Your guess is as good as mine. Cal said today. That's all I know." She grimaced and shook her head.

"Well, send her in when she gets here."

"Will do, boss."

He went inside his office and closed the door, tossed the mail on his desk, and went to the window. He had a nice view of the front of the ranch and the tree-lined driveway. His office had originally been part of the living room. His grandfather's chair had been exactly where Brian's chair now sat.

Sometimes, if he closed his eyes, he could see him, feet propped on the footstool, pipe on the small round table.

"Now let me tell you the story about when I was a young fella. Times weren't near as easy as they are now," he'd say. Then he'd laugh and tell him and Cal a story. They would be enthralled with his descriptions of the way things used to be.

Man, he missed him a lot.

Or maybe it was just the family atmosphere he missed. Hearing his grandmother humming softly in the kitchen as she baked. Grandma had loved to cook and no one had ever been able to duplicate her rolls. He missed her homemade breads. He missed a lot of things.

It was good that Cal was home, even if he'd be leaving soon. And Brian knew he would. Cal liked the country but he wasn't passionate about it. His enthusiasm lay in sports. Brian guessed everyone needed something that he or she cared deeply about.

The sound of a car pulling up in the circular gravel drive-way drew his attention and he glanced out the window again. His eyes widened. At least he thought it was a car. The only thing holding it together was rust. At one time it might have been green, but it was hard to tell.

The person inside cut the engine. The car rattled and shook before backfiring, exploding a cloud of thick black smoke out of the tailpipe.

Whoever it was had to be lost. And down on his or her luck. He only hoped the person's car had enough get-up-and-go to make it off the property. The car looked totally out of place, surrounded by the manicured lawns and the three-tiered fountain that spilled water over each rim.

Then she emerged. A vision in flowing robes, her hair tied back in a vibrant purple scarf. She stood beside the car, took a deep breath, and raised her arms toward the sun as if pay-ing homage.

Or maybe she was just thankful she'd made it without her car exploding.

Brian didn't even realize he was holding his breath until she turned toward his window. There was no way she could see past the dark screen, but for just a second it felt as though she could.

She was beautiful, ethereal, and she didn't just walk to the front door and out of his line of vision. No, it was more like she glided on air.

Was she a guest? The people who stayed at the ranch were from various walks of life.

Could she afford to stay here? His prices were reasonable, but from the shape her car was in, he didn't think she could pay the price. Hell, after just one look he was tempted to comp her room. The woman had literally taken his breath away.

A moment later, his phone buzzed. He moved to his chair and sat down, pushing the intercom button. "Yes, Shelley."

"Your massage therapist is here."

He looked out the window, then toward his door. Damn, that was the last thing he'd expected.

"Send her in." He had a feeling his vision of loveliness was about to become a problem. He didn't need another problem.

A few seconds passed before Shelley opened the door and ushered the woman inside his office. She breezed past Shelley and took the seat he motioned toward.

"You have a wonderful office." She smiled and her whole face lit up.

He guessed her to be in her early twenties, maybe twenty-two. Not much experience for a massage therapist. He wanted someone like Amy, his last one, who'd abruptly moved away. She'd given only a few days' notice, which had left him in a bind.

Okay, so maybe he didn't want someone exactly like Amy.

But in everything else, Amy had been reliable. She'd been in her late thirties and had worked as a therapist for over ten years. This girl couldn't have more than a year or so under her belt. One thing he prided himself on was offering only the best for his guests.

"Thank you," he said. "I designed the room myself."

He might as well be friendly before he sent her on her way. He'd make sure she had money and he could probably get Jake at the filling station to check out her car. He didn't want to think about her stranded on the side of the road.

"No," she said. "It's more than that."

He raised his eyebrows. Or she could've escaped from the nuthouse.

She laughed. A light, musical sound. It was almost as though she'd read his thoughts. That was impossible, of course, but she was cute.

"I can feel the love in this room."

How the hell could she know what this room used to be? Goose bumps popped up on his arms. "It's an office." A real nutcase, that was all she was.

She shook her head. The silver hoops in her pierced ears swung hypnotically back and forth. "No, it's much more than that." She closed her eyes and breathed in deeply. "I can smell the remnants of pipe tobacco."

Now she was starting to worry him. "I don't smoke."

"Someone did. I can feel the love emanating from the spirit this person left behind." She opened her eyes. "People leave a part of their spirit behind. Did you know that? That's why we occasionally catch a glimpse of someone who's crossed over or hear their laughter or even smell a pipe they used to smoke. That's part of who they were. I think this person loved very deeply and he must've been very kind to leave such a strong reminder behind. Do you know this person?"

He cleared his throat. "My grandfather used to smoke a pipe. I'm sure there's a lingering odor. It's hard to get the smell out."

"I see." She bowed her head slightly.

"What do you see?" This was one strange bird.

"You don't believe in ghosts."

He twitched. Not that much, but he could see in her eyes that she'd caught his nervous movement.

"Or do you?"

"Of course I don't." Cal was right: he'd only imagined he'd seen something at the cabin. "You're looking for a job?" he asked, steering the conversation back to why the woman was here.

"I already have one."

"Then why are you here?"

"You hired me."

He pinched the bridge of his nose. He could already see this was going to be a very long day. "I don't think we'd gotten to that point yet."

She nodded. "There was a Dallas newspaper at the truck stop. I saw the ad and called about the job. You hired me. I finished what I needed to do yesterday, then left very early this morning to get here." Her brow knitted in worry. "Are you going to tell me I don't have a job?"

For the first time since she'd gotten out of her car, he saw her confidence falter. That's when he noticed the dark circles under her eyes. Just smudges, but they were there. Damn, he felt bad that he couldn't hire her, but the woman was obviously delusional.

"We didn't talk on the phone," he gently told her, hoping she would understand.

"You're not Cal?"

Of course. Cal. He should've guessed. His brother could have told him he'd hired her. He was going to kill him. Slowly and with great pleasure.

Business was business and Brian only hired the best. Tamping down the pity he felt, he looked at the young woman. "You can rest in the previous therapist's room and I'll have someone take a look at your car, but I think you're too young for what I'm looking for. You can't have that much experience."

"There's good experience and bad experience. Good massage therapists and bad. For the record, I'm twenty-eight. And you don't have any idea what I can do until you try me."

She was right about that. He still wasn't sure. And she looked younger than twenty-eight. No more than . . . than . . . okay, maybe she did look twenty-eight. Why did he feel so much older when there was only three years' difference?

"I'll give you a massage. That should convince you."

He thought of her hands kneading the taut muscles in his back, moving lower and lower.

Her giving him a massage wasn't going to happen. It had been too damned long since he'd even been out with a woman. Cal was right. He'd been working too many long hours. He cleared his throat and shuffled through some papers on his desk. "I have work to do," he said.

She nodded. "I can see you've already convinced yourself I won't work out. Thank you so much for your time."

When she stood, she weaved just a little and grabbed the back of the chair to steady herself. It was almost imperceptible, but he saw it.

"You can't drive in your condition."

She raised an eyebrow. "I assure you, I haven't been drinking."

"No, but you're so tired you'll probably fall asleep at the wheel and kill yourself or someone unfortunate enough to be on the road." Damn, why did she have to be his responsibility? Didn't he have enough as it was?

And he still didn't have a massage therapist. He looked at her. She was right: he didn't know if she was any good or not until she started working.

He made a quick, and hopefully not stupid, decision. "Okay, I'll give you the job, but it's on a trial basis only."

"Thank you."

"What's your name?" He might need to know that since he'd officially hired her.

Her gray-green eyes sparkled. "Celeste Star."

He had a feeling he was going to regret this.

Chapter 10

Cal looked up when he heard the soft pad of footsteps behind him. He had to blink so his vision cleared. For a moment, he wondered if he'd died and God had sent an angel down to get him, but then he thought about his life and didn't figure he'd get an escort. At least not one who was this pretty, and he had a feeling it would be debatable which direction he'd be going.

"Good morning," he said.

She studied him for a moment. "You're Cal Braxton, the football player."

"The one and only."

He was surprised she knew who he was. She didn't look the type who watched sports. His gaze swept over her. She didn't look like a guest, either. Not like any who came to stay at the ranch, anyway. Not this young and pretty, anyway.

The outfit she wore was long and flowing, in a rainbow of colors. Hues ranging from deep purples to brilliant oranges ebbed and flowed when she moved. She reminded him of a little fairy—like Tinker Bell.

She smiled and the room lit up. "I'm just surprised I didn't put two and two together when we spoke on the phone. You scored five touchdowns last year against KC. Not bad, not bad at all."

People had been surprising him all year. Cynthia, when

she'd announced to the world they were getting married, even though he hadn't asked, and didn't plan to ask. Nikki, he hadn't expected a barracuda to look like her or feel quite as soft. Now this woman whose delicate beauty made her appear angelical, and yet she talked as though she was a fan of contact sports. Maybe the world had moved off course and screwed everything up.

"We spoke on the phone?" he asked. If they'd talked, he was almost certain he'd remember.

"I'm the new massage therapist you hired. A trial basis, that is. Mr. Braxton thinks I'm too young." She smiled, then shrugged. "Age shouldn't be measured in years but in the wisdom one accumulates along the way."

She was an interesting creature. "Are you older than you look? I mean, in wisdom."

"Aren't you supposed to be resting?" Brian stood in the hallway, a sheaf of papers in his hand. "Where's Shelley? I thought she was showing you where you'll be staying? Did you get lost?"

"I'm right here," Shelley chimed in as she came around the corner. "I had to take a bathroom break."

Brian frowned. "Oh."

"And you're right, I'm very tired. As soon as I get to my room I plan to take a short nap." Celeste nodded toward Cal. "It was nice talking to you again."

He watched until the two were out of sight, then turned to his frowning brother. "Why are you looking so grumpy? You've replaced the massage therapist. This one is a lot cuter than your last one. I'd think you'd be overjoyed."

Brian's frown only darkened. Now what the hell had he said? His little brother really needed to lighten up.

"No, you hired her. Without telling me."

"Did I forget to mention that? Sorry."

"Yeah, remorse is written all over your face."

"If you don't like her, fire her."

Brian waved the papers at him. "You saw her. She's so

tired she's about to fall over. And there's no telling how long it's been since she's had a decent meal. And I won't even mention her car or the fact that the only thing holding it together is a prayer. So, no, I couldn't tell her to go away and come back in a few years—like say, ten."

"Maybe she'll work out." Cal studied his brother. "You really shouldn't take things so seriously."

"Like you?" He snorted. "Look at the mess you've gotten yourself into. And I've seen the tabloids, too. You change girls as often as you change underwear."

He grinned. "Jealous?"

"I'm trying to make the ranch a profitable venture."

"You have. Maybe it's time you relaxed a little. Take a vacation. I'll take care of everything while you're gone." He couldn't believe he'd just said that. He didn't want to be tied down.

Brian frowned again. "Stay away from her."

"Huh?" Ah, crap, he'd met Nikki despite his attempt to keep the two of them apart.

"You heard me. Celeste is too young for you, and she seems to be a sweet kid."

He let out a sigh of relief. Not Nikki. But it was awfully interesting the way Brian was warning him away from Celeste.

Cal downed his head. "You're right. I'll keep my distance."

Brian cleared his throat. "Good. I'm glad you see that we're in agreement. She's not used to someone like you. You saw how delicate she looks."

"Someone like me?" He frowned, not caring for little brother's attitude right now. "What's that supposed to mean?"

"You date a different breed of women. Women who know the score. Celeste is like a fragile flower that would wilt around you. Anyone can see that."

"I'm hurt you have such a low regard of me," he joked.

"Not a low regard," Brian said quietly. "Never that. I'm proud to call you my brother."

When had Brian grown up? It was right after they'd captured the big oak in the south pasture. The one with limbs that reached to forever then back. It had been their fort, a place all their own. Cal had started high school and Brian junior high. The old tree was forgotten, as were all their old haunts. He missed that time in their lives.

"Back at you, little brother, and Grandma and Grandpa would be proud of you, too, and what you've made of the place." He meant every word. "Hey, what say you and I go riding this week?"

"I need to catch up on some things."

The businessman was back, but he couldn't really blame Brian too much. The ranch meant a lot to him. He nodded. "Yeah, sure."

Brian looked as though he was weighing his options. "How about Friday? I'll tell you about the brood of children Wanda Jo and Ape Man have."

Cal grinned. "That will be perfect."

Maybe he didn't like the country as much as Brian, but he liked the memories, and he liked knowing he had family. That wasn't a bad thing, not at all.

And he realized that Celeste hadn't answered his question. Was she older in wisdom? He had a feeling there was a lot more to her than met the eye. It might be interesting to see what transpired between her and his brother. He knew damned well he'd caught a spark of interest coming from Brian—even if little brother didn't realize it yet.

Things were definitely not boring at the Crystal Creek Dude Ranch anymore. His gaze moved toward the window, toward the old homestead.

Things had definitely gotten interesting.

Had making love ever been that good? Nikki didn't think so. Not that all her experiences had been bad. They just hadn't been this damned fantastic.

It was a little scary since she was here under false pretenses. Cal said he believed in honesty. She didn't think he'd appreciate her lack of it with him.

Was she developing a conscience?

That wasn't good. She hadn't been given the award for best journalist of the year two years in a row because she'd had scruples when it came to lowering the boom on dirty politicians. Nikki Scott, developing a conscience? Yeah, right, when hell froze over, maybe.

But apparently, she wasn't quite good enough. She'd subtly questioned him after they'd had sex. He'd planted a good one on her lips, and while she was still trying to recover from the fire that had begun to build, he'd rolled out of bed and told her he'd promised to meet his brother.

Before she knew what was happening, he'd dressed and gone out the front door. She felt as though she'd lost another round. A smile curved her lips, but what a way to lose.

She stretched her arms over her head, then strolled toward the kitchen, stopping at the door and staring at the black beast, but the longer she stared the more frightening it looked. She didn't need a psychic to tell her she'd be taking another cold sponge bath.

Her stomach rumbled, reminding her that all she'd had was a PB&J sandwich yesterday. That last town she'd gone through wasn't that far away. She needed a few things anyway and surely they had a fast-food joint of some kind. It felt as though she hadn't eaten in months.

But after that, look out. They didn't call her The Barracuda for nothing. She'd beat Cal at his own game. She grabbed clean clothes and after a quick wash headed for her car. Oh, yeah, she was on top of the world.

It was only a twenty-minute drive into town but it seemed longer since she had to maneuver around all the potholes. This time she noticed the town's sign as she drove past it. Frog Hollow—population 1,625.

Frog Hollow? Who named a town Frog Hollow? She

drove down Main Street—which looked like the only street. Where were the fast-food places?

Wait, there was a café. She pulled in front of it and parked her car and just sat there for a moment.

Oh, yeah, this should be good, she thought as she read the faded sign: THE CHICKEN COOP. She really hated chickens and more especially roosters, but she was so hungry it felt as though her stomach was about to cave in. Maybe she'd get a little revenge and have fried chicken.

She glanced at her watch. Almost eleven. Please let them be serving something . . . anything.

The bell jangled over her head as she went inside. The aromas of home-cooked food assailed her nostrils and her stomach rumbled in anticipation. It looked clean. There were ruffled black and white checkered curtains on the windows and yellow Formica booths with matching vinyl seats. No rips or tears, no silver tape patching holes, and the black and white tiled floor practically sparkled.

It felt as though she'd stepped back to the fifties. She wouldn't be at all surprised if Don Knotts strolled into the café. She slid into one of the booths.

A girl, who looked barely out of high school, came over, gum smacking, blond hair swinging in a ponytail, and handed her a menu.

"Sweet convertible. I bet it really looks nice when it's washed," she said as she glanced out the window.

"Texas dust."

"Yeah, we have a lot of it around here. Back-country roads and all. My name's Jenny, by the way, and I'll be your waitress." She chuckled. "I'm the only waitress, actually. Middle of the week, slow time. The crowd won't start to come in until after five."

This town had a crowd? Nikki tried but couldn't visualize it. She opened the menu and glanced at the offerings. God, she was so hungry.

"Can I get you something to drink?"

Wine was probably out of the question. "Soda. Coke?"

"Sure thing. Back in a minute."

Could she order everything on the menu? She could probably eat it, as well as the menu. Her stomach rumbled again. She wanted something fast. No fried chicken or thick, juicy steak this time.

Her perusal stopped on cheeseburger. She bit her bottom lip to keep from moaning. A big, fat, juicy cheeseburger loaded with onions and a side of fries. Oh, yeah, that was living.

"Here you go." Jenny set the drink, along with a straw, in front of her. "Do you know what you want?"

She nodded, then gave Jenny her order and the girl left to pass it along to the cook.

Nikki glanced out the window. From her viewpoint, she could see the gas station she'd stopped at for directions when she came through town, an abstract office, the post office, and a pharmacy.

"You just passing through?" Jenny asked.

"I'm staying at the Braxton ranch."

She nodded, looked at the convertible, then back at her. "Tourist."

"Sort of. I'm from Fort Worth."

"Cal still home?"

Nikki immediately went on alert. "You know Cal?" She casually picked up the straw and removed the white paper before sticking the straw into her drink.

Jenny grinned. "Everyone knows him. Star football player, a handsome devil." She blushed. "My oldest sister went to school with him. I think every girl had a crush on him and his brother, Brian. They hated when Cal got engaged, but that's all over now."

"I'm sure he was hurt by the breakup."

Jenny snorted. "I don't think so. He came in last week and was flirting with Sandy Fairfax and she was practically drooling all over him."

"He was flirting with her?" For some reason, the thought of Cal flirting with someone irritated her.

Jenny frowned. "It might've been more flirting on Sandy's part. But the way you hear her talk, Cal was falling all over himself to be sweet to her." She frowned. "Come to think of it, Sandy was the one acting like a dog in heat—excuse my phrasing."

"Order up," the cook announced.

"That's your food." The waitress hurried over to get it.

"Since I'm the only customer that's obvious," she muttered *God, I'm such a bitch when I'm starving.*

Jenny brought Nikki's food over and set it in front of her. "Is there anything else I can get you?"

"No, I'm fine."

She managed to get a little more information. Jenny seemed to think Cal might have been the one to end the relationship since he didn't seem to be in pain over the breakup. Interesting. Maybe she'd have another chance to question her.

But first, food.

As Jenny walked back to the counter, Nikki took a huge bite of the burger, closing her eyes as her taste buds went into overdrive. Better than sex.

Well, maybe not sex with Cal, but a hell of a lot better than the last couple of men she'd had sex with. The cheeseburger was absolute heaven. She closed her eyes again as she savored another bite of grilled-to-perfection hamburger.

Catsup. She had to have catsup. She grabbed the bottle that was on the table and dumped at least half a cup on her plate, then dragged a French fry through it.

Oh, yeah, heaven.

Ha! The Barracuda was back. She'd be damned if she'd starve or live the next week or so on PB&J. What Cal didn't know wouldn't hurt him.

She didn't think about anything else. In fact, she didn't do anything except savor each bite of food until she swallowed the last morsel of burger, ate the last French fry, then sucked down the last drop of her soda.

"I don't think I've ever seen anyone inhale one of Jim's burgers that fast." Jenny laughed.

"It was fantastic," Nikki said. "I'm stuffed."

"Sure you won't try some peach cobbler with a scoop of vanilla ice cream? Jim's wife made it herself and there's none better."

Maybe she wasn't that stuffed.

She finished half an hour later, then paid out. Jenny had been right: the cobbler was the best she'd ever eaten. The young waitress hadn't given her any more information that she could use, but she pointed her in the direction of the dry-goods store and the grocery store.

Ye-haw, she thought as she walked inside. She admitted the smell of leather was kind of nice, but she wasn't into spurs that jangled or purses with tiny saddles on top of them. She did buy four pair of jeans, a pair of boots, and a week's worth of tops, though. She didn't plan on needing to stay any longer and hoped it wouldn't take her that long.

A trip to the hardware store yielded solar lights, along with a few more items she thought she might need.

The grocery store was her diamond in the rough, though, as she grabbed ham and cheese, bagels and cream cheese, and chocolate. Gourmet food it wasn't, but it was better than nothing.

Coffee was another story. She might have to break down and light the black beast after all. Then again, she wasn't *that* addicted to caffeine. Sodas might be able to give her the fix she craved.

She grabbed a few toiletries that she hadn't thought she would need, but did, an armload of air fresheners in all shapes, sizes, and forms, and then paid out. She'd stash her goods and Cal would never know she'd cheated. A satisfactory smile curved her lips. She was just too damned good.

And she made sure she kept every receipt. Marge was going to owe her for this one. She figured at least two weeks off. Her parents would probably tell her that was too long, but dammit, she deserved it. And she didn't care what Marge thought, either.

Her cell rang as she shut the trunk. She brought it out of her purse and flipped it open.

"Hi, Mom." Why was her mother calling her? Her mother never called. What if her father was ill? Or worse. "Is everything all right?"

"Finally—I've tried to call you several times, but it wouldn't go through. And yes, everything is fine now that I know you're okay. Where are you?"

Her mother was worried about her? Strange, but it felt nice to know she cared so much. And she had sounded generally upset. Actually, that scared Nikki even more.

"Is everything okay?" her mother asked.

"Yes, I'm doing great. I'm on assignment in the boonies. There's limited service here."

"Another politician?"

She cringed. "Not exactly. A football player."

"Steroids?"

"No." She knew her mother wouldn't leave off until she knew the whole story, so she quickly told her the details.

"Your editor sent you to do a piece about the love life of a socialite and a football player? What could she have been thinking? Your talents are going to waste."

"It's a nice change."

"And you're staying in a nice hotel."

She cringed. "Not exactly. More like a cabin on a dude ranch. It's . . . rustic."

"I know you better than that, dear. If the living conditions are primitive, then you must feel as though you're in hell."

She thought about making love with Cal and knew she wouldn't exactly say everything was hell. But she didn't want to tell her mother that.

"I'm tough, so I think I'll survive."

"That you are, dear."

"Why did you call?" Her mother never had said.

"Our second Saturday meeting is this month but I'm afraid we'll have to cancel and I wanted to give you plenty of notice."

They never canceled. Again, fear coursed through her. "Why?"

"I have exciting news. We're thinking about moving to Washington. The Stanleys have been after us for years to move up there. Jack already has an established practice and he wants us to come in as partners."

"You're moving?" All of a sudden, Nikki felt as if she was being abandoned.

"You have a fabulous career, dear, and you don't need us so much anymore. We'll still meet once every couple of months except you'll fly out. It'll be exciting. You'll see."

Her mother was right. Nikki drew in a deep breath. She was a big girl and could take care of herself. And it was probably a fantastic opportunity for her parents.

"If you and Daddy are excited, then so am I. I hope everything works out the way you both want."

"I knew you would understand, dear."

"Of course I do. You raised me right." But it didn't stop the sadness from flowing through her. Sometimes she wondered if a career was worth the toll it took on one's personal life.

They rescheduled their dinner date and said their goodbyes.

Nikki got into her car and started it, but she couldn't shake the lonely feeling.

Chapter 11

Nikki knew she could do this. How hard could it be? She'd mapped out her strategic plan and was ready for any unforeseen complications that might arise. All she had to do was talk herself into doing it.

This was utterly ridiculous. She'd never lacked courage. She was the one who was always first to take a chance. She could do this, too. She closed her eyes and slowly counted to ten. She opened her eyes knowing there was no turning back.

She made sure the nose clamp was firmly in place. She'd found that little lifesaver at the hardware store, of all places. It was the kind swimmers used. Yeah, she was good.

Armed with a can of air freshener in each hand, she was ready. At least as ready as she'd ever be.

She leaned back and cautiously opened the door of the outhouse with the toe of her shoe and began spraying as she stepped forward, holding her breath, eyes closed, face turned away, and arms stretched out in front of her. The door closed behind her, but she continued to spray.

A white fog began to surround her. Oh, Lord, she needed air! Her lungs were about to explode. She stuck her head outside the door and drew in a quick, gasping breath before facing the interior once again.

She sprayed the inside of the outhouse with spicy apple air

freshener for another good minute, then set the can on the floor, reached into the brown paper sack just outside the door, gasped another breath, and pulled out more ammo.

"I am The Barracuda and I don't lose," she said with fierce determination, except her words sounded like someone with a bad cold, since she still wore the nose clamp.

She peeled off the backs of the shiny foil stick-on scented fresheners to expose the sticky side and plastered them all over the walls. She'd bought every cinnamon-scented and spicy-scented room deodorizer they had in the store. She hadn't even cared that the clerk had given her a strange look. Let him think what he would.

She slapped the last one on the wall. The outhouse looked as though an infestation of a new species of techno insects had infiltrated the walls. The smell was almost—*almost*—bearable if one didn't linger, and she had no intention of staying any longer than she had to.

As she let the door slam behind her, she removed the nose clamp and scooped up the sack with the solar lights and the hammer. She walked down the path and hammered the lights in place. Three on one side and three on the other.

Let there be light.

And there was.

Well, there would be as soon as it got dark. Cal couldn't find fault in her wanting to light the way to the bathroom. And if he did, so what?

She stepped up onto the porch and surveyed her handiwork. It almost looked homey. Yeah, right, as if she would ever feel like Suzy Homemaker. No way would she get used to a place this secluded. She liked the hustle and bustle of the city. The restaurants, the plays, the glitter of the nightlife. She didn't care if she knew the people around her or not; at least there were people.

Not that she felt that alone here. She glanced over her shoulder into the dark interior of the kitchen. A cold chill ran down her spine. She didn't think Cal had been joking when he'd said there was a ghost here. It was as though she could feel a presence.

Was there really such a thing as ghosts? Maybe her parents were wrong. Sure, there were special effects in the movies, but what about real life? There weren't any out here in the middle of nowhere.

Maybe there was a ghost.

A series of guttural grunts made her jump. She slapped a hand to her chest and waited for her racing pulse to slow. Off to her right Bandit waddled toward a tree.

Okay, not a ghost, only the stupid raccoon, but she still had a creepy feeling about the old house. Probably because it was about to fall down around her ears; the wind whistled through it, making weird noises; and it had a musty smell that no amount of air freshener could get rid of.

Of course there was no such thing as ghosts.

There were only wild animals. Yeah, right. Now she felt a lot safer. She stayed on the porch but kept her eyes on the raccoon, curious to see what it would do.

Bandit was sort of funny to watch, the way his weight shifted back and forth like someone on a boat for the first time during rough seas. Not that she wanted to get to know the raccoon or anything. As long as he kept his distance, they would get along just fine.

Another sound drew her attention.

A vehicle.

Cal maybe?

She couldn't see from where she was, but the pickup didn't stop out front anyway. Whoever was driving kept going until he was beside the barn.

It was just one person, Cal, and he pulled a trailer behind the pickup. Nikki crossed her arms in front of her and frowned. *Oh, goody, what does he have for me now? The excitement is almost too much*, she thought sarcastically. She could barely contain herself, she could . . . actually, her body did tingle at the thought of seeing him again.

But she wasn't all that enthused with what he might have brought her. She had a feeling whatever it was, she wouldn't like it.

He still had no idea she wanted to do a story about him. No, he thought she really wanted to know about country living. Like that would ever happen—not in her lifetime.

She stepped off the porch and wandered over to the pickup. He didn't even look up as he unfastened the back door of the trailer, even though she knew he'd heard her.

"Hi," he said.

Hi? That was it? Just hi? Not that she wanted him to drop to his knees and profess his undying love or anything, but she'd expected a little more than a bland "hi."

She drew in a deep breath and regrouped her thoughts. "Did you bring me another cow to milk?" she asked.

He stopped with his hand on the door. His gaze slowly traveled over her. Before the fire inside her could begin to sensuously burn out of control, he turned away and opened the gate.

"Just a calf to put on Bessie so you won't have to milk at night."

Had he forgotten the fabulous orgasm he'd given her? He acted as though nothing had happened between them. That bothered her more than she wanted to admit. She'd been taken to new heights, soared to the heavens on a hazy cloud of intense delight, experienced a sexual awakening.

She frowned.

Maybe it hadn't been that good for him. He'd given a lot more than he'd received, but that wasn't really her fault. She'd wanted to be more in charge, but that hadn't happened. Cal had taken complete control of the situation—boy, had he. Her body sizzled as she remembered just how much he'd taken control.

She leaned against the side of the open trailer, pretending interest in the calf, but in truth, she needed something to hang on to as visions of them making love flooded her mind.

The way he'd caressed her body, kissed almost every inch of it, the way he'd plunged inside her, in and out, in and out.

She was sweating. A droplet slid between her breasts. She hunched her shoulders when it tickled. What the hell was happening to her? Had Cal cast a spell over her like all the other women in his life?

Of course he hadn't. *Shake it off! Deep breath.* She was The Barracuda.

Story, think story. Yes, that's what she needed to do to take her mind off their lovemaking.

But the story didn't interest her. She didn't want to think about it or the fact that she had zilch information. It was a fluff piece. Besides, she was starting to feel as though she shouldn't be doing it at all. Cal seemed like a nice guy, and what she planned to do wasn't right.

Oh, God, she *was* developing a conscience.

No, that couldn't be it. She'd been working too much on other stories. After she'd turned them in, she should've taken a few days off, but Marge had talked her into doing this story. The article about Cal and Cynthia was at the bottom of her list of things to do while Cal was at the top. And she so wanted to do him again.

Except the man seemed immune to her charms. Sure, she knew he'd enjoyed their morning romp, but apparently it didn't mean nearly as much to him. She frowned as she wondered why.

But Cal once again drew her attention as he lifted the calf out of the back of the trailer, his arm muscles tightening before he set the animal on the ground. It bleated like a sheep and looked up at her.

Okay, so what if the baby cow was cute. She was more interested in the man. But the calf wobbled over to her. She stared down at it, wanting to tell the animal to go away, but she petted the tiny head instead.

Maybe it was a little more than just cute.

Nikki looked up. Cal was watching her. She blushed. She

could feel the heat rise up her face. She never blushed. Dammit, though, she needed to know what he thought about their time in bed.

"I enjoyed this morning," she pressed. She didn't want an award for best sex or anything, but she'd like to know what he took from the experience, and maybe if he wanted to do it again in the future. Near future preferably.

He aimed the calf toward the gate. "Milking the cow or gathering the eggs? Both were good research."

Her forehead puckered. "No, I mean, sure, the research was great. I was talking about after that."

He nudged the calf inside the enclosure. Bessie Two was already at the fence looking at it. She sauntered closer, sniffing the tiny creature. The calf bleated again. The cow bumped the calf with her head, aiming it in the right direction. As if on instinct, the calf went right for a teat and began to suck.

Cal closed the gate, then looked at Nikki. "Oh, you're talking about when we had sex. Sure, I enjoyed myself."

That's all? He *enjoyed* himself? She had expected a little more from him.

"The cream is probably ready to be skimmed off the milk. You'll love churning butter. Pioneers didn't need all the fancy gyms they have now. Not when they had to work just to put food on the table."

"I'm looking forward to it." The pioneer women all looked like drudges, too, from the pictures she'd seen.

He eyed her. "Have you managed to work the stove?"

She quickly put her hands behind her so he wouldn't see them tremble. "Are you joking? I was made for this kind of life." What he didn't know wouldn't hurt him. And she hadn't really lied. Okay, maybe she had.

An hour later, Nikki was wishing someone would amputate her arms. God was punishing her because she'd lied about using the stove. No, that couldn't be it. If that were the case, she'd have been churning milk into butter long before now.

This was torture, though. Cal had poured the cream into a large glass jar and screwed a lid on it that had wooden paddles and a handle. When she turned the handle, the paddles spun through the cream.

There wasn't a lot to it, at first. But then the cream began to thicken, and even though she frequently changed sides, her arms felt as though they might fall off any minute. They ached all the way across her shoulders.

Cal opened the door and stepped inside the kitchen. "I put the calf up so she won't get tomorrow's milk."

Don't do me any favors!

"Great." She smiled at him. If nothing else, she was a damned good actress.

Cal smiled back, not buying her performance for one second. An actress, she wasn't. And he still wasn't sure she'd really used the stove. It didn't look as if it had been lit in months. She had to be getting tired of PB&J sandwiches by now. This story must be real important to her. He hated that she was going to be disappointed.

He almost laughed when he remembered how she'd tried to find out what he'd thought about them having sex. He'd intentionally downplayed how much he'd enjoyed it and was rewarded when her forehead wrinkled in disappointment. She'd quickly covered it up, though. Nope, he wasn't about to tell her it was the best sex he'd ever had.

He watched for a few seconds as she turned the handle. He remembered when his grandmother had stuck him with this chore. He'd rather clean stalls all day than churn butter, and he'd never acquired a taste for fresh butter, either.

"The cream is churned," he said. He'd cut her a little slack. It might not be good publicity for the ranch if her arms fell off.

"Oh, it is. I was having fun, too."

"If you move your hand off the handle, we can unscrew the lid and get it into the molds."

She grimaced, then took her other hand to free the one holding the handle. "It seems to be locked in this position." She laughed without humor. "Unused muscles, I suppose."

"You'll toughen up; don't worry." He patted her on the back.

She sucked wind.

"Think of all the research you're getting. I bet you'll write a hell of a book."

"Oh, I'm sure before I leave here I'll have everything I need."

That's what you think.

But Cal only smiled. He planned to show her all there was to know about the ranch, but that was the only information she'd have when she left. For now, he'd leave her to her own devices, but after he left, Cal found it was a lot harder to stop thinking about her.

It took him a long time to fall asleep that night.

Chapter 12

Celeste opened her eyes. It was dark. Confusion settled over her like a cold and unwelcome blanket. She reached out and felt the bedside table and the small lamp, then the switch that turned it on.

The low-wattage bulb cast a warm glow in the room. At least she was no longer in the dark.

Where was she this time?

The room was unfamiliar, but that was a normal occurrence with her. She'd traveled a lot over the years—different towns, different states, never staying long in any of them. She didn't regret not having a permanent home. The adventures she'd had were amazing. Nothing else mattered.

She rubbed the sleep from her eyes and waited for the fog to go away. Then she remembered where she was—Crystal Creek Dude Ranch—and she was the new massage therapist, even if it was on a trial basis. That was okay, too. She had a good feeling about this job.

She glanced at the clock: just after midnight. Her nap had lasted a long time. All day and into the night. Her forehead wrinkled. That's what she got for going so long without sleep. Brian probably thought she was lazy. Not a good way to start her employment.

Her stomach rumbled, reminding her she'd missed lunch and dinner. God, she was so hungry, too. What had she eaten yesterday morning? A package of crackers and washed it down with a soda that had been only lukewarm. Her eating habits weren't the best even in good times. Much like everything else she did in her life, she ate on the go.

She stretched her arms above her head as she glanced around. This was a nice room, comfortable, and it had a bathroom. No tub, but it did have a shower. She'd rather soak in scented bathwater inhaling her relaxing herbs.

Beggars couldn't be choosers, though.

And hopefully she wouldn't have to resort to begging Brian to let her keep this job. No, she wouldn't think like that. She was a good massage therapist. Fate had brought her here, so why in the world would fate have Brian fire her?

It would be a trial basis only until Brian felt more comfortable. Then he would see what she could do, and the job would be permanent. At least, as permanent as she wanted it to be. It would always be her choice.

She needed to settle in one place for a while. Her money had run low. So low that she had less than a hundred dollars, and even she knew her car was on its last tires. She doubted it would take her another five miles. It was time to trade it in, and that was okay, because she was beginning to dislike the car tremendously, especially when it backfired and belched out black smoke. Lord, how embarrassing was that?

She would just have to prove to Brian that she was great at what she did and only hope it didn't turn out like her last job. A shudder swept over her. No, she didn't even want to go there right now.

Instead, she grabbed her robe. Would Brian care if she wandered the ranch at this time of night? Her stomach rumbled again. It seemed her body was making the decision for her. Surely he wouldn't mind if she went to the kitchen and found something to eat.

She eased out of her room and quietly shut the door. She'd passed the kitchen, so she knew the direction it was in.

The ranch was quiet as she wandered the halls, only the

dim light from wall sconces lighting her way. The dining room was eerily empty, but there was a light from beneath the swinging doors that led to the kitchen area.

There was a sign on one of the doors: EMPLOYEES ONLY. She was an employee, even if she was here on a trial basis. A very hungry employee. Maybe there were some crackers or something she could munch on. That should hold her until morning.

But when she pushed through the double doors, she wished she'd stayed in her room. Brian sat on a stool at the long counter. He had a sandwich in front of him but it didn't look as though he'd eaten any of it yet.

Something fluttered inside her chest and she knew it wasn't hunger pains. The same feeling had happened earlier, when she'd first laid eyes on Brian. Not that anyone would blame her. He was a nice-looking man.

Before she could ease back out of the room, he looked up.

"Don't go," he said as though he'd read her thoughts and knew she was going to flee.

"I was hungry." That sounded so lame.

"Me, too." He stood and went to the cabinet, took down another plate. "Sit."

She moved to one of the stools, keeping one between them.

"Do you like sandwiches?"

She nodded when he looked at her.

"Good, because that's all I could find without having to heat anything up."

"Right now I think I could eat a horse. I missed lunch and dinner."

"I know."

Of course he would. He probably knew everything that went on at the ranch.

He cut his sandwich in half, then slid one portion onto the empty plate and set it in front of her.

She took a bite. A steak couldn't have tasted any better than the slice of ham. She barely restrained herself from cramming the whole sandwich into her mouth. Brian didn't say anything until she'd almost finished the sandwich.

"Tell me about yourself," he said.

"What do you want to know?" she hedged, picking at the crust on her bread. Then she took another bite of the sandwich. She didn't want to answer questions. She hated questions.

"What was your last job?"

Okay, she could skirt around that one. "My last job was in a hair salon."

"As a massage therapist?"

"Not exactly."

He raised his eyebrows.

She shrugged. "There wasn't an opening, so I worked as a receptionist."

"I'll need references."

She cringed. She'd known it was coming. Just not this soon. "I was fired from my last job." She glanced at him out of the corner of her eye and saw his back stiffen. That didn't bode well for her.

Please let me get through this and still have a job.

"Some money came up missing," she hesitantly continued. "I didn't take it, but I was the new employee and I made a good scapegoat. The charges were dropped because of lack of evidence. I doubt the owner will give me a reference." She pushed her plate away, suddenly losing her appetite.

Brian tapped his fingers on the counter as though he was thinking about everything she'd said, then stood and took their plates to the sink.

"I really didn't take it. The owner's son did." Which was the last thing she should've told Giselle. No mother wants to know her sixteen-year-old son is a thief. But Celeste had seen him shutting the cash register. He'd only looked at her with a snide grin on his face. Her sinking feeling had been a premonition of what was to happen next.

"You'd better get some sleep," Brian said. "First day on a new job is usually stressful."

She jerked her head up. "Then you'll still give me a chance?"

Brian had to be losing his mind, but she looked pretty broke to have stolen money. And she looked innocent. Probably because she still had that sleepy look about her. Her blond hair hung down her back in a tumble of soft waves.

He still wasn't sure she hadn't lied about her age, though. Right now, he'd guess her to be closer to twenty than thirty. The way she was all tucked inside her heavy terry cloth robe reminded him of a little pixie. Sweet, adorable.

He cleared his throat and his mind. He wouldn't get caught up in feeling sorry for her. "A trial basis is what I told you and I meant it."

"Thank you." She hurried from the room. Had her eyes sparkled because of unshed tears? Or the way the light had hit them?

He had to be crazy to keep her after her confession. He was usually a good judge of character, though, and she just didn't look like a thief. He only hoped that he wasn't making a huge mistake.

He turned off the light a few minutes later and walked out of the kitchen. He was tired all the way to his bones, but there had been things that still needed doing before he could go to bed. It seemed his days were getting longer and longer.

Cal was right: he needed a break, but he didn't think he'd take his brother up on his offer to run the place so he could take a vacation.

He glanced down the hall and caught a glimpse of Celeste right before she turned the corner.

No, Brian had a feeling Cal had made more trouble when he'd hired the girl. There was something about her. Not that he thought she was a criminal, but then people became desperate when they needed money. No, there was something else about her. A feeling that she might be lost.

A completely ridiculous notion, of course. She'd found her way here, hadn't she?

But as he made his way to his room and his bed, he had a gut feeling that he'd done the right thing by hiring her. He only hoped his gut was right.

Chapter 13

"Cock-a-do, cock-a-do!"

Nikki came straight up in the bed, groaning in pain when every muscle screamed out. Who would've thought she could ever be this sore. She was swearing off milk and butter for life. She flexed her back as she tried to get the kinks out.

What woke her, anyway?

"Cock-a-do, cock-a-do!"

"Good Lord!" She jumped.

What damned time was it? She blinked several times, then rubbed the sleep out of her eyes. She stared at the illuminated dial on the wind-up clock. Five o'clock.

"Not again," she moaned.

"Cock-a-do, cock-a-do!"

She eased back down and pulled the pillow over her head.

"Cock-a-do, cock-a-do!"

It didn't help, and the bad thing was, the rooster now sounded like a man who'd gotten his balls caught in a vice that was rapidly getting tighter and tighter.

She flung the covers to the side and stomped out of the bedroom and out the front door and stood on the porch. It was damned chilly. The sun was just barely peeking over the horizon—*again!*—and casting a deep orange over the land.

Awestruck, she just stared at the beauty of it all for a moment.

About fifteen seconds was all it took to realize she needed another three to four hours of deep, uninterrupted sleep.

"Cock-a-do, cock-a—"

"Shut the fuck up!"

Squakkkkk!

The rooster jumped a good two feet off the top rail of the fence flapping its wings, then landed on the ground, fell over on its side, then got up, wobbling back and forth.

She noticed only two hens were admiring Romeo this morning. Okay, she felt a little guilty that since he'd become disabled he'd lost some of his audience. It wasn't exactly fair kicking a . . . a rooster when he was down.

Romeo continued to flap his wings as he drunkenly headed for the barn, the two hens close on his tail feathers like groupies chasing after an aged rock star.

Nikki shoved her hair out of her face and stomped back inside.

"Damned rooster."

He shouldn't be waking people up this early in the morning. She crawled back into bed and pulled the covers up to her chin, wondering if there was a chance raccoons ate roosters.

Probably not.

Besides, she didn't really want anything to happen to the damned bird. Hell, she'd already done enough damage. She just wanted Romeo to crow at a decent hour—like in the afternoon. Late afternoon.

She closed her eyes and let sleep overtake her.

When she next opened her eyes, she groggily looked at the clock: seven. Still too damned early, but something had woke her. She lay in bed listening.

Was that a whistle? Not like when a person whistled, but more like a deep sigh or wind blowing through the house. Of course. That had to be it. The cabin was drafty. It could only be the wind.

Or a ghost.

She was certainly wide awake now.

She flung the covers away and sat on the side of the bed, raking her fingers through her hair. She flinched. How the hell could she be this sore? She flexed her fingers, then rolled her shoulders. And she had another day of milking to get through.

Damn, she needed at least a gallon of coffee.

She glanced out the window as she stood. There was a tree not far away and nothing was moving on it. Not one little bit of wind to cause the eerie noises she'd heard.

Okay, that made her feel a whole lot better—not.

Her robe was on the end of the bed so she grabbed it as she made her way to the kitchen. She really needed caffeine.

After washing her face, Nikki grabbed a diet soda she'd hidden deep in the icebox. It was supposed to have something like ten times the amount of caffeine the other ones had. A Twinkie from her stash and she was all set. It wasn't the healthiest breakfast, but, oh well.

She took a long swallow of the drink. Oh, good Lord! The bitter, syrupy taste clung to her taste buds. She grimaced. Did people really drink this stuff? She wasn't so sure the caffeine was worth it.

After pouring the foul-tasting drink down the sink, she dug out a normal diet soda. She could live without her regular jolt of caffeine for a few days. And she didn't need to light the stove, which was fine by her.

Laughter bubbled out of her. Damn, she was good. So good that she ate another snack cake, then quickly disposed of any evidence.

"I am The Barracuda."

As she went back to the bedroom to dress, she realized she'd better come up with a game plan. She was tired of the cabin, and as much as she liked Cal, she was ready to get back to Fort Worth: traffic, pollution, and people.

Ah, but she would miss him. And the sex had been pretty good, too.

She stopped at the bedroom door. The closed bedroom door. Now dammit, Nikki knew she'd left it open. This wasn't funny. Not one little bit.

"There are no such things as ghosts!"

The door slowly opened a crack, all by itself.

She hugged her middle, then nudged the door open the rest of the way with her foot. The bedroom still looked the same. There were no mists floating around.

God, she was being so ridiculous. It had to be the wind. That was all it could be. The cabin sat on a hill and the window was open. The door had probably caught a little bit of breeze.

She quickly pulled on a pair of shorts and a top, then made her way to the outhouse. The deodorizers were doing their job. No one would get the better of her. She'd show Cal a thing or two.

Not that she wanted to linger, though. She quickly exited the structure, then went inside and washed her hands at the pump.

Thinking of Cal reminded her of something: he was in and out yesterday. She smiled at what that thought conjured, then quickly sobered. She would need to keep him more in her company today if she was going to get any information. She had to get him talking about Cynthia. That shouldn't be too difficult. Not for The Barracuda.

She went back outside and grabbed the milk bucket off the back porch and made her way to the barn. Bessie Two let out a low moo of welcome. Nikki stopped at the fence and patted her on the neck. She had to admit she kind of liked the cow.

Oh, God, that was priceless. Her friends would laugh themselves silly if they knew she was going soft over a cow. Not that they had anything against animals, but they knew it wasn't her thing. The closest she'd ever come to a cow was when she'd bought her leather sofa.

Oh, yeah, now she felt better. That could be Bessie Two's mother Nikki was parking her butt on.

Bessie mooed.

On second thought, it was Italian leather, so she really doubted it was one of Bessie's relatives.

"Hey, girl, you ready to let me milk you?" She hoped the cow was in a good mood. She started toward the barn but turned at the last second. "Go to the bathroom first or I might not give you any breakfast."

Before she stepped inside the barn, she let her eyes adjust. No crazy roosters or a waddling raccoon that she could see. Cal had said two scoops of feed. She could do this. She wanted to do this.

Actually, *wanted* wasn't exactly the word she would use, but she had a feeling Cal would show up this morning and she was ready to prove she could milk. Besides, it would make her lie about why she was here seem more plausible.

Two scoops of feed, then she would milk the damned cow if it was the last thing she did.

But after ten minutes, she began to wonder if she could buy a gallon of milk in town and fill the bucket. Would Cal notice? Yeah, probably. He'd been right when he'd said fresh milk didn't smell the same as milk bought at the store.

Before she managed to get a quarter of the bucket, she heard the familiar sound of Cal's pickup. She smiled when she heard the cabin's front door slam, then slam again. And a few seconds later, his heavy tread as he walked inside the barn. Nikki bet Cal had thought she would still be in bed.

Damn, she was good.

She looked up. "Good morning." She feigned cheerfulness. "You were so right when you said I'd enjoy my experiences on the ranch. I think I'm getting the hang of milking, but I'm still not as fast as you."

He frowned as though he was surprised she was still there, let alone milking Bessie Two.

"I'll finish if you'd like."

She laughed. She was definitely the consummate actress. "I think you might have to. The cow would probably be grateful, too."

When he sat on the stool with his back to her, she shook out her arms and fingers. She'd had no idea her fingers could ache this much. And she didn't even want to think about churning more butter, but her smile was wide when he looked at her.

She should've been on the stage.

"I thought you might like to go riding today," Cal said, not buying her smile for one minute. She hated milking and it was as plain as the nose on his face. Revenge could be sweet. And it was about to get even sweeter.

Horseback riding would be the straw that broke the camel's back. Bye-bye reporter.

"Riding?" Her voice squeaked. She cleared her throat. "On a horse?"

He chuckled. "That's the usual way when you're on a ranch, and you did say you wanted to experience everything."

Her smile looked pained. "I'd love to, if you don't mind that I've never been on a horse."

He liked the way she accepted a challenge, though. "Of course. You might want to change into a pair of jeans, though. You did say you were going shopping?"

"Yes. I bought jeans."

They took the bucket of milk to the house and strained it. "You'll have time to gather the eggs before I get back with the horses."

Her smile was still pasted on. Her face kind of looked like those of some of the actresses he'd dated who'd had Botox injections one too many times.

She nodded. "I'll meet you on the front porch."

"Great."

Boy, did he have her number. She didn't want to ride a

horse, but she was trying hard not to let her fear show. Not that he'd let her get hurt or anything.

He went out the door and climbed inside his pickup. He had a feeling the rest of the day was going to be as interesting as it had started.

Chapter 14

Celeste snuggled down in the bed. It felt so good to sleep on luxurious sheets and . . .

She pushed the cover down and glanced at the clock. Drat! It was after eight. Being late her first day on the job wasn't good. Not that Brian had actually set a time. She was pretty sure it wouldn't be noon, though.

After a quick shower, she pulled on a pair of white slacks and a bright yellow top. As much as she loved her robes, they had a tendency to get in her way when she was giving a massage.

There was only one more thing she needed to grab before she left the room. And what she needed was in her suitcase . . . somewhere.

She dug around inside until she found the herbs she was looking for. There they were. Right at the very bottom, of course. She brought out the small bag that contained other small bags. Inside, she found what she needed. Her supply was getting low and would soon need replenishing.

She left the room, closing her door, and walked back to Brian's office, stopping at the secretary's desk. Shelley glanced up.

Shelley smiled. "Good morning. Amazing what a good night's sleep will do. You look radiant."

"Thank you. I feel a lot better."

She studied her for a moment. "You're dressed different, too. The outfit you're wearing is . . . nice." She tapped her pencil on her desk. "I might just have to tough out this cold to see what'll happen today. Amazing what a change of style can do." When Shelley smiled she looked like a cat who'd just found a bowl of cream.

"Is this okay to wear?" Celeste looked down at her clothes. Maybe she would have to wear a uniform, which was okay; she didn't mind.

"Oh, no, what you're wearing is fine. Who would've thought you would have a figure like that underneath the loose robe you wore yesterday."

Celeste had no idea what Shelley was talking about. Maybe the cold had made Shelley a little spacey. Her figure was okay, nothing spectacular in her opinion.

She decided to change the subject away from what she was wearing. "The bed was wonderful. I slept like a baby," she said.

Shelley started to say something but her words turned into a cough. She quickly covered her mouth. "Ugh, this cold is driving me crazy. I just can't shake it. Sorry about that. I hope no one else catches it."

That reminded her. "I brought you some herbs." She held up the small bag.

Shelley eyed it skeptically. "Herbs?"

Celeste nodded.

"What kind of herbs. I don't do drugs or anything."

Laughter bubbled out of Celeste. "Neither do I, but a . . . a relative taught me about them. Trust me, they'll help with your cold."

"What is it exactly?"

Her brow wrinkled in thought. "Elder flowers, thyme leaves and a few other herbs. Just put it into a teapot and add a couple pints of boiling water. You'll want to let it steep for about thirty minutes then strain off the herbs and drink it. It can be bitter so sweeten it with honey. Thyme honey if you happen to have any."

"And it will cure my cold?"

Celeste laughed. "If I could cure a cold then I'd be rich. No, it won't cure your cold, but it'll ease the symptoms."

Shelley nodded. "Okay, I'll try it."

The door behind Celeste opened and Brian stepped out. His eyes narrowed when he saw the baggie of herbs. He looked up and their gazes collided. His mouth dropped open, and for a moment he didn't speak as he looked at her. Really looked. She could feel herself blushing. What was it with people today?

"You're awake, and you look different." He waved his arm toward her. "You're not dressed the same."

"Oh, my clothes. I don't wear my robes when I'm working. As much as I love the freedom of movement, they kind of get in my way."

He frowned.

Her stomach growled. "I don't suppose you'd have something to eat? The sandwich I shared with you last night has worn off."

Shelley started to cough.

Brian's frown only deepened. "I told you to stay at home if you were still sick. Take the rest of the day off, and if you're not one hundred percent better by morning, I don't want you to come in."

"But . . ."

"I'm the boss."

Shelley rolled her eyes. "Okay, if I'm not feeling better, then I'll stay at home. I'll get Beth to cover me. She's back from vacation." She smiled at Celeste. "It was nice meeting you, and thanks for the herbs."

"What exactly did you give her?" Brian asked as he and Celeste walked toward the kitchen.

"I could tell you but then I'd have to kill you."

He stopped and looked down on her. She suddenly realized how much he towered over her, and right now he didn't look happy. And he was still her boss.

"Herbs—that was all. They won't hurt her and they might help with her cold."

"You're trained in the use of herbs?"

"Yes. Don't worry, I wouldn't give her anything that would cause her harm."

"This is the dining room that you went through last night. Meals are provided for guests. We have one cook, one assistant, and two servers." He walked past the tables, then through the swinging doors into the kitchen.

A woman looked up as they entered. Her gray hair peeked out from under her red cap. She wore a matching red apron that had "Kiss the Cook" emblazoned across it in black letters. When she saw that someone was with Brian, she smiled a smile that enveloped Celeste in a warmth of welcome. Celeste immediately liked her.

"This is our new massage therapist, Celeste," Brian told the older woman. "At the moment, she's starving."

"Hello, Celeste. Have a seat at the bar and I'll fix you right up with some breakfast. We can't have you starting your first day on the job starving to death." She continued to smile. "You can call me Betty."

"When you finish eating, come back to my office and I'll show you where you'll work." He turned and left without another word.

"He doesn't say a lot, does he?" Celeste asked as Betty went to the counter and began to fix a plate of food. Celeste took a seat at the island, hooking her tennis shoes on the bottom rung of the stool.

The kitchen looked a lot different in the light of day—less forbidding. Maybe because Brian had left the room. It just seemed homier. And very clean. The tan granite countertops were free of clutter and complemented the creamy white cabinets.

There was an industrial-sized stainless steel stove and re-frigerator. Except for the larger appliances, it could have been anyone's kitchen.

"Brian's got his head full of everything he has to do here at the ranch," Betty said, and Celeste turned her attention back to the cook. "It wasn't always making a profit like it is now. He had to put in a lot of long hours to make this place what it is today."

"But it's doing well now?" Her last boss not only had ac-cused her of stealing but hadn't paid her what she had com-ing. Not that she thought this would be the same situation. At least she hoped not.

Betty set a plate of food in front of Celeste, then went back for silverware. "Oh, yeah, the ranch is doing a lot of business now. We're nearly always full. We have eight couples here this week. Two have kids. And one single woman up at the old homestead." She shook her head. "Why anyone would want to pay good money to stay in that shack is beyond me. But Brian sees to everyone and makes sure they get what they came here for."

She nodded as she took the fork and knife that Betty handed her. "Except I have a feeling he's forgotten how to relax." Darn, had she just said that aloud?

Betty laughed. "Are you going to show him how to have fun, child?"

Apparently, she *had* spoken aloud. She really needed to re-member to think before she talked. "I doubt I could show anyone much of anything."

Betty was thoughtful as her gaze wandered over Celeste. She shifted in her seat. Why was everyone looking at her as if she'd grown two heads or something?

"There's a sadness about you. I can't quite put my finger on what it is, though."

"I slept a long time. I'm still not quite awake."

Betty shook her head. "Nope, it's more than that." Her eyes narrowed. "Be careful. Brian always has liked to fix things whether it be a toaster or a pretty girl, but he shies away from commitments just as much as his brother, Cal. Don't be getting more hurt piled on those pretty shoulders."

Their conversation was getting just a little too personal. Celeste took a bite of her eggs. She didn't need fixing, but she could certainly see how a girl could get her heart broken around here. Brian was a handsome man.

"These eggs are wonderful," she changed the topic.

Betty beamed. "That's because they're fresh."

Celeste had a feeling she was going to like it here. Aside from the fact the people were a little strange, they still seemed friendly. She only had to remember that Brian apparently wasn't a morning person. He'd frowned an awful lot.

Brian went straight back to his office. He didn't breathe easy until he was sitting at his desk.

What the hell had happened to the delicate, wraithlike creature he'd hired? In her place was a sexy, sensual, vibrant woman. How was he to know she would look all curvy beneath those robes?

This wasn't going to work. She would be too much of a distraction. He'd just have to find a way to tell her that he couldn't use her after all. He'd give her enough money to last her a few weeks, a glowing recommendation, and . . . and what? Buy her a car?

No, he wouldn't do any of that. He'd seen the look in her eyes when he'd told her she could work here on a trial basis. She'd been excited.

He stood and went to the window, staring out at the past.

The first job he'd ever had was for Mr. Miller at the feed store. He'd been thirteen and Mr. Miller had told him he was too young. But Grandpa had hurt his back and couldn't work. Cal had gotten a job in town, but it still wasn't enough.

After a lot of pleading, Mr. Miller had given Brian a chance and the family had managed to make it through the summer. He still remembered how it felt to be able to pull his own weight. He kind of figured Celeste felt the same way.

So maybe he'd keep her at least until she proved whether she could do the job or not.

He sat back down and started going through the mail. Who said he even had to be around her? Rhonda managed the spa. If there were any problems, she could handle them. He'd just show Celeste around.

But there had been something different about her. He wasn't sure, but she almost seemed lonely. He wondered if she had anyone—a relative or a friend. Everyone needed someone.

Brian snorted. Cal would be laughing his fool head off if he knew the direction Brian's thoughts were going. Always trying to fix something, Cal would say. He'd be right. His habit had gotten him into more trouble more times than he wanted to think about.

Like Wanda Jo. He'd tried to fix her, but she'd turned the tables and showed him a whole lot more than he'd ever expected. Yeah, like he needed to think about her when she was happily married to Ape Man.

He sat forward in his chair and cleared his mind of the past, glancing at his watch. Celeste should be almost finished by now. He tapped his fingers on the desk, then picked up the mail. A couple of bills, a brochure on a horse sale coming up next month. Nothing that couldn't wait. He tossed the mail to the side and glanced at his watch.

Then he realized how anxious he was to see Celeste again. He was a fool. But that didn't stop him from jumping when the buzzer on his phone went off.

"Yes?"

"Celeste is back."

He could feel his heart racing inside his chest. No, he wasn't just a fool. He was a complete idiot. Anyone would think he was a virgin. It had been so long since he'd been with a woman, he felt like one.

Brian didn't say a lot as he walked Celeste out the back of the main house and toward the east side. A stone path led the way to the building he'd had built a couple of years ago. He hadn't planned to have a spa, but so many of his guests asked about one that he decided it made good business sense.

"It's very serene," she said.

He looked around. Yeah, he guessed it was. He'd paid to have it landscaped. There were trees on each side of the path, small ones. The landscaper had called them Japanese plum trees. They were kind of neat looking the way the trunks twisted, and combined with music from hidden speakers, it was nice.

"You pay for what you get and I only have the best." He held the door and let her go in first. The foyer was circular. Something about peace and harmony. A load of B.S. if you asked him, but his guests enjoyed it.

He watched Celeste from the corner of his eye. She was taking everything in, and from the expression on her face, he had a feeling she liked it, too. For some odd reason, that pleased him. And he admitted the entrance was impressive.

Celeste couldn't believe she was going to be so lucky to work in a place this tranquil and beautiful. Pale yellow walls and music like gentle rain greeted her. She liked this area of the ranch. It made her feel relaxed and welcome.

"Hello, Mr. Braxton." A woman, who was probably in her fifties, spoke from behind a desk.

"Rhonda, this is Celeste, our new massage therapist." His gaze moved back to Celeste. "Rhonda is the brains of the spa. She makes sure everything runs smoothly. If you have a problem, she's the person to talk to, and if there's anything you need, just ask her, and she'll get it for you." He turned and abruptly left.

"Wow, you'd think his tail feathers were on fire. I don't think that man ever slows down." She turned her attention back to Celeste. "You'll love it here, though."

Rhonda was pretty, with deep auburn hair, and she had a good aura surrounding her.

"Right now, I'm only temporary. Brian thinks I'm too young and can't have very much experience, but he felt sorry for me and is using me on a trial basis." She had a sudden sinking feeling in the pit of her stomach. "I'm not sure he'll keep me. He seems upset with me about something this morning."

Rhonda's gaze swept over her. "Oh, honey, you certainly don't look too young, and that may be the problem. Brian hasn't dated anyone in a long time."

She could feel the heat rise up her face. "I really don't think he's attracted to me."

"Oh, yeah, he's attracted. Any man would be—if he was straight, that is. And by the way, experience isn't everything. Amy had experience, the last massage therapist, and she was good, but she lacked that certain extra something. Brian thought she was suited for the job and kept her."

"Hopefully, I'll make this a permanent job."

"I hope not."

Celeste's eyebrows shot up. "I beg your pardon?" Had she run up against more opposition?

"You may be very good at what you do, but you're too young and pretty to be stuck way out here in the middle of nowhere. Unless, of course, you and Brian hit it off."

She relaxed. "I think I'll like staying here until I do move on, and believe me, Brian isn't at all interested." Angry, a workaholic, dry—but interested? No, not a chance. Although it wouldn't be difficult to imagine his arms pulling her close.

And she'd better get those thoughts right out of her head.

"I hope you'll be around for a long time." Rhonda stood. "Come on, I'll show you the rest of our little spa. I'll tell you, this is the most relaxing job I've ever had."

"Do many people use the spa?"

"Enough, but as busy as we get, I still feel a sense of renewal while I'm at work. If you ever want to practice massages, let me know. I'll willingly take one any day."

"I'll remember that."

"We have two women on staff who do pedicures and manicures: Jill, you'll meet her later, and Lillie, who also does hair. They're in the salon area, which we fondly call the gossip room. The guests usually get to know each other fairly well while they're getting pampered."

"It sounds like fun."

"Oh, we can create quite the party atmosphere."

They walked down a hallway. Rhonda opened a closet door. "Here are all your lotions, towels, there're even stones. Brian ordered a lot of stuff that Amy never used. She wasn't much into a lot of the New Age stuff. What about you?"

"I'm in to it."

"I think you're going to work out just fine." She walked a little farther down the hall and opened another door. "This is where you'll do the massages."

The room was painted a calming beige and the music was piped into this room. A cushioned table was in the center, and there was another door. "What's behind that door?"

Rhonda chuckled. "You have to see it to believe it."

Celeste followed as Rhonda went inside and opened the door. "Oh my."

"You can say that again. Brian spared no expense to pamper his guests."

"It looks like something out of a Roman bath." Tall pillars, a sunken jetted tub that looked more like a small swimming pool. The tiles were an old-world design in soft gold and white.

"Besides the tub, there's a steam shower. By the time the guest does the shower, the whirlpool, and then has a massage, they're down for the count."

"Heaven."

"You got that right." She sighed, then seemed to remember she was showing Celeste around. "I hope you don't mind, but Ms. Darnell wanted a massage. She should be getting here in about ten minutes. I've been helping out and giving them, but only because Mr. Braxton was in a bind. I've had a little training but it's not really what I enjoy."

"I'd love to start."

"Just take what you need out of the supply closet. I have to get back to the phones. I suspect once word gets out that we have a new massage therapist, it'll start ringing off the wall."

As soon as she left, Celeste walked back to the bathing area. A place where she could soak. She smiled. Surely Brian wouldn't mind if she used the facility after hours. She was so going to love working here.

She gathered a few things from the closet and went back to the massage room. She set everything down on the counter, then lit the aromatherapy candle. For just a moment, she let her mind empty as calmness stole over her.

"I'm early."

Celeste jumped.

"Sorry, Rhonda told me to come on in."

Had she been lost in meditation that long? Apparently. The woman wore a white terry cloth robe, her bright red hair pulled up on top of her head, and she looked worn and tired.

"I'm Katie Darnell."

"Hello, Ms. Darnell. I was just meditating."

"Do I need to come back?"

She shook her head. "Not at all."

"Good. This is my escape time while Jim watches the boys. They're going horseback riding and then looking for arrowheads, then swimming, all in the hopes that the boys will expend enough energy they'll fall asleep by eight tonight and Jim and I can have a little time alone." She frowned. "I only hope Jim doesn't fall asleep early."

Celeste laughed.

"I talk too much, don't I?"

She shook her head. "Not at all. You've only absorbed some of your sons' energy."

"Did I mention they're twins? I don't feel as though I have any energy."

"It's not the same thing."

"I didn't think so. I should be so lucky to have even half of what they have." She paused, her face suddenly glowing with warmth. "But I do love them."

What would it feel like to know that kind of love?

Chapter 15

Cal rode up to the cabin, leading the horse he'd brought for Nikki to ride. Just as she'd told him, Nikki was sitting in the rocker waiting. Yep, she didn't give up easy. If he wasn't careful he could really start to like this woman.

When she stood, his heart began to pound. Man, oh man, he'd just thought she'd looked hot before. What was there about a woman who wore tight-fitting jeans? If he didn't know better, he'd think she was country born and bred.

Good thing he knew better about a lot of things when it came to Nikki and too bad she probably wouldn't be staying very much longer.

"This is Tornado," he said, indicating his horse.

"He's beautiful."

"Tornado's a she."

"At least you didn't name her Bessie."

He really liked her sense of humor. "And this is Taffy." He tugged the reins of the other horse, bringing the animal forward. "And yes, I named both of them."

Nikki warily eyed the horse. "She looks sweet. Is she? I mean, she's not going to throw me off or anything?"

"Taffy is a gelding and no, the horse is gentle."

"Good for her."

"A gelding is a male. It means he's been cut."

Her eyes widened in disbelief. "You cut the horse?"

Cal chuckled. "So he won't breed."

"You steal the chickens' eggs and scramble their offspring, the horses are eunuchs—what the hell else happens on a ranch? On second thought, I don't think I want to know."

Yeah, she had a real nice sense of humor.

Her eyes narrowed. "Are you sure we couldn't just sight-see from your pickup? I know women in the nineteen twenties rode in pickups."

"It's not the same as when you're on top of a horse breathing in the fresh country air."

She mumbled something about the fresh country air not being that sweet, but he couldn't quite make out her words.

He swung off Tornado in one easy motion and stretched his legs. It had taken him about a week to get over the soreness of riding once he came home. It sure wasn't the same as when he was a kid growing up on the ranch. Back then, he'd loved to ride and practically lived on a horse. Not so much now.

Nikki was about to find out firsthand what it was like to ride a horse. She didn't look too happy about the prospect.

"Come on, I'll give you a leg up," he said.

"Are you sure I can't walk him for a while? Just until he gets used to me."

"Not afraid, are you?"

Her chin jutted out. "Of course not."

Much better. He liked her feisty. Brought the color to her cheeks and made her eyes flash. Besides, Taffy was gentle. The horse that Brian put all the kids on.

"Grab the horn," he said, sliding his fingers along her arm and taking her hand to the front of the saddle. His movement brought her closer. The heat of her body swirled around him in a haze of teasing pleasure, sending an aching need all the way down to his midsection.

"And then what?" she asked breathlessly.

"Raise your foot."

She did and he bent, guiding it to the stirrup. As he stood, his hands glided up her calves, over her thighs, and cupped her bottom. She leaned against him. He lost himself in the sweet scent of her perfume, and the heat emanating from her.

"Now what do I do?" Her whispered question fanned the hairs on his arm, showering him with ripples of pleasure.

"Push off with your other foot and pull on the saddle horn. As you come up, swing your leg over the horse." His words were husky as he fought the passion that flared inside him. He refused to let her win in the game she'd started.

In one fluid motion, she was sitting on top of the animal. Cal handed her the reins. Their fingers touched. Hers trembled. Maybe she wasn't as much of a barracuda as people thought.

"It's really high up here."

"It'll be a nice, easy ride," he told her and wondered if he was talking about the horse, or something else, and did she know it? But then, she didn't like it easy. He cleared his throat. "Ready?"

She nodded.

He climbed back on Tornado and they started at a walk. After about a quarter of a mile, he knew she was more relaxed. "Are you ready to try a faster pace?"

"Yeah, sure."

She hadn't sounded sure. Nope, he didn't think she looked nearly as confident as she pretended. "Raise up a little in the stirrups, and then nudge him with your heels. Try to go with the rhythm of the animal."

She lightly kicked the horse's sides. Taffy moved into a nice, easy lope. She grabbed the saddle horn.

"You're doing fine," he told her.

"It doesn't feel like I am."

"Try to relax."

"What? I don't look relaxed?"

He grinned but stayed close, watching as she did exactly as he'd explained. She picked up the movement of the horse and adapted to it.

The wind blew through her hair as they sped by trees on each side of them. He saw fear change to excitement and knew she was enjoying herself. She wasn't supposed to have fun. His plan was backfiring. But had he really wanted her to be afraid of riding a horse?

When Cal slowed Tornado, Taffy matched the other horse's pace.

"That was fantastic," Nikki said, laughter in her voice.

Yeah, it had been even though he didn't want to admit that he'd enjoyed her reaction. It did make him wonder what the hell kind of childhood she'd had.

"Didn't you ever go to an amusement park, feel the rush of wind on your face when you rode the roller coaster?"

"Like Six Flags?" She shook her head. "No. My parents had their reasons, but we did travel most of Europe. The art museums were wonderful."

They'd traveled Europe. He would've loved sightseeing when he was a kid, especially art museums. Yeah, right. Not that he'd had a choice. His grandparents hadn't had that kind of money.

But where she'd traveled wasn't his concern. He refused to feel sorry for someone who wanted to drag his reputation through the mud, but maybe he would show her a few things—like what sightseeing on a ranch was all about.

"There's a spring-fed pond not far from here. I used to practically live there during the summer. We can water the horses. Want to see it?"

"I'd like that."

"I'll race you."

"You're on!"

She lightly kicked the sides of her horse. Taffy leapt forward and she had to grab the saddle horn to keep from falling off, but she didn't slow down. An amazing woman—but still a reporter.

He chuckled as he sat watching her. Damn, but she was something else. She had plenty of determination and stubbornness. But that's why she'd been nicknamed The Barracuda, and he needed to remember that.

"Are you going to let me win?" she yelled over her shoulder as she reined the horse in.

He grinned. "You're going the wrong way!" He twirled Tornado to the east and nudged her forward.

"That wasn't fair," Nikki told Cal when she caught up to him, but she had to bite back the laughter that threatened to bubble out of her. That was the most fun she'd ever had in her entire life. Who knew riding a horse could be that exhilarating?

"Yeah, I know. But you enjoyed every second of it, admit it."

She cocked an eyebrow. "It was fun. There, are you satisfied?"

"It's okay to enjoy life."

"I enjoy life very much. Do you think I don't?"

"I wondered. You're stuck in the nineteen twenties doing research, you've never been to an amusement park, and you've apparently never celebrated a holiday."

She cringed at the lie about why she was really here, but it wasn't as though she could tell him the truth. Now that she really thought about it, her life had been tame, except for her job. There'd never been anything tame about the stories she went after—well, except this one, and she didn't really want to think about it right now.

They rode the rest of the way in silence, stopping when they came to a stand of trees.

Cal swung his leg over Tornado and jumped off. She swung her leg over Taffy and jumped to the ground, too. Immediately, her legs buckled. Before she could fall, Cal caught her up against him.

"Did I forget to mention riding a horse is a lot like going from a ship to land? You have to get your balance back." There was laughter in his voice.

"I believe you did leave out that minor detail."

His arms were firm as they held her close. If she raised her head a fraction, and circled her hand behind his neck, she could pull his face down to hers so their lips would meet.

Except she was still pissed that he hadn't seemed quite as excited about their lovemaking as she had. She hoped he got a killer hard-on and suffered a great deal of pain. Then and only then, she might relieve him of the discomfort.

"I'm fine now." She pushed away. Her legs actually wobbled more. Oh, yeah, she'd really punished him. This was kind of like cutting off her nose to spite her face.

"The trail is narrow here, but it'll widen out when we get to the pond. We can walk the horses to it."

Was there sweat beading his forehead? She didn't get her hopes up. It was getting warm, and they'd been riding for quite some time. It was nothing more than that. The last time she'd looked at her reflection she'd looked pretty hot. So why did he seem so uninterested?

He led the way and she followed.

When she reached the pond, she stopped. An oasis in the middle of rolling hills. Curtained off by trees and framed with lush green grass, the secluded location presented a pretty picture of peaceful serenity. Her irritability evaporated.

"It's beautiful."

"Brian and I used to pretend it was the place where fairies lived. Magical people for a magical place." He took the reins from her and led the horses closer so they could get a drink.

"Fairies?" she asked, raising an eyebrow.

"If it makes you feel better, there were a couple of dragons, too." He shrugged. "We were kids with vivid imaginations. Didn't you ever pretend you were in a different land with magical creatures?"

"No." Her parents had told Nikki fantasies were great time wasters. If you wanted something, you went after it by working hard. The dreamers were the ones who usually had nothing.

Odd, but Cal had quite a lot, and he'd reached his goals even though he'd apparently had strange musings. She felt as though she'd missed something along the way while she was growing up.

"Do you swim?" he asked as he loosely tethered the horses to a bush so they could eat the grass without running off.

Swim? She used the pool every day she went to the gym. "I'm a very good swimmer."

"The water is nice this time of year."

Her pulse quickened. "I'm not wearing a suit."

"You don't need one out here. Don't tell me you've never been skinny dipping."

The water looked inviting. Swimming was her passion. The heat of the sultry Texas sun beating down on her shoulders was a great inducement and she knew exactly what it would lead to.

"Skinny dipping?" Nikki asked, eyeing the dark waters with more than a little trepidation.

"You look nervous," Cal said.

She frowned. "Not about getting naked. I'm not in the least ashamed of my body."

"And you shouldn't be." His gaze swept over her in a way that made her body tingle. "If you're afraid of the water, don't be. There's nothing in there that'll hurt you."

Okay, she'd try just about anything once even if she wasn't so sure what was beneath the murky water. She wasn't a coward. She unbuttoned her shirt and tossed it across a bush. Her bra followed. She looked at him. Cal wasn't doing anything but watching her.

"You are planning on swimming, aren't you?"

"Oh, yeah, that and a whole lot more."

Chapter 16

Nikki was glad she and Cal were on the same page, because she wanted to do a whole lot more, too. Except that he wasn't getting naked.

"You aren't going to take off your clothes?" Now that would be a shame.

Cal reached for his top button. "I'm enjoying the view."

"Is that so?" She grinned as she toed off her boots, then unbuttoned her jeans and slowly slid the zipper down. She kicked out of her jeans, leaving her black lacy thong on as she tugged off her socks. Then slowly, seductively, she removed the thong, too.

"Have you ever had sex in the water?"

It wasn't so much a question as it was a promise. Her nipples tightened as a familiar ache swept over her.

"I think I'm about to."

Nikki walked to the water's edge and hesitantly stepped in. It was cooler than she expected. The bottom was smooth, soft except for an occasional rock. Okay, she could do this. She waded out a little farther.

Not long ago, she would've laughed if anyone had told her she'd be swimming in something other than a pool, or living on a ranch in a cabin without utilities. Or milking a cow, gathering eggs, or churning butter.

Or that she would meet a very incredible man and they would have fantastic, mind-blowing sex.

Or that she would be deceiving the man in the hopes of getting a story.

Drat, why did she have to think about that now? She quickly pushed that thought to the far recesses of her mind. She'd worry about the consequences of her actions later.

When she was waist deep, she dropped down until the water covered her head. Cold enveloped her, but different from a winter day. It was more exhilarating and exciting and . . . fun. She pushed with her feet and shot back up, shoving the hair from her face as she turned toward the bank.

No, she wouldn't think about the story she was trying to get. Not right now, not when Cal's passion-filled gaze captured hers.

His heated look started at the top of her head, lingered on her breasts, then moved downward as if he could see past the shadowy water to her legs, which trembled so hard from need she could barely stand.

She didn't take a breath until he turned away to untie the leather strips at the back of his saddle. He brought the blanket that had been rolled up and laid it on top of a large rock.

Tossing his hat to the side, Cal grasped the bottom of his black T-shirt, and in one movement, he tugged it over his head. A fine sheen of sweat covered his sun-bronzed skin. Nikki swallowed hard to remove the lump that had formed in her throat. Heat coursed through her body like hot wax dripping down the sides of a melting candle.

Entranced, she found herself unable to look away as his hand slid down his stomach, over his six-pack abs, and down to the first button of his jeans. He tugged it through the buttonhole and continued with the second, third, and fourth. Hooking his hands into the waistband, he pushed the denim down, revealing white briefs.

There was enough exposed skin to make her muscles turn to the consistency of pudding. She tried to drag her gaze away, to think about anything besides the fact she wanted him so bad she'd probably raised the temperature of the water at least a degree. But she could only stare as he performed his striptease.

No, she didn't look away. Hell, she had an incredible urge to yell, "Take it off, take it all off!" But she already knew he would. He was stripping for her and it was a hell of a turn-on.

He hooked his thumbs in the waistband of his briefs and smiled. A slow, sexy smile that said he knew exactly what she wanted. Then when she was about ready to launch herself out of the water and throw herself at him, he pushed his briefs downward, revealing his incredible erection. Her mouth went dry; her body burned for him.

He grabbed a condom out of his jeans before dropping them behind him, and sliding it on in slow motion. Her hands itched to be the one to do that, to caress him. He stepped into the water and advanced. She took a step toward him, wanting to feel his arms around her.

He grinned devilishly, then dove into the water, a ripple the only sign of where he'd been.

Now where was he?

Water splashed. She whirled around. He stood before her, water dripping down his face. Cal laid a hand on her shoulder, slid his fingers down until they curled around her arm, and tugged her toward him. She trembled, knew he felt her reaction. His eyebrows arched upward as his other hand brushed across the fullness of her bottom lip.

"Do you know how incredibly beautiful you are? The first time I saw you, I wanted you." His words scraped against her skin.

He lowered his head until his mouth covered hers. She drew in a quick, sharp breath and tasted his need. His tongue stroked hers. He brushed a strand of hair from her cheek, his touch sending a spasm of pleasure over her.

"I want you," he murmured.

"I want you, too." He drew her closer, and she pressed against him.

Cal knew this was wrong, but it felt too damned good to stop. When he gazed into the golden-brown depths of her eyes, he could only think of how right it felt. He wanted her like he'd wanted no other woman. He'd sensed the fire inside her from day one. And even knowing he'd probably get burned, he had to have her again.

A groan escaped his lips when he cupped her breast, the nipple already hard from the cold water. He rolled it beneath his thumb.

She gasped.

"You're so perfect."

Her body shivered.

"Are you cold?"

"Just the opposite. You make me hot. I think you've cast a spell over me, Cal Braxton."

"Good." Slipping his hands beneath her arms he brought her out of the water. She grasped his shoulders, wrapping her legs around him. He took his time as he lowered her.

He nipped a breast, then circled the orb with his tongue before sucking the pebbled nipple into his mouth. She moaned, arching toward him. He lowered her farther, his tongue tasting her skin, wanting even more. His mouth found hers again as their bodies began to join. She tightened her legs around him, pulling him deeper inside. Hot liquid fire filled him. He cupped her buttocks, rocking her against him, groaning with pleasure.

She nipped his neck with her teeth, then licked across the tiny wound. He sucked in his breath, pulling her closer, crushing her body against his. The heat of her body scorched him as she kissed his face.

"Look at me," he said when her glazed eyes began to drift closed.

Slowly, her eyes opened and their gazes locked. He wanted to watch her. To know the very moment she was ready. He wanted to see the passion flare in her eyes. It had to be as good for her as it was for him. He'd settle for no less.

"Now." Her arms tightened around his neck as her mouth moved over his.

"Not yet. Soon." Cal wanted every one of her senses to explode when she came. He nibbled her ear; his tongue plunged inside.

She cried out. "I need you."

He ignored her pleas for release. "I want to taste you again. All of you." Cal raked his teeth along her neck. He looked deep into her eyes. "Next time you'll let me. Promise me that you'll let me kiss your sex, that you'll let me lick every inch of it."

"Yes," she cried as her body trembled. "I need . . . I need . . ."

He thrust deeper.

She gasped and pressed closer.

Water splashed around them, slapping their bodies and intensifying the motion. The strain of holding back became too much as her hardened nipples brushed against his chest. Spasms clutched his body. The muscles in his legs grew taut as every part of him became a roaring fire burning out of control. When the explosion hit, it rocked him to the core of his being. He clasped her tighter against him, cupping her butt and pulling her in closer.

She cried out her pleasure when she came. Their ragged breathing echoed in the silence. Still holding her close, he moved to shallow water, and sank to his knees. Water lapped around their waists in gentle caresses.

Right now, he knew if Nikki asked him about what had happened between him and Cynthia, he would tell her every blasted thing there was to tell.

Yeah, he was in deep shit.

He drew in deep mouthfuls of air. No woman had ever made his legs tremble like this—hell, his whole body.

They finally waded to the bank. He spread the blanket and they collapsed on it.

"I could sleep the rest of the day," she said, stretching as she rolled to her back.

Without really thinking, he cupped her breast, lightly massaging.

"Or not." Her laugh was shaky.

He realized what he was doing and stopped, moved to his back as he lay on the blanket. "Sorry."

"I'm not." She moved into the crook of his arm, resting her head on his chest.

He stared at the tree limbs crisscrossing above him. This was nice, and he didn't regret anything they'd done, either. He'd told himself after he discovered Nikki was a reporter out to get a story, he didn't have to give her one, and he wouldn't.

"I can't believe you don't have a girlfriend," she said, breaking the silence.

And the moment was destroyed. One little sentence and she'd killed it.

"I'm a free agent," he said.

"So you've never been engaged?"

Damn, if he didn't know who she really was, he'd probably be spilling his guts right now. Telling her things that would end up in an article for the world to read. Except he did know better.

"I was engaged once, but it didn't work out," he said. Before she could probe further, he asked a question of his own. "What about you? Ever gotten close to the altar?"

"No. Marriage is way down on the bottom of my list of things to do. So, who was she?"

"Who was who?"

"The girl you almost married."

"I didn't marry her and that should be all that matters."

"I guess every woman wants to know her predecessor."

Cal turned in a way so that she was half beneath him. His lips found hers. She moaned when he deepened the kiss, but he abruptly ended it before he could go very far and jumped up instead.

"I promised Brian I would help at the ranch this afternoon."

She frowned. "I think most of the afternoon is already gone."

"So I guess I'd better get back." He pulled on his briefs, then his jeans.

She didn't look too happy, but she stood and reached for her clothes and began to reluctantly pull them on.

Damn, she was temptation. He quickly averted his eyes and grabbed for his shirt.

As soon as they were dressed, he helped Nikki mount. He played the perfect guide on the way back to the homestead, pointing out different kinds of trees. Once a jackrabbit popped his head up, long ears straight in the air. He kept the conversation going so she wouldn't have a chance to ask any questions about Cynthia.

She didn't look happy when he left her at the cabin. But she also didn't have any fodder for a story, either.

Damn, he was good. He was still smiling when he rode up to the barn at the ranch. Barracuda, yeah, well she'd just met a shark.

Chapter 17

Brian walked around the side of the swimming pool, careful not to get too close to the little Darnell boys, who were splashing wildly. Jim Darnell was lazing in one of the lounge chairs but keeping a watchful eye on his sons. The boys' father actually looked as if he were half dead. It must have been an active day for them.

"Do you remember when we had that much energy?" Jim asked without moving from his seat.

Brian looked at the boys. For just a second he saw a pasture with trees and low hills. He saw him and Cal racing across the space until their lungs felt as though they would burst from lack of oxygen.

Yeah, he remembered.

He also remembered Cal had wanted him to go riding, and for a moment, when they'd been talking, Brian had recaptured something that had been lost between them.

But then he'd thought about canceling when something business-related came up. He'd need to go out of town on Friday. It hadn't even been that big of a deal, and he wondered why he'd even considered leaving. Cal was right: Brian needed to relax more, and maybe he wanted to spend a little more time with Cal. They hadn't done a lot of things together since his brother arrived.

"It would be nice to have an overabundance of energy,"

Brian told the father as he returned his attention to the young family. "Did you have a good day?"

"We went on an arrowhead hunt. I think your foreman took us over nearly all of the south end of the ranch on horseback, and now swimming." He nodded toward his sons. "They're like that battery bunny rabbit."

They laughed. Yeah, he had a feeling his grandparents had felt the same way about him and Cal.

Katie Darnell came out to join her husband and sons. There was something different about her. She practically glowed. She didn't look nearly as tired as when they'd first arrived. Apparently, she'd had a good day, too.

Jim studied her. "It looks like you enjoyed your massage. You look beautiful."

She smiled. "Celeste was wonderful. Not only did she have the most intoxicating fragrance filling the room, but after my massage, which totally relaxed me, she brewed me a cup of tea that she said was a special blend and had the cook send over some cookies. I felt very pampered."

Tea? Cookies? Brian could feel the color drain from his face. Had she brewed one of his guests something she'd concocted from her herbs? Oh, hell. Visions of a lawsuit filled his mind.

"In fact," Katie continued, "I've never felt this good ever. It's almost as though she added something to the tea to make me feel so wonderful." She laughed.

Great, drugs. Hell, Celeste had even looked liked a hippie when she'd first arrived. Brian gritted his teeth and drew in a deep breath.

"I'm glad you enjoyed your time at the spa," Brian told her. "I'll be sure to pass on your compliments to Celeste. In fact, I'll do it right now. If you'll excuse me." He opened the French doors and went inside.

What if Celeste had given Ms. Darnell some kind of narcotic? Hell, it wouldn't just be a lawsuit he'd be looking at. He could see the cops showing up in a late-night raid, all that he'd worked for destroyed. Damn it, he'd been afraid something like this would happen.

His jaw began to twitch as he strode inside the spa. For once, the tranquil atmosphere did nothing to calm him.

"Mr. Braxton, did you need something?" Rhonda asked as she looked up from behind her desk.

"Celeste?"

"In the therapy room."

He didn't stop but walked right toward it and went inside. Celeste was putting clean sheets on the table but looked up when he entered. He shut the door behind him, hoping whatever was said would go no further than this room. He'd give her enough money to leave and he'd make up something to explain why she'd taken off.

But first, he had to know what was in the tea. "What did you give Ms. Darnell?"

"Katie?"

"That's the only Ms. Darnell that I know, so yes, what did you give her?"

"A massage." She tucked in a corner of the sheet.

"After that?"

"I had Betty send over some cookies."

He counted to five. "The tea. What was in the tea?"

She was beginning to look a little worried, and so she should. He couldn't have an employee drugging his guests.

"I'm not sure. It was your tea."

"My tea?" Some of his anger began to dissipate.

She nodded, then reached behind her for a box. "Spicy chai tea." She pointed to the words on the box. "Special blend. I thought it sounded good so I brewed us a cup. Is something wrong with Katie? I feel fine, and Rhonda had a cup."

"My tea?"

"It was in the supply closet. Apparently, Amy ordered it but never used it. I thought Katie needed extraspecial attention because she seemed so frazzled. After the massage, I had Rhonda brew the tea and Betty send over a plate of cookies.

I think Katie just needed some female conversation to feel like a woman again. I thought it had worked." She worried her bottom lip.

"That's all you did?"

She nodded. Man, how wrong could he have been?

"I'm sorry."

"For what?"

"For thinking . . ." His brow creased.

Understanding slowly dawned on her face. "You thought I'd drugged her?"

But rather than being insulted, she was smiling, then laughing at his misconceptions about her. And why shouldn't she? He'd made a total ass out of himself.

"Again, I apologize."

"Apology accepted. It's not like you know that much about me, so it's okay that you'd be a little suspicious."

"Not good enough."

Her eyebrows rose. "Excuse me?"

"Have dinner with me this evening. I have a private dining area. I'd like it if you'd join me."

"Do you think the boss would mind?"

Now she was teasing him. He guessed it was better than her throwing something at him.

"Please."

"Okay," she said as she smoothed her hand over the crisp white sheet and tucked it a little tighter at the corner. "I have a few ideas for the spa that I'd like to talk over with you. Nothing major. I asked Rhonda and she thought they were good ideas."

"You have ideas already?"

"Oh, it's a great spa. I just think if you added a few things it could be better."

"Like tea and cookies?"

The warmth in her smile filled the room. "Yes, like tea and cookies . . . chocolates."

"Then I'll see you about six and we'll discuss your ideas."

"Six it is."

There wasn't any reason for him to hang around. He'd blundered and apologized. Then he'd invited her to dinner. Dumb excuse, but he did want to make it up to her.

And maybe he wanted to find out more about the woman who had made such a big difference in Katie Darnell's day.

He left the spa area, his steps lighter than they had been in a long time. He glanced down at his watch as he walked inside the main building. He didn't have that long to wait, either.

"You look like you're in a good mood," Cal said.

Brian looked up. "I'm always in a good mood." His gaze swept over Cal. "Your hair's wet."

"I went swimming in the pond."

"We have a pool."

"I like the pond. Remember when we used to go there?"

Brian smiled. "I remember how we used to get in trouble for going there. Grandma was afraid we'd drown."

"That's three times."

Cal had finally lost his marbles. "Huh?"

"You smiled the day I arrived, when we walked up from the barn and you were telling me about Wanda Jo, then just now. I was afraid you'd forgotten how."

"Funny."

"Seriously, you need to slow down a little and enjoy life."

"You're right," Brian agreed.

"I am?"

"Yes, you are." When Cal grinned, Brian remembered just how much his big brother meant to him. Speaking of which. "How's it going with that reporter? I hate that you're having to deal with all this crap. Say the word and I'll toss her off the property."

"I think I can handle her."

"Good."

"I'll see you at dinner tonight."

Brian could feel color flooding his face. "Actually, I have other plans."

Cal gave him a questioning look.

"I'm having dinner with Celeste. She wants to discuss some ideas she thinks will improve the spa."

"Ideas?"

Brian couldn't stop his grin. "Yeah, ideas. Now go so I can finish my work." But as Cal walked away, Brian heard his chuckle.

Brian found himself looking at his watch again and wondering why time was moving so slowly.

And then it was a quarter to six and he could feel his pulse speed up. When he stepped out of his office, Celeste was there, waiting for him.

"I would've come to your room," he said.

"I didn't know this was a date. I thought it was an apology, and so we could discuss some ideas."

A smile tugged at the corners of his mouth. She had him there. "You're in Texas, ma'am. A gentleman always meets a lady at her door."

"Is that right?" She still looked skeptical.

"Absolutely."

"I'm from California."

"I won't hold it against you. I'm sure you got to Texas as quickly as you could."

She cocked an eyebrow. "That's so not funny."

"Then I'll just hope you're hungry."

"Starved."

"Good." He led the way to the secluded alcove away from the dining room. This was his private spot. The bay windows looked out onto the back pasture, reminding him of what it had been like years ago, before he'd opened the ranch to the public. French doors led to a private patio.

There was no more spectacular view than when the sun was setting as it was now. Soft oranges blended into a darker red, then spread across into a wide open deep blue sky with threads of a light gray weaving through the palette of magnificent colors.

"You really love it here, don't you?" she said.

"Does it show that much?"

"And then some."

"I grew up here—me and Cal. It was our grandparents' place. Our parents were killed in an accident and they raised us."

"I'm sorry about your parents."

"I didn't really know them."

"Then I'm doubly sorry."

For a moment, he saw pain etched on her face and he wondered if she was remembering something from her own past, but he didn't press because one of the young men who helped serve in the kitchen arrived with glasses and a bottle of wine that Brian had arranged for earlier.

"I took the liberty of asking Betty to fix us something special. I hope you enjoy the meal."

She smiled and again he marveled at how she seemed to brighten the room.

"I'm sure I will."

The waiter returned a few minutes later with salads and a basket of bread. For the first time in his life, Brian didn't know what to talk about with a woman. Celeste saved him from stuttering like a fool.

"Tell me about life on the ranch."

Okay, that was a safe topic as long as he didn't mention Wanda Jo. "We have a ghost." Oh, that was smart. Now she'd think she was having dinner with a lunatic.

"Really? I thought you didn't believe in them."

He shrugged, feeling the heat move up his face and was glad they were eating by candlelight. "I've never seen it or anything."

"Sometimes you don't have to. You can sense they're there. Is it the person who smoked the pipe?"

"No, that was Grandfather. He loved his pipe." He cleared

his throat. "The ghost is at the old homestead. My grand-mother said a young woman died there."

"Oh, how sad that her spirit is trapped."

He frowned. "I never thought about it like that." He took a drink of his wine. "We have a guest staying there."

"Will she free the ghost's spirit?"

He laughed outright at that. "I don't think so. She's a re-porter trying to get a story."

"What kind of story?"

"About Cal." When she still looked confused, he contin-ued, "My brother plays professional football."

"Yes, I know, and he does it very well."

"She's trying to dig up some dirt on him."

Celeste frowned. "I hope she doesn't print anything that will hurt his career. This reporter doesn't sound like a very nice person."

"I don't think she is. Cal said Ms. Scott looks like an old nag our grandfather used to have." He laughed and shook his head at the description Cal had used. That had been a really ugly horse.

"So why does he let her stay? I would think you'd throw her off the property."

They stopped talking when the server brought their main course. As soon as he was gone, Brian continued.

"If it had been up to me, the reporter would already be gone." He shrugged. "I think he wants to teach her a lesson about messing with other people's lives."

"I hope he does."

He studied her. "Do you really like football?"

"I love it."

An amazing woman. He nodded toward her plate. "How's the steak?"

"Perfect."

They finished eating and both declined dessert. He refilled her glass and they stepped to the terrace. A fountain bubbled in the background.

"It's so tranquil here." She looked up at the sky. "And so many stars. They seem so bright and so close I could almost imagine that I could reach up and grab a handful."

He followed her to the edge of the patio, and when she turned to look up at him, he could only stare.

"What?" she asked.

"You're so beautiful."

She raised her glass to her lips and took a drink. He could handle that, but when she ran her tongue across her lips to catch that last drop of wine, he couldn't resist leaning forward and brushing his lips across hers.

"Sweet," he said, stroking her neck.

She took a step back. "I'm . . . I'm sorry if I gave the impression that there would be more to this than . . . than sharing a meal and discussing the spa. Maybe we should leave our talk until tomorrow." She hurried away before he could stop her.

"No, I'm sorry," he muttered. Why the hell had he kissed her? But, then, he thought he knew the answer. She was young and beautiful and like no one he'd ever met.

And he'd ruined it by acting like a fool.

Or maybe not. For just a second he was almost certain she'd returned his kiss.

Chapter 18

Nikki dragged her eyelids open and stared at the clock as she waited for her eyes to adjust so she could read the numbers. It was seven. Something was different about this morning. But what?

She shoved the cover back and forced herself to sit on the side of the bed. Oh, Lord, every muscle in her body ached. Who knew riding a horse could make a person this sore. She'd only thought milking and churning butter was bad. Okay, churning butter was still a horrible memory.

It suddenly occurred to her what was different. The rooster hadn't crowed. She came wide awake.

Oh no, what if it had died during the night? Guilt washed over her as she hobbled out of bed and stumbled to the front door, sighing with relief when she saw the bird.

Romeo strutted back and forth in front of Bessie Two's pen. Well, as much as he could since he still listed to the side. But he was alive, and that's what counted.

She stepped to the front porch. The fresh air was crisp and there was even a clean freshness carried on the light breeze.

Birds were singing and a squirrel jumped from tree to tree. Warmth spread through her. So maybe the country wasn't so bad after all.

Yeah, as if she didn't know the real reason why she felt as

if she were walking on clouds: Cal. He'd brought something new and wonderful to her life.

Fantastic orgasms!

No, no it was more than that.

She closed her eyes for a moment and remembered how it felt to have him hold her close, brush his lips across hers, and make sweet love to her while skinny dipping in the pond.

Life was suddenly very, very good. More than reporting the news, more than going after the story. More than the cutthroat world. Excitement bubbled inside her and she just couldn't keep it bottled up a second longer.

She swung her arms wide and welcomed this new day with joy. "Good morning, world!"

The rooster jumped three feet off the ground, turned and saw her, then began to squawk in his soprano crow.

"Cock! Cock! Cock!"

Wings flapping he made a beeline around the side of the barn.

"Moooooo," Bessie Two reprimanded.

The birds grew silent and the squirrel stopped to look at her as though she'd lost her mind.

Nikki slunk back inside the house. Okay, so maybe she'd been a little too energetic in her appreciation of the start of a new day. It was all Cal's fault that she was so giddy. He'd cast some kind of spell over her.

She wouldn't let the way he made her feel sway her from the reason she was here. Maybe she was just discovering there was more to life than her job. She could have both. Couldn't she—relaxation and work? Yes, of course she could.

She quickly pulled on clothes and made a fast trip to the outhouse. She was back in the cabin and just finishing off a soda and a Danish when she heard Cal's pickup. She quickly shoved the last bite in her mouth and downed the rest of her drink before throwing her trash into a bag and hiding it in the cabinet.

She was just too damned good, although she was starting to get tired of ham sandwiches for lunch and dinner, and pastry for breakfast.

She grabbed the bucket and went to the front porch. "I was just going to start the milking," she lied. "Isn't it a beautiful day?" And it was, so she really wasn't lying about that.

But she couldn't help thinking somebody somewhere was sipping a latte in a tiny bistro watching the traffic whizz by and thinking the same thing about it being a beautiful day.

He grinned and they walked toward the barn. "Yeah, it is," he said.

But that person in the city wasn't with Cal. Had she ever met a man more handsome? She didn't think so. And he was so nice to show her everything there was to know about a long-ago era. If she had wanted to know about it, this would be the ideal situation.

"I didn't ask—how long will you be visiting your brother?"

"Who knows? Maybe longer than I thought."

"Don't you have to get back? Isn't there some kind of football training you have to go to?"

Silence.

She stopped and looked at him. "You're still on the team, aren't you?" He stopped walking, but didn't answer. "I mean, you didn't quit or anything, did you?" What if Cynthia's father had gotten him fired? Her daddy was a powerful man.

"I've been thinking about retiring, taking things a little easier. A person can get knocked around only so many times before the body begins to protest."

Now that was a juicy tidbit for her article.

"Any thoughts about marriage and kids?"

He started walking again, so she was forced to keep up with his longer strides. "Are you applying for the position?"

She laughed. "No. Like I said, that's on the bottom of my list of things to do in this lifetime."

They walked inside the barn and toward the back.

"No, just curious." She smiled, sure she presented the picture of innocence. But when he looked at her, for just a brief second, she felt a pinch of guilt.

"Tell you what, you get the feed and I'll start the milking," he said.

He didn't have to twist her arm. Besides, she needed to put a little space between them. She couldn't feel guilty. That emotion was not allowed in her line of work. She was here to do a job, to get a story. If she started feeling guilty about what she needed to write, her career would soon be down the tube.

She took a deep, steady breath, trying to regroup her feelings. "You're sure you want to do the milking?"

"Yeah." Cal scooped some water in the bucket and squatted beside Bessie and began to wash her udders.

There was something different about Nikki but he couldn't quite put his finger on what it was. She was still probing for answers, but that was nothing new. There for just a brief second, she'd looked a little . . . guilty?

Yeah, sure, he needed his eyes checked. Jeff was right about her being good, and Cal was seeing firsthand just how good.

But when they made love, he could forget all about why she was here. He had a feeling she did, too. He knew damned well she wasn't faking her responses to his touch.

But what the hell was he doing offering to milk the blasted cow?

As though he didn't know the answer to that one. When she'd walked out on the porch and the sun had bathed her in morning light, it had been all he could do to breathe. She was the most beautiful woman he'd ever seen.

And for that moment in time, he'd pushed away the truth. That she was only here for a story and as soon as she got it, she'd leave in a flash. All the time they'd spent with each other would mean absolutely nothing to her. He was only a means to an end. The sex was great, but bye-bye, adios, so long. Just like all the other women he'd dated.

He finished washing the cow's udders, tossed the water, and sat on the stool.

As he started milking, he thought he should probably have his head examined for thinking for one second she'd change her mind about writing her article, and until she'd started asking her questions this morning, he'd thought exactly that. Nikki was a reporter and she was just like all the rest of the reporters with whom he'd crossed paths.

Except she was The Barracuda.

He covertly watched her out of the corner of his eye as she put the lid back on the feed bucket, making sure it was on good and tight.

"Tell me about your books," he said when she leaned against the fence.

For a moment, she didn't say anything. Her expression changed from relaxed to guilty. Maybe not guilty, probably not guilty, but he'd at least made her damned uncomfortable.

"Uh, what exactly do you want to know?"

"Is this your first?"

"Yes."

"What do you do when you're not writing? I'm guessing you have a job. Some way to support yourself."

"Of course I have a job."

He waited to see what kind of lie she would come up with this time.

"I work in a library. I'm the . . . head librarian."

He covered his snort with a cough. "Now why didn't I ever get lucky enough to have a librarian who looked like you? The only ones I knew were old or married."

Her smile was wobbly.

Yeah, she was full of lies and he was a fool if he fell for them. Maybe it was time to up the ante and see just how important getting the story was to her.

He finished the milking and stood.

"I thought we might spend the day together . . . and the night," he said, letting his fingers trail down her arm, then taking her hand.

Her pupils widened, desire flaring. "I'd like that."

"Good." He took her hand and handed her the milk bucket. "I have it all planned out. Have you ever been camping?"

She shifted the bucket to her other hand. "Camping?" Her expression showed surprise.

"Yeah, pioneer women did it all the time." He frowned. "I'm surprised that you've never experienced sleeping under the stars. You haven't run across camping out in your research?"

Her face lost some of its color. "Well, yes, of course I have, but I would've needed a guide and there wasn't really anyone . . . uh . . . available."

He grinned. "It's a good thing we met then. I'll be able to show you all about camping."

"But who'll milk Bessie Two?"

"One of the ranch hands. Believe me, you'll enjoy this as much as you do the chores here at the ranch."

Her smile wobbled. "Oh, goody."

Yeah, The Barracuda had met her match. He had a feeling after camping out beneath the stars, she'd be more than ready to cry uncle and give up on her pursuit to expose his private life.

"We're going camping, Marge! Did you hear me? Camping!"

"Both times." Marge sighed across the phone. "Okay, that's it. I want you to give up the story and come in. You don't belong on a ranch, let alone doing everything you've had to do. You'll feel lots better when you sink your teeth into a nice, juicy politician."

No, she wouldn't, because Cal wouldn't be there. "Listen, I'll give it a couple more days and see what happens."

"If you're sure."

No, she wasn't. Not anymore. But she'd never given up on anything in her life and she wasn't sure how to let go of this story.

"Yeah, I'm sure."

"You don't sound sure."

"I'm sure."

"You haven't fallen for this guy or anything, have you? He's one of the ten most eligible bachelors in the area. Hell, the whole country. I think he's even ranked number three or something. I doubt it would be very hard to fall for him."

She straightened. "Of course I haven't fallen for him. You know me better than that."

"Good. Cal left a string of broken hearts when he hooked up with Cynthia, and now she's been added to the list. I'd hate for your name to be on it as well."

"Have you forgotten who you're talking to? I'm The Barracuda."

"You're right." Marge laughed. "Just be careful. I'd hate it if you got eaten by a bear."

Nikki's head jerked around. "They have bears in Texas?"

"Beats me."

Great, one more thing to worry about. They said their good-byes and Nikki flipped her phone closed, then quickly moved away from the outhouse.

She wasn't looking forward to camping at all. Cal would be able to protect her from wild animals, wouldn't he? It wasn't like he hadn't grown up here. He knew the land.

She snorted. If he knew her real reason for being here he'd probably gladly feed her to the bears.

She went back inside and threw a few things into a bag. Cal said to pack light and suggested using a bag so it could be tied on the packhorse. This trip was not sounding good.

As she started to turn away, she caught sight of a blue fog forming in the corner. She froze. Gas leak? Doubtful since there was no gas, only wood-burning stoves and a fireplace.

There was a deep, sad sighing, and then the mist faded away. A cold chill ran down her spine.

She grabbed her bag and hurried to the porch, deciding to wait for Cal there. As the screen closed behind her, she looked over her shoulder. Nothing. But she knew she hadn't imagined what she'd seen.

Ghosts didn't exist, dammit. If they did, then everything she'd grown up with had been false information. The whole structure of what her life was about would be in question. But was she ready to start believing in what she couldn't taste, see, or touch?

Would she start to question other things as well? She didn't think she was ready to delve deeper than the surface of what her life was about. She was afraid of what she might see.

Celeste bypassed Brian's office and took the long way around to the spa. She couldn't believe that he'd kissed her last night or that for a split second, she'd kissed him back. Heat rushed up her face.

Or that she'd enjoyed it so much.

And then she'd done the unthinkable: she'd run away as though she was a virgin or something—which she wasn't. Why couldn't she have said something intelligent or witty? She'd traveled all over the country, seen a lot of things—she should have had a zippy comeback.

Except she'd never been the type of woman who could be provocative. What you saw was what you got.

Maybe she wouldn't have to face him today. One could only hope.

She opened the door and stepped inside the building and was surrounded by peace and serenity. Boy, did she need that this morning. She waved to Rhonda, who was on the phone.

Rhonda mouthed something, but she couldn't understand

what she was trying to tell her, so she just held up one finger to indicate they'd talk after Rhonda got off the phone. Then Celeste went on toward her room.

Yesterday had been busy as she learned the lay of the spa. She'd also met the other two women and some more of the guests. Her first massage wasn't until later this morning, but she wanted to go through the supplies to see exactly what she could use. But first she wanted to light her candle so the warm vanilla fragrance could fill the room.

But when she opened her door, she realized what Rhonda had been trying to tell her.

Brian looked up, holding the candle to his nose. "Nice fragrance."

"Vanilla," she said. What was he doing here? She didn't want him here. But the wild beating of her heart gave lie to her thoughts.

"Come in and close the door."

She hesitated.

"Please. I won't try to kiss you."

Heat rose up her face as she closed the door. "I didn't think that you would." No, she'd been too busy thinking about the kiss they'd already shared.

"It was inexcusable."

She wouldn't go quite that far.

"Believe me, I don't usually pounce on my employees."

She studied him. "Why did you kiss me?"

He hesitated. "You're a beautiful woman." He set the candle down. "It's been a long time since I've been out on a date. I guess I got caught up in the moment. It won't happen again."

He started toward the door, and as he passed her, she caught the scent of his aftershave. It wrapped around her, daring her to let him walk out of the room without saying anything.

She knew she would have to make the next move. "I enjoyed the kiss. It startled me, was all."

He paused with his hand on the doorknob. "You did?" He grinned and Celeste saw the change in him. Suddenly he wasn't her boss or even a businessman—he was just a man, and a very handsome one at that.

"Yes, I liked it very much."

He frowned. "I don't date my employees."

Fear coursed through her. Was he going to fire her? "I don't date ex-bosses," she quickly said.

"Don't worry, I won't let you go. I think I'll have to make an exception to my rule." He turned serious. "Your job will never hinge on what happens between us, though. I want you to understand that."

"I do." And she meant it. From the little things she caught from the other people who worked for him, Brian was honorable.

He left and she let her breath out. Okay, that had gone well. Warm fuzzies began to swirl inside her. She liked the way they felt.

Chapter 19

The Scotts did not give up. They only bared their teeth and advanced. That thought didn't keep Nikki's gaze from darting around. She expected a ferocious rabid bear to jump out from behind a tree and eat her at any minute. If there were ghosts, then there were probably bears. At the very least, aliens ready to swoop down and kidnap her.

She was losing it.

How the hell was she going to survive the camping trip? She was beginning to think maybe everything her parents had tried to teach her might not exactly fit with this situation, either. They hadn't taught her anything about survival in the wilderness. Nikki didn't even watch the reality shows. She'd only seen the occasional commercials. A lot of good that would do her.

If something happened to Cal would she have to exist on worms to stay alive until someone discovered her malnourished body? She'd read somewhere that worms were pure protein. Starving sounded a lot easier then eating a worm.

"How are you doing back there?" Cal asked.

"Just fine. Great, in fact. I don't suppose you brought a compass with you or a radio of sorts?"

"Don't need them."

So in other words, if something happened and she perished

out here, she could justify placing all the blame on her parents.

Great, now she was starting to question everything she'd been taught. If not for what she'd learned from her parents, she wouldn't be where she was right now. She'd done damned good as a reporter, risen to the top in record time. She wasn't about to let this silly little article be her downfall.

She grimaced. Sitting in the saddle was another story, though. God, her thighs felt as if they'd been rubbed raw. The Thigh-Master had nothing on straddling a horse and riding up and down hills all morning. She'd probably scraped off a good two layers of skin.

"We're almost there."

Since they'd been riding for at least three hours, she would hope so.

"It's over that hill."

Oh, good, another hill. That really stretched the muscles. Feel the burn.

But she and Taffy made it up the hill. And Cal was right again. It was beautiful. From this viewpoint, she looked down on the river and the lush greenness of the area. The water was so clear she could see the rocks on the bottom. And the trees must've been hundreds of years old, with limbs that stretched far and wide.

Taffy was surefooted as he made his way down the hill. It was all she could do to hang on, but they made it without her tumbling over headfirst. And then she could hear the water flowing over the rocks. There was a crisp freshness about the air, too.

Something stirred inside her, but she quickly tamped it down. She was not going country. It might be a nice place to visit but she certainly didn't want to live there.

When they stopped beneath a tree, Nikki gingerly swung her leg over the saddle and eased her feet to the ground. She gripped the saddle horn until she thought her legs would hold her up, then turned and gritted her teeth as she smiled at Cal. "That was fun."

He chuckled. "The soreness will go away."

Okay, so he'd seen through her act.

"It happens to the best of us," he said.

At least she knew why cowboys were bowlegged. It was from all the calluses they built up over the years on their thighs. Cal pulled a small jar out of his saddlebag and tossed it to her. She caught it, then frowned.

"Liniment," he said. "It'll ease the soreness."

"Thanks." For nothing. He was the one who'd made her sore. Oh, she wasn't even going there. At least not right now. But later—look out!

She watched for a moment as Cal unbuckled his saddle. Something was bothering her. She glanced around. "Where's the cabin?"

"Cabin?"

"Yeah, you know, where are we going to sleep?" If there was a cabin here, it must be hidden in the trees.

He pointed toward the extra horse that carried supplies. "Everything we need is right there."

"No cabin." Unless he'd brought an inflatable one. She didn't think that would keep any bears out.

"Sleeping bags," he said.

"Are there bears?"

He shrugged. "I've never seen one."

"But that doesn't mean there aren't any."

"Used to be black bears around. Like I said, I've never seen one."

She breathed a sigh of relief.

He looked at her. "I'd be a lot more worried about mountain lions. Now they can get real nasty if you're not careful."

Great.

Her stomach suddenly rumbled. It had been a long time since her morning Danish and she was starved.

"What's for lunch?" she finally asked as she watched him remove Tornado's saddle and set it on the ground. It had to be way past noon.

"Fish."

Fish? Oh, Lord, her mouth began to water. She could almost taste the succulent, tender meat. Her gaze went to the packhorse and the two fishing poles that were strapped to the horse.

"In the river, right?" she asked.

"You catch on real fast."

"Yeah, I've been told that before." She frowned.

"Not exactly like the pioneer women would've done it," he continued. "Most of the time all they had was a cane pole, string, and probably a safety pin for a hook. We'll have to pretend."

"Darn."

Taffy turned and looked at her as if to ask when he was going to get his saddle off. Another guilt trip. The horse had carried her all this way without complaint. She wasn't that heavy, but she wouldn't want to carry someone on her back for three hours.

How hard could it be to remove a saddle? Nikki pulled up on the strap to unbuckle it like she'd seen Cal do. Except nothing happened. She gritted her teeth and pulled harder.

"Need some help?"

"No," she managed to say. Just another inch. There! She gripped the leather tightly with one hand and let go with her other one, unhooking the strap.

The leather straps through the metal rings were all that held the saddle on. She pulled up and loosened them—much easier than the other strap. Now all she had to do was remove the saddle.

She stretched on her toes and did exactly as Cal had done, sliding one arm under one end of the saddle and her other arm under the other end. She pulled the saddle toward her and slid it off, taking the weight.

The weight of the saddle surprised her. She staggered back and landed on her butt in the grass. Ow! Who would've thought a saddle would be that heavy?

"You okay? Need some help?"

She blew the hair out of her face. "No." She wiggled out from under the saddle and stood, then bent at the waist and picked it up, but this time she was ready for the weight. She staggered over and dumped it beside Cal's.

Then she smirked at him, except he wasn't even looking. He was unloading the packhorse. Not that his approval mattered. She didn't need it. The saddle was off the horse and she'd done it without his help.

He finished unloading the camping equipment from the packhorse, putting everything to the side, then scooped up the reins. "We'll water the horses, then see if we can catch a fish or two."

As empty as her stomach was, it would take more than one fish to fill her, but the sooner they watered the horses, the sooner they would get to eat.

She grabbed Taffy's reins and walked beside Cal to the river. The body of water was wide and didn't look very deep. If she wanted, she could walk right out into the middle of it and never get more than knee deep.

She only hoped there were plenty of fish. She didn't see any.

When the horses finished drinking, Cal staked them out so they could eat the grass but not wander off.

"Have you ever fished before?" he asked.

She shook her head.

"You're in for a treat then."

Hadn't he said the same thing about milking?

Cal grabbed the poles, bucket, and a small shovel. Okay, her curiosity was getting the better of her. "What's the shovel for?"

"To dig the worms."

Of course—she should've guessed. Great, she thought sarcastically. The worms would be sacrificed to the fish, and then the fish would fill their stomachs. She had a feeling the worms got the short end of the stick. After all, they weren't hurting anyone as they dug through the earth. Not that she cared at this point in time. She was hungry. But not hungry enough to eat a worm. Hopefully, the fish would find it a tasty treat.

She watched as he dug through the earth and brought out fat worms, dropping them in the bucket. When he apparently thought they had enough, he stood.

"Let's see if we can catch our supper."

"And if we don't?"

"Then we'll dine on a can of pork and beans and beef jerky."

She hoped she caught a fish. At least now she knew she wouldn't have to exist on worms if something happened to Cal. Not that she thought anything would happen to him. One never knew about those kinds of things, though.

They walked to the water's edge again and Cal set the bucket down. He handed her a pole, unhooking the hook so the line would swing free.

"Okay, grab a worm out of the bucket and put it on your hook. Then I'll help you throw your line out."

She knew damned well fishing would not be the treat he'd said it would, but she refused to let him see just how squeamish she was. So, with more bravado than she was feeling, Nikki reached into the bucket and brought out a worm. It curled around her finger as if it was clinging to her for dear life, and actually, she supposed it was, but right now all she could think about was how much she'd like to throw it on the ground. As it was, it took a supreme effort on her part not to let her body convulse into shivers of repugnance.

"Here's the worm," she said, stretching her hand toward him, hoping he'd do the honors of attaching it.

"You have to put it on the hook."

She took the hook between her fingers, then looked at the worm. "How does it stay on?"

"You have to thread the worm onto the hook."

She raised an eyebrow. "You're joking, right?"

He shook his head.

She looked at the worm, then at the hook. How hard could it be to ram a sharp hook through a fat, helpless worm? She swallowed past the lump in her throat and wondered if worms had pain sensors.

"It won't be long until dark and you still have to catch a fish."

"Okay, okay."

She took the worm and threaded it onto the hook, knowing Cal saw that her hands shook. She wanted to whisper to the little worm that it was going to a better place but kept her lips firmly clamped together.

"Now what?"

"We cast your line into the water." He stood behind her, wrapping his arms around her, and she suddenly forgot about her empty stomach or the demise of the worm as new sensations swarmed through her.

"You bring your arms back like this," he said close to her ear as he showed her.

"Okay." Her words came out raspy and she wondered if he knew what he was doing to her.

"You hold this button down. That will release the line."

He flicked the pole with barely any movement except for his wrist. The fishing line whistled as it flew through the air. There was a small plop when it landed in the water. Ripples circled out from where the sinker had landed.

Cal moved away and went to his pole. Nikki's anticipation of what was about to happen died. Not that she really wanted to skip food for sex. Food first, then sex. But it had been nice when he held her close.

He threaded a worm onto his hook, then tossed his line

out the same way he'd shown her. Now what were they sup-posed to do? Just wait until a fish grabbed the worm on the way by? It seemed pretty boring and time-consuming if you asked her.

"How long does it take to catch a fish?" she finally asked.

He shrugged. "We might not catch one."

"After I sacrificed a worm? You're telling me the worm might have died for nothing?"

He chuckled. "It happens sometimes."

"And you enjoy fishing?"

"Yeah, I do."

"Why?"

"It's that first tug on your line. It's the fight. It's landing a fish after you hook it."

She didn't see the enjoyment in it, and after ten minutes passed, she was having doubts that she would have more than pork and beans and jerky for supper.

There was a tug on her pole. The current, nothing more. It stood to reason that if the water was moving, she would feel movement from time to time on her line. There was another tug, but harder.

Her pulse sped up. Her line pulled again, even harder. She gripped the pole. "I have one! I have a fish! I think. What do I do?"

Cal dropped his pole and ran to her. "Hold on tight. Don't let it get away."

"Of course I'm not going to let it get away." The fish was all that stood between her and starvation. "What do I do?"

"Reel it in. Turn the handle on the side. Not too fast."

It wasn't as easy as it looked. The fish was really putting up a fight. She was sure she'd snagged a forty-pound shark.

"Play with the fish. Drop your pole a little, then bring it back up as you reel the fish in."

"I don't want to play with it. I want to eat it."

"And you want to keep it on your hook."

"Whatever." But she did as he said.

Okay, she admitted to herself it was kind of exciting. Who would've thought fishing would be this much of a thrill.

Cal ran into the water and grabbed her line. The fish flopped up in the water. He grabbed it.

"Don't drop it!"

"I won't." He held the fish up for her to see.

She frowned. "That's it? I thought it would be a lot bigger." It had felt huge.

"It's big enough to keep."

Damned right it was. But it didn't look as if it was big enough to share. She might be forced to give some of it to Cal since she had no idea how to cook a fish and there wasn't even a black beast of a stove out here.

Cal put a string in the mouth of the fish and tossed the fish back into the water, then staked the other end firmly into the ground. It was kind of sad. The poor fish would probably think it was free.

Death Row.

Her stomach growled. But it was going to a good cause: her empty stomach.

Nikki reached into the bucket and got another wiggling worm. "It'll only hurt for a minute," she said and quickly threaded her hook. The worm wiggled and she stabbed herself.

Retaliation. She should've guessed the worm would exact some measure of revenge. Not that it did it any good. She reared back and flung the pole forward.

Nothing happened.

Well, except the worm became a trapeze act without a trapeze as it went flying through the air.

Fly away, fly away worm and be free. She watched until it made a little plop in the water. A fish flopped near where it had landed. Maybe not exactly free.

Crap. Now she would have to start over.

"You didn't push the button down."

"Oh." Darn, she'd forgotten that step. She threaded another worm on the hook, and this time when she threw her line out it actually went into the water. She was starting to like the whistle it made as the line stretched out across the river, then plopped down and disappeared.

"Got one," Cal said and began to reel his line in.

Excitement flittered through her. Who knew she would have just as much fun watching him reel in a fish as she had when she'd snagged hers. And even better, now she wouldn't have to share her fish.

"It's a big one," he said.

She frowned. Bigger than hers? Maybe he'd share his fish with her since hers was kind of small.

"Don't lose it," she said.

"I don't plan to."

"Good."

He raised his pole, turning the reel, then brought it down and repeated it again. The fish flopped out of the water, its body twisting and turning before it went beneath the surface again.

"It's huge," she said.

He looked at her and grinned. "Bigger than yours."

She cocked an eyebrow. "I'm not through fishing, either." She might be a rookie fisherwoman, but she was a fast learner and she didn't give up easily. She'd get her fish and the story. Her parents had taught her the value of winning and she didn't take losing without a damned good fight.

Chapter 20

Nikki felt a tug on her line. "Ha! I have another one." She'd started to worry there weren't any fish left in the river. That little fish she'd caught earlier had started to look smaller and smaller.

"Don't lose it," Cal said, then smiled.

She smiled back, then repeated what he'd told her, "I don't plan to."

She did exactly as he had and reeled in as she brought the pole up, then gave the fish a little bit of line as she lowered it.

"You're doing good."

She grinned. "Yes, I am, aren't I?"

Until she reeled it in and saw the fish was about the same size as the last one she'd caught, but it had put up a bigger fight. Not that it mattered that much. It was enough for a meal.

Cal caught two more, smaller than his first. Okay, so maybe she didn't beat him, but at least she'd given it her best shot.

"I'm starved," he said as he raised the stringer. "What about you?"

She nodded, reeling her line in. "I could eat a horse." Taffy raised his head and whinnied. They both laughed. What were the odds?

"We'll need to get a fire started," Cal said. "Why don't you do that and I'll clean the fish."

Starting a fire sounded much better than cleaning. "What do I need?"

"Some rocks about this size." He made a fist. "And some wood, small branches and a couple of bigger ones. Don't get anything too green. You want it as dry as possible so it'll burn better."

The task wasn't that difficult. She had a feeling he was cutting her a little slack, which was fine with her. Looking at fish guts would probably be a whole lot harder than threading a worm on a hook.

She'd just as soon not see the fish die, either. She glanced over her shoulder and watched him for a moment—well, until he began to slice open the fish they'd caught. Bleh. She'd never look at fish on a menu in quite the same way.

And they called her The Barracuda? Some tough predator she was. It wasn't as though she'd never eaten fish before. She loved fish—as long as it arrived on her plate fully cooked and minus its head.

But fishing had been fun—more than she wanted to admit. She was a city girl, but it certainly didn't mean she couldn't like country—to an extent. She sat down on a rock and picked up a stick, and aimlessly drew circles in the dirt.

She liked a whole lot of things, actually. Maybe she should just drop the article. Marge wouldn't kill her if she didn't write it. Her boss had even told her as much. Not that Nikki thought Marge had really meant what she was saying. Not when she'd made it sound like a challenge.

Marge might not bother her so much, but what would her parents think? They would look at each other and shake their heads, that's what they would do. Even if it was a fluff piece, it was still the principle of the matter that counted. She'd taken the job and she had to follow through.

And now that her mother knew about it, she'd want to know what happened. They might not see each other very often but they knew what the other was doing in her career.

So maybe she would write the story just to keep everyone off her back.

She was so confused. Damn, she'd never been one to linger on the fence. She always knew what side she was on. Indecision didn't sit well with her at all. Before the end of this trip, she would decide exactly what she was going to do one way or the other.

Nikki quickly gathered some of the broken branches that were on the ground and went back to camp, not even glancing in the direction of where Cal was still preparing the fish.

By the time she'd gathered rocks along the bank of the river and returned, Cal had finished with the fish.

She watched him as he quickly put a fire together and marveled at how enterprising he was. "I feel as though I'm on an episode of *Survivor*," she said.

"Brian and I used to come here a lot to fish and camp out. Sometimes we'd stay for a week."

"You love your brother a lot."

He looked up. "We don't spend nearly as much time together, though. He doesn't get to the city as much as I'd like, but yeah, I enjoy his company. We've always been close."

"And do you miss all this?"

He looked around. "I do. There's a peacefulness out here that you can't find in the city."

Hadn't he said his brother worked too hard? Apparently, the ranch was left to both of them since it had belonged to their grandparents. Cal had said he was thinking about retiring. She wondered if that meant he'd be going into business with Brian.

She glanced around, absorbing the quiet. Nothing moved, not even a leaf. Sure, fishing had been fun, but she certainly wouldn't want to make the country her home. It was as she'd first thought: she and Cal were total opposites.

"Do you have brothers or sisters?" Cal asked, breaking the silence.

She'd welcome any conversation right now. "No. It's only me and my parents."

Nikki sat on the ground, crossing her legs, but as soon as she felt the muscles pull, she uncrossed them and stretched them out in front of her instead. You'd think working out in the gym would have kept her from being so sore.

"Do you see them often?" he asked.

"I guess. We meet the second Saturday every other month. We usually take in a play and go out to eat." She smiled. "Quality time."

"They live out of town then."

She frowned. "Well, no, but they're very busy. They both have successful careers."

"But they make an appointment to see you."

She came to her feet. It wasn't that comfortable sitting on the ground. And how the hell had he turned the conversation to her life? He wasn't the reporter; he was a football player.

"It's not like that," she said.

"If you say so."

"I do." But now that she thought about it, he was right. They made appointments to see her. It was the same way during holidays. She went to their house at Christmas and spent exactly four hours there. They opened their one present—something practical—then went to a restaurant and ate dinner.

But she enjoyed her time with them and she really hated that they might be moving to Washington. Damn it, he was making her question her life again and she didn't want to examine it too closely.

Because she was afraid of what she might see?

"I think I'll take a walk."

"You okay?" He didn't look up.

"I'm going to the bathroom." She wasn't, but she really doubted he would ask her anything else if she used that as an excuse. Men usually shied away from that sort of thing.

Cal watched her walk away and was riddled with guilt.

Why had he pushed her about her parents? How the hell was he supposed to know her family had a business arrangement with her?

Maybe he'd suspected it from the little things she'd told him here and there, but he hadn't realized it was as bad as what she'd just told him. What was worse, she didn't seem to mind.

No wonder she'd gotten the nickname The Barracuda. Look at how she was raised. He shook his head and went back to preparing their meal.

Once the fire was burning good, he set the skillet in the center and waited for the oil to get hot. He'd already rolled the fish filets in cornmeal.

When he thought about families who made appointments to see each other, Cal realized that he and Brian were getting close to doing the same thing. They'd made an appointment to go riding on Friday.

No, it wasn't the same as Nikki and her parents. He and Brian still had meals together and they dropped in on each other all the time. They didn't have to schedule time to see each other, but apparently Nikki did.

What? Did he feel sorry for her now? Was he going soft? No, Nikki wanted a story and she'd do anything to get it. He wouldn't forget that fact, either.

He glanced up as she returned and couldn't help but notice the rise and fall of her breasts, the gentle swing in her hips. Maybe it was a good thing he didn't know any state secrets because it wouldn't take much to make him guilty of treason.

He focused on placing the fish in the skillet. They sizzled when they hit the hot grease. "Hand me a plate," he said.

"Do you and your brother come out here often?" she asked after she handed him a couple of plates.

She eased to the ground. She was still sore. Maybe he'd rub the liniment in the places she wouldn't be able to reach. He closed his eyes and counted very slowly to five.

"Not as much as we used to," he said.

"Why?"

"No time, I guess."

"Am I the first girl you've ever brought out here?" she asked as she looked around.

Nikki might have put her pole down but she was still fishing. "You're the first."

"Then I'm honored."

He busied himself opening the can of pork and beans, then dumped them into a pan.

"Tell me about football. When did you get started playing?"

Was she planning on dragging his career through the mud, too?

"I started in peewee. I was eight."

She smiled. "I bet you were cute."

He relaxed. Maybe she just wanted to know more about him. "Why would you think that?"

"Because you're a handsome man. Did all the cheerleaders start drooling when you walked by after you got older?"

"Who said they ever stopped?"

She laughed. "Oh, that was bad. I didn't know you had an ego that big."

Something about her was different. He couldn't quite put his finger on it. He wondered if she sensed the change, too. Maybe she would get her story, but he had a feeling she would get a whole lot more than just an article about him and Cynthia.

Cal finished frying the fish and set the pan of pork and beans on the fire. As soon as they were warm, he poured some on the two plates and added a filet of fish to each. "Here you go," he said and handed her a plate.

"Is this how people traveled a long time ago? A couple of tin plates, a couple of forks, a spoon, and some iron pans?"

"I don't know, but then I'm not the one doing research. I'm sure they didn't have it this good, though."

She looked down, unable to meet his eyes. That's right,

feel the guilt. Maybe he should just tell her that he knew who she really was.

"This is so good," she said as she closed her eyes and took a bite.

She acted as though she hadn't eaten a hot meal in days. And she probably hadn't. He had a feeling she'd bought some food when she went shopping because the stove at the cabin still hadn't been used. All the wood was still in the pile. Nope, she didn't fool him for a second.

But she was right about the fish. It had been a long time since he'd eaten fresh fish and it tasted as though the best five-star chef had cooked it.

They didn't speak again until they'd finished off the last of the fish and almost all the beans. Cal set his plate down.

Nikki looked up and caught him studying her. "I guess you probably think I'm a pig for eating so much."

"You have a healthy appetite." No, he was thinking a lot of things, but it wasn't that she ate too much.

"Most men are put off by a woman who eats too much."

"It doesn't bother me."

"Good."

"Would it bother you if it did?"

She grinned. "No, I love to eat and I don't care who knows."

"I didn't think it would bother you. Not much does."

"I'll take that as a compliment." She set her empty plate on top of his. "So why did you and your last girlfriend break up?" she asked out of the blue.

Just when things were going well, too. "Is it important?"

She shrugged. "Maybe I don't want to do the same thing."

"Is our relationship that important to you?"

When she looked at him, he could almost believe that it was.

"Isn't it to you?"

He thought of her milking Bessie for the first time, or

Bessie Two, as she called the cow. Then he remembered the excitement on her face when she rode a horse for the first time. Skinny dipping, making love. Even fishing today.

And then it hit him. The reason why he made excuses to be around her. He liked watching her reaction to everything she did and saw. He liked her tenaciousness. He liked a hell of a lot about her.

"Yeah, I think it could be," he said.

"Then tell me about her. Did you love her?" She set her plate down and lay back on the grass staring at him.

And looking oh so innocent, except he knew better. He picked at a blade of grass. If he told her the truth, Cynthia would become a laughingstock. There were some people who would like that. Cynthia was certainly no angel and she'd pissed a lot of people off in her thirty-one years. But he wouldn't tarnish her reputation any more than it was already tarnished.

"She broke it off with me."

Nikki raised her eyebrows.

"Why? Do you snore or something?"

"I guess you'll find out tonight."

Before she could ask any more questions, he stood, then reached a hand down to her. "Come on, we'd better wash the plates before it gets dark."

She followed him down to the river, but then she surprised him by taking off her shoes and socks. He wondered just how far she would go. Hell, he already knew the answer to that.

But much to his disappointment, she rolled up her jeans and waded into the water.

"It's cold!" She tiptoed out as quickly as she'd gone in.

"This river has always had the coldest water. I think that's why the fishing is always so good." He set the plates down and toed off his boots. His socks were next. He needed to let them dry out anyway since he'd been in the water with them on. If his grandmother were still alive, she'd give him what for.

"Okay, where's the soap to wash the dishes?"

"We don't need any." Cal picked up one of the tin plates and walked into the water. She was right about it being cold. "This is how the pioneers washed the dishes." He bent over and scooped up a handful of sand off the bottom of the river and began to scrub the plate.

"You're washing our dishes in mud?"

"It has a built-in scouring pad and the fish eat all the stuff at the bottom of the river so it's clean."

He glanced at her. She still didn't look like she bought what he was telling her. He set the plate on the bank and grabbed the bean pan, then handed it to her. "Try it."

"Oh, yeah, give me one of the pans," she said, but she was smiling.

She dipped the pan in the water, scooped up sand off the bottom, and began to clean the pan. "We may have something here. If we market it just right we could come up with a new cleaning product."

He laughed. "Like what? Clean with the cleaner solution—mud."

Her laughter joined his. "You're right, that might not work. Darn, and there go my visions of making millions."

They quickly finished washing the dishes and turned them upside down on the bank to dry.

"My feet are freezing," she said as she hurried the short distance back to the camp.

She sat in front of the fire and stuck her feet close to the dying embers. He sat down next to her and grabbed her feet then began rubbing them.

"Better?"

"Much." She lay back, pillowing her head with her arm. "I could get used to this."

"Are you saying you're starting to like the country?"

"I don't think I'd go that far."

He worked his massaging motions up her leg, kneading the calf, then repeated with the other one.

"Umm, right there," she said.

"I want to make love with you," he said.

"I know. I want the same thing."

Nikki was in way over her head. Maybe she didn't realize what she was doing or that she was getting in deeper than even she realized, but Cal knew when a woman was more than interested.

"It probably won't work out between us," he warned. That was the closest he'd come to telling her he knew the real reason she was here.

"I understand."

Their gazes locked. Without losing eye contact, she brought her hand from beneath her head and slipped the metal button of her jeans through the buttonhole.

It was as though something had passed between them, a silent understanding. No recriminations, no regrets.

Chapter 21

"You're sure no one is at the old homestead?" Celeste asked Brian.

"Positive. Cal took Nikki camping. The only thing here is a few animals and, of course, the ghost."

Celeste had to admit she'd been curious about the place where Brian's great-grandparents had lived. Well, more about the ghost he'd told her haunted the place. When she'd mentioned she'd like to have some fresh mint to make one of her specialty drinks, he'd told her that mint grew wild up by the old place, then offered to take her.

Brian had liked her idea of a small area where they could make tea or fruit smoothies and gourmet coffees. Betty was even making tiny cupcakes and cookies. So far, the guests loved the little extras.

He stopped the pickup in front of an old house that wasn't much more than a shack and got out. "I haven't been here in ages."

She eyed the weatherworn building with trepidation as she got out of the pickup. It was worse than she could've imagined. "I can see why."

He was frowning when he looked at her.

She laughed at his disgruntled expression. "What I can't understand is why anyone in their right mind would want to stay here. It looks really bad. That reporter must be regretting her decision to do the story on your brother. I know I would, and I've stayed in some really run-down places."

He looked at her curiously for a moment and she knew she'd said a little too much about her past.

"Yeah, she must want it pretty bad," he finally said.

She breathed a sigh of relief and glanced around, taking in the pen, the cow, and the calf. "I can't see anyone staying here, die-hard reporter or not." She liked the idea of getting back to nature but this was even a little too much for her.

"The guests are rare. I think they enjoy the absolute quiet."

"Cock! Cock! Cock!"

She jumped, throwing her arms around Brian when a possessed rooster drunkenly flapped across the yard as it made a beeline for the barn. Her heart jumped to her throat.

"Damn! Scared the hell out of me, too," Brian said as he held on to her as tightly as she held on to him.

"Was that the ghost?" she asked.

"That was the rooster, but something is seriously wrong with it. It acts rabid."

"Or psycho." She looked up at him, and suddenly, the rooster didn't matter. His blue eyes were fastened on her lips in a way that made her think he wasn't thinking about the rooster, either.

"You said you enjoyed my kiss, right?"

"Yes," she whispered.

"Good, because I'm going to kiss you again." He didn't wait for her answer but lowered his mouth to hers. At first he only brushed his lips across hers.

Celeste trembled from head to feet, then pressed closer and parted her lips. His tongue stroked hers. She tightened her arms around his neck, pulling him closer, wanting more, needing this connection. She returned his caresses with a passion she hadn't known existed inside her. When he ended the kiss, they were both breathing hard.

"Wow."

That was all he said. Just wow. But it was enough for her

to know he was affected by the kiss as much as she had been. She stepped away, putting a little space between them. Heat rose up her face when she realized just how she'd reacted to his touch.

"I . . . I'm sorry," she said, stumbling over the words.

"I'm not," he told her.

She couldn't meet his gaze but chose to look at the ground instead. "I usually don't act like this around people . . . around men. I mean, I'm not a virgin or anything, but I don't have a lot of experience, and I guess you think that's probably crazy. . . ."

He pulled her back into his arms and hugged her close. "It doesn't matter."

Warmth spread through her but not like the heat of a moment ago. No, this was as though the sun shined down on her. It was a good feeling, not as good as kissing, but she enjoyed it.

He let go of her but kept holding her hand. "Come on, I'll show you where the mint grows."

She looked at the cabin. A shadow moved across one of the windows. "Can we go inside?"

"The cabin is technically rented."

She looked at him. "I promise I won't bother anything."

He shrugged. "I guess so." A slow smile curved his lips. "But I won't guarantee you'll see the ghost."

"How did you know I was curious to see if there was one here?"

"I don't know. Wild guess?"

Her eyes narrowed on him. "I bet I'm not the first girl you've brought here." When his face turned a nice shade of red, Celeste had her answer and couldn't stop her smile. "Shame on you."

"What is it about girls and ghosts? They always want to check out the haunted houses."

"It's walking toward the unknown."

He waved his arm in front of him. "Knock yourself out. I'd just as soon know where I'm going."

"You're not coming?" It was one thing to go in with Brian and another to go in by herself.

"This is what gets men in trouble," he said on a sigh. "How can we say no? Okay, come on."

They walked up the steps. The well-oiled hinges on the screened door didn't make a sound when he opened it.

"Hello?" Brian called out.

"I thought you said no one was home," she whispered, hugging his arm.

"There isn't. I just wanted to see if the ghost would answer." He laughed when she frowned.

Cold air washed over her. She squeezed his arm a little tighter.

"You don't have to be scared. I don't think there's really a ghost here."

"Yes, there is."

"Huh?"

"I felt her."

He scanned the room. "What do you mean, you felt her? How do you feel a ghost?"

"I felt a rush of cold air."

"Then what you felt was cold air."

She shook her head. "No, it was the ghost." She was certain of it.

"What? Are you telling me you're psychic?"

"No, but I can sense things." She looked around the room. "Some people call it a gut instinct. Everyone has it, but most people don't trust their feelings."

"But you felt a ghost here?"

"I felt something."

A window in another room crashed shut. They both jumped. He grabbed her hand and pulled her out of the cabin. Not that Brian really had to pull very hard because she was right on his heels. This would not be a good time for her to linger.

"Enough ghosts for one day?" he asked when they were safely standing in the yard again.

"I think so."

They looked at each other and laughed. She marveled at how much younger he looked when he was away from the business side of the ranch.

"Maybe we should grab some mint and head back."

"That's a good plan." She followed him around to the back of the cabin. "A lighted path to the outhouse. You spare no expense for your guests." It was all she could do to keep from laughing at her joke.

"Cal or Nikki must've put them up."

They got the mint and went back to the pickup, but Celeste couldn't resist one last look at the old house as they drove away. Her breath caught in her throat. Was that a woman standing at the door? If she was, it looked as though she might be crying.

"Tell me about the ghost," she suddenly said.

"I don't know a lot. For a long time, I thought I was imagining things, and I'm sure that's all it was this time. The house is old and the window probably chose that moment to slip and crash shut."

"I saw her at the door."

His head jerked around and he stared at her. "Are you sure?"

She nodded. "It looked as though she was crying."

"Okay, that's it. I'm not letting anyone else stay there. Not if it's haunted. The ghost might hurt someone."

"We should have a séance."

"You mean go back up there and sit around a table and intentionally call the ghost?"

"Not scared, are you?"

"No . . . yes." He frowned.

"But don't you want the poor girl's spirit to be set free?" She sighed. "I feel sorry for her."

He pulled in at the stables. "I don't. She used to scare the hell out of me."

"Maybe you needed the hell scared out of you. I mean,

you were bringing girls up there to make out with." She laughed when his frown deepened.

"I was a teenager."

"And I was teasing you."

"I guess I have been spending too much time on ranch business."

"That's okay. I can help you relax," she joked, then realized the way her words sounded.

He let his gaze roam over her. "I think you can."

His implication was clear. Celeste could feel herself blushing all the way to her roots.

"That wasn't what I . . . uh . . . meant."

"Now who doesn't know when someone is joking?" He grinned.

She relaxed. "You're right. Maybe we both need help."

They got out of the pickup.

"Hey, we had a new colt born this morning. Want to see her?"

"I love horses! I once lived with some people who had a horse. They let me take care of brushing her and I was in seventh heaven."

"How old were you?"

"Thirteen," she said as she stepped inside the barn. She stopped and waited for her eyes to adjust to the dim light.

Brian paused at the door. Why would she be living with a family that she wasn't related to when she was only thirteen? He watched her as she walked to one of the stalls, then stopped before she peered inside and turned to look at him, a question in her eyes.

"Where were your parents?" he asked.

Her face paled.

It made him wonder what her life had been like before she came here.

Chapter 22

There was nothing sexier than a woman sliding the zipper down on a pair of cowboy-cut jeans. Cal's hands stilled in the middle of rubbing Nikki's feet. Her passion-filled eyes told him exactly what was on her mind. When she started to shove the jeans down over her hips, he reached up and grasped the waistband, tugging them down. He was thinking the same thing, and who would blame him?

"There's a freedom in making love out in the open," she said, her words soft and seductive. "I like the way it makes me feel—decadent and a little naughty."

He liked naughty, and Nikki wore it well. "You've never made love outside before. Before the pond, that is."

She shook her head. "My partners were always afraid we'd get arrested for having sex in one of the parks. It certainly wasn't for lack of trying on my part, though."

He laughed. "They just didn't know the right parks."

One eyebrow rose. "And you do?"

"I'm not sure I would now, but yeah, I know a few places where you can make out without getting caught. The way the press hounds me, it wouldn't be smart to get back to nature."

"Are . . . they that bad? I mean, they must help your career, too."

"Some do."

"Then you don't despise all reporters."

"No, there are a few I actually like." He watched her closely and saw the look of relief on her face. It made him wonder why she would care what he thought, but as soon as she sat up and began to unbutton her shirt, it didn't really matter.

Cal followed suit and unbuttoned his but kept his gaze on her as she slipped off her shirt and the only thing left was a wispy red lace bra.

"I always thought it would be nice to vacation in a nudist camp," she said, the laughter back in her eyes. "What about you? Ever think it might be fun?"

He shrugged. "Half the time Brian and I ran around in cutoffs and that's about it. It was almost like being naked, and when we went swimming we were usually in the buff. I guess I enjoyed the freedom. I never really thought about it. It just seemed to be a part of growing up."

"It sounds like fun."

He couldn't take it anymore. Naked sounded real good to him right now. He reached behind her, unclasped her bra, and slipped it off. She had the most perfect breasts and they just fit in the palms of his hands. He lightly squeezed them, scraped his thumbs across the nipples. They tightened.

"That feels good," she said as she moved to her knees. She raised her arms above her head and stretched, arching her body toward him as she begged for more.

He moved to his knees. "You like that?"

She nodded. "You're very good at making a woman feel great about herself."

When she brought her arms down, she wrapped them around his neck and drew his head down to hers. Their lips touched. Her tongue scraped along his before delving inside his mouth stroking, caressing him.

She slid her hands down his arms and cupped his ass. He drew in a sharp breath. She pressed closer, her breasts rubbing against his chest.

He pulled her even closer, running his hands down her

back, bringing her in tighter against his erection. She wiggled her body. There was only a scrap of silk between her and his jeans. It was a hell of a turn-on knowing what she must be feeling right now.

He began to lightly massage her ass, kneading and squeezing. "What about this? Do you like what I'm doing? Do you like the way it feels to rub your tender clit against my rough jeans? But that's right, you said you liked it rough."

"Yes, but I want more."

She surprised him by scooting back and unbuttoning his jeans and tugging the zipper down. He didn't mind a bit letting her have her way with him. She shoved his jeans and briefs over his hips, freeing him. Cool air caressed his dick.

"This is what I want," she said, and brushed her fingers over the tip of his penis. She placed small kisses on his chest, working her way up his neck. "I want you. I want to lick you and suck you inside my mouth," she said, her words raspy with need.

His mouth went dry. He knew exactly where she wanted to put her mouth.

She didn't wait for him to answer but leaned down and took him inside her mouth, her tongue swirling across the tip of his dick before she sucked him deep inside.

A rush of fire swept through him, settling in his stomach. He arched toward her as his fingers curled in her hair. "Oh, damn, yes. That feels fucking fantastic."

He didn't think it could get any better, until she began to lightly knead his balls. He couldn't focus as the strength was drained from his body. He sat back on his heels. She continued to suck and lick his dick, sliding his foreskin down, then back up.

"I can't hold back," he said.

"Then don't." She squeezed up close to him, sliding her thong to the side until her sex fit tight against him. "Did you like when I sucked your cock?" she asked as she began to rub her sex against him.

"You know I did," he barely got out as he tried to take a deep breath and couldn't.

"I liked it, too. The hard length, the soft tip, running my tongue over it." Her movements increased.

He moved to a sitting position, pulled her in closer, making the connection tighter. She bit her bottom lip and closed her eyes.

"Oh, damn, this feels good," she said. "Oh, oh, I think I'm almost there."

Her words seemed to come from a tunnel as his world exploded all around him. He sat straighter, grabbing her ass and holding her against him. She cried out as her orgasm swept over her.

Their breathing was ragged in the quiet of the late afternoon. Had he ever had such incredible sex as he'd just experienced?

He didn't think so.

She laughed. He frowned.

"Is that another good laugh or a bad laugh?" he asked.

Nikki leaned away from him and stared into his eyes. "Definitely good." Her smile was wide and mischievous. "But very, very messy. I think I need a trip to the river."

"Good idea." She frowned. "I'm starved, too."

"It hasn't been that long since we ate."

She shrugged as she stood. "Sex always makes me hungry. What can I say?"

"Okay, but leave your panties here."

"Why? So you won't be the only naked one? Are you embarrassed?"

He shook his head as he let his gaze roam over her. God, she had a magnificent body. "No, this is Camp Braxton and you're not allowed to wear clothes."

Her smile was slow. "I think I like this camp." She removed her thong and tossed it to the side.

It didn't take them long to wash up since the water was ice

cold. When they returned to camp, Cal dug out a bag of marshmallows and found branches. He took his knife and trimmed the ends of the branches until he had a sharp point on each.

"Oh, we're going to roast marshmallows. Cool. I've always wanted to know what they taste like."

He looked at her. "Don't tell me you've never roasted marshmallows?" He added more branches and had flames in no time.

She shook her head. "No, but I always wondered what it would be like to go to camp and do all the things that other girls were doing."

He studied her.

"Not a nudist camp. Well, not until I got older." She grinned. "No, I always wanted to go to a summer camp. My parents thought it would be a bad influence."

"Well, I'm here to round out your education, but fair warning, I am a bad influence."

"Oh, I'd say you're certainly that."

When Cal returned her smile, warmth washed over her. Not the sexual kind she usually experienced when he looked at her. This was different. It made her feel good on the inside, but it worried her, too.

Cal handed her a stick with a marshmallow on the end. She dutifully stuck it in the fire, like he was doing with his. When it burst into flame, she quickly blew it out.

"It's burnt," she said.

"That's the best part." He pinched off the burnt part on his and stuck it in his mouth.

It didn't look very appetizing but she'd try just about anything once. The burnt part slid right off. She blew on it before sticking the gooey mess into her mouth.

"So?"

"Okay, it's good, but now my tongue is stuck to the roof of my mouth." She laughed.

"The hazards of eating roasted marshmallows." He grinned, then brought another one out of the fire. "Have you ever been serious about anyone?"

"Why?" Where was he going with this conversation?

"You want to know more about my past affairs, it's only fair you tell me about yours."

"But you haven't told me anything about yours except your fiancée broke up with you."

"You tell me and then I'll tell you."

She was finally getting somewhere. Nikki thought back to the last guy she'd fallen for. Her forehead wrinkled.

"Have you ever been serious about anyone?" he asked.

"Of course I have." Had it been that long ago? There hadn't been anyone she would say that she'd been serious about in college. There had been a guy in high school, though. "His name was Phillip. We were seniors in high school. I went to the prom with him."

"High school?"

"I'm picky about who I get serious with."

"What happened?"

She shrugged. "We went to different colleges."

"So distance didn't make the heart grow fonder." Cal blew on his flaming marshmallow, then popped it into his mouth.

"He wasn't that good in the backseat of a car. We couldn't afford a motel room." She remembered back. "I think we had more of a connection talking about what we wanted to do with our lives. He wanted to be a rocket scientist."

"Pretty lofty aspirations. What did he become?"

She stabbed two marshmallows onto the end of her stick. "A rocket scientist." She stuck her stick into the fire, then looked at Cal. "He works for NASA."

"You're serious?"

She nodded. "We've kept in touch over the years. He married and had a couple of kids."

"And you haven't been serious about anyone since high school?"

The way Cal put it, it did seem like an awfully long time. She'd been busy with her career and hadn't had time to date anyone seriously.

"No one has made your heart beat faster?"

Only Cal. As soon as the thought hit her, her heart began to thump so loudly she thought he would probably hear it. She swallowed past the sudden lump in her throat.

"Pathetic, aren't I?" Nikki tried for a smile but didn't think she pulled it off, so she concentrated instead on burning the marshmallows on her stick.

She wasn't falling in love with Cal. She barely knew the man. There was a lot she liked about him, sure, but there was a wide gap between like and love. Besides, he'd kill her if he knew the real reason she was at the ranch.

The thought that he would find out made her stomach churn. He would eventually when he saw the story she'd write, and she would write it. She'd never given up on a story yet. That's why they called her The Barracuda. Her job defined who she was. She had to do the article. Her shoulders slumped. But it didn't mean she had to like it.

"I wouldn't say pathetic." He laid his stick to the side. His gaze drifted over her. "Maybe you haven't been looking in the right places for love."

"What if I don't want to find it," she said. "I have too much happening right now with my career. I don't want to settle down."

"Your librarian career?"

She drew in a deep breath. "And my writing." It wasn't really a lie, she told herself. Yeah, right, then why did she feel bad?

"You don't have a ring on your finger, either," she said, changing the topic back to him. She would get the blasted story and be done with it.

He leaned back on his elbow. The fire cast him in shadows and light and it was all she could do not to stare. He was magnificent in all his naked glory. His tanned muscles were as firm as they looked.

"I plan on getting married someday, having a few kids, but I'm not in any hurry," he said.

"But you never did say why your fiancée broke off the engagement," she prodded. "Why was there no happily ever after?"

He raised his gaze to hers. "I wasn't always the good guy, Nikki."

She felt the color drain from her face. What? Did he beat women? Take steroids? Illegal sports betting?

Did she want to know? And if she did, would she be able to write about it?

She had a feeling her life was about to get a lot more complicated, and not in a good way.

Chapter 23

Brian watched Celeste as she stood in front of the stall. Her back had stiffened. He almost wished he hadn't asked about her parents.

"I had foster parents," she finally said.

She glanced over her shoulder, then looked away, but there was something in her eyes—so much pain.

He had a bad feeling in his gut. "Did they abuse you?" He couldn't imagine anyone hurting Celeste. Just the thought made him furious.

"No, they were very good to me."

He relaxed a little. At least they hadn't hurt her.

"I never really felt as if I belonged, you know," she went on. "I always felt as though I was on the outside looking in. They were nice, but it wasn't the same as being part of a family. Somewhere in the back of my mind, I knew if I did something wrong or if circumstances changed, I could be shipped off to another family."

"What about your parents?" he asked softly.

She was silent.

"Hey, it's okay. You don't have to talk about it. My parents were killed when I was a baby. I know what it feels like to grow up without a mom and dad, although my grandparents were great, and I had Cal, too."

She took a deep breath. "My father is in prison. He has

been since I was eight." She faced him and there was such sadness on her face that it tugged at his heart.

"What happened?"

"He murdered my mother."

Ah, damn. He took a deep breath. "Where were you when it happened?" He clenched his hands. He'd never expected her to tell him that her father had murdered her mom. He couldn't even imagine how hard that must've been.

"At school. When I came home, Daddy was sitting at the kitchen table, the gun beside him, just staring at it. My mother was lying in a pool of blood on the kitchen floor. I rushed over to her. Her eyes were open but I think I already knew she was dead. I ran out of the house crying. The police came and that was the last time I saw my father."

"You don't know why he did it?"

She seemed to snap out of the past. "When I was older, I looked up the newspaper articles. We were well off—some said rich—but my father apparently made bad investments, and then he lost his job." She hugged her middle. "He killed her because he'd lost his job and they were going to lose everything. They say he planned to kill me, then himself. But when I came home, he didn't make a move toward the gun. He just kept sitting there staring at it."

Brian walked toward her, then took her into his arms. "I'm sorry."

"My foster parents gave me a letter from him once. I was nine. He'd apparently tracked me down." She raised her face. "I remember what he was like, what our life was like, and it had been happy. We lived in a big house and I took music lessons. I even had a dog, but when they took me away, I never saw her again."

For the first time in his life, Brian felt utterly helpless. All he could do was hold her close.

"I threw the letter in the trash without reading it. My mother was a kind and gentle woman. If I listen hard enough, I can hear her laughter and sometimes I see her smile. He ripped her from me. He took everything away."

"Not everything," Brian told her. "You're still alive and you have heart and spirit. No one can take that from you."

Celeste laid her head on his shoulder. He wanted to make it all better, but he knew she would always live with her pain. Damn, that's why she'd only had one suitcase and a junky car. She probably didn't want possessions to rule her life like it had her father's.

He kissed the top of her head just before she pulled away. Her expression was mortified.

"I can't believe I opened up like that. I've never just spilled my guts before. I didn't even talk about my father with my foster families. And I barely know you."

She started to turn away from him again, but he clasped her arm. "It's okay to talk about what hurts, and we might have just met, but I feel as though I've known you forever. I can't explain it. Maybe I'm crazy, but I want to get to know you a lot better."

"Even though my father is in prison?"

"But you had nothing to do with the choices he made. He ruined your life, your mother's, and his. I don't care about your past. I don't think that's who you are."

"I think I could like you a lot."

"Would that be so bad?"

"I don't know. I don't stay in one place very long," she warned.

"You don't have to run away from here. You're safe now."

"Safe. I'm not sure I know the meaning of the word."

"I'll teach it to you."

When she looked up at him, he couldn't resist pressing his lips to hers. His kiss was gentle, meant to tell her she didn't have to be afraid around him, but it was all he could do to keep from crushing her to him. Dammit, he had to think about something else.

He pulled away and drew in a deep breath. "Want to see the colt?"

"Yeah." Just the whisper of a smile touched her lips. She seemed happy that he'd changed the subject.

Brian led her down to the end of the barn. There were six stalls on each side. The barn was open on both ends today, so there was plenty of light inside.

"Does someone take care of all this for you?" she asked.

"My foreman manages the day-to-day operations of the ranch. We cut and bale our own hay—we're self-sufficient."

"But what if you had a bad year?"

"We could survive more than one bad year." He knew why she asked. She was afraid if he went under, he might do what her father had done. "I'm a survivor, Celeste. I would find a way to make it in this world if things took a turn for the worse. Nothing would ever be so bad that I couldn't find a solution." He took a deep breath. "And even if I lost all this tomorrow, I could always go to work for someone. Possessions don't rule me."

She nodded, then moved closer to the stall. "Oh, look," she said as she peered over the top rail. She stared at the mother and colt. "It must be wonderful to experience the birth of something so precious."

He stood next to her. "One of the things I love about the country."

"I know that you could never do what my father did," she quietly told him.

He squeezed her arm. Maybe she would stop running away from her past now that she was here. Either that, or he'd look around one day and she'd be gone.

That thought left an emptiness inside him.

They walked back to the ranch in silence.

"Have dinner with me," he said.

Her hesitation was brief. "Okay."

"I have some work to take care of first. Is seven okay?"

"That would be fine."

Once inside, they parted. Celeste went to her room. For a long moment, she stood in the middle of the room. Then she went to her suitcase and pulled out a worn photo album. Her fingers lightly caressed the dark green leather that bound the book.

It had been a long time since she'd looked at the pictures. She sat on the bed, then opened it. Her mother stared up at her from the first picture. She was beautiful and she was smiling.

In the next picture she was holding Celeste's hand. Sometimes she could close her eyes and feel the softness of her mother's skin. She turned the page and her father stared back at her. He was pushing her in the swing. She still didn't know why she'd kept the pictures of him.

She carefully closed the album. The man sitting at the table that day, staring at the gun, hadn't been her father. He was the man who'd killed her mother. That day her father had died in her heart. She hated him, but she loved him, too. For years she'd felt guilty but then realized it was okay to love the father he'd been and not what he'd become.

She put away the album and looked around the room. She was tired of running away from the past. Afraid that she'd look over her shoulder and the man who'd killed her mother would be right behind her, gun aimed at her head.

It was time she stopped running. Tiredness enveloped her. This was a good place—she could feel it in her heart—and Brian was a good man. She didn't know where their relationship would take them, but she wanted to hang around long enough to find out.

She walked to her closet and took out a long white dress that had been worn only twice. She'd bought it on a whim because it was so pretty, that and she had matching white heels. Tonight would be a good night to wear the dress.

As soon as she soaked in the tub. Her spirits lifted. Rhonda had said they were closing early today because most of the guests were going on a hayride. She would have the place all to herself. She could already feel her body relaxing.

Brian glanced at his watch. He knew he'd told Celeste seven, but he couldn't wait any longer. He left the office and went in search of her, but she wasn't in her room.

Fear coursed through him. Had she packed up and left? He knew she didn't stay in one place very long, but would she leave without saying good-bye?

He walked back down the hall and out the back door, breathing a sigh of relief when he saw her car. Okay, so where was she? He glanced toward the spa building and saw a light on. He knew everyone had already left for the day, so Celeste was probably there.

His steps were light, and he was grinning like an idiot when he walked inside. She wasn't in the front area, but she'd turned the music on. Celtic, he thought. It was nice, peaceful.

He went to her massage room, frowning when she wasn't there, either. He started to leave but heard a noise coming from the bath area.

When he tapped on the door, no one answered, so he pushed the door open. His breath caught in his throat. Celeste stood in the roman bath, drying off. She'd pulled her hair up on top of her head, but some of it had come loose and the moisture in the room had caused tendrils to curl about her face.

She looked up and froze, clutching the towel against her naked body.

"I'm sorry. I knocked," he said, but his words were raspy.

"I didn't hear you."

"I should go." But he couldn't make his feet move.

"Don't. Go, I mean. I don't want you to." She stepped out of the sunken tub and walked toward him. "I've been running for a long time and I want to stop, at least for a little while." She stopped in front of him, then dropped the towel. "I need you."

She didn't have to say anything more. He took her into his arms and covered her mouth with his. She tasted sweet, like honey, and passionate all at the same time. He couldn't get enough of her.

"I've waited a lifetime for you," he finally said after he ended the kiss. He caressed her hair, her neck.

"I need you so much," she whispered.

He knew she wasn't just talking about sex. "Me, too."

She leaned back and looked at him. Her smile was shy and seductive.

"Have I told you how beautiful you are?" he asked.

"I think you've mentioned it. But did I tell you that I think you're handsome?"

He shook his head. "I want to make love to you."

"I want it, too."

"Are you sure? We can wait if you need time."

"I'm sure and I don't think I can wait much longer. My body feels as though it's on fire."

"God, I'm glad to hear you say that."

He would've had to soak in a tub of ice cubes if she'd wanted to wait. Even then, it might not have put out the flame of passion roaring inside him.

He lifted her up and carried her into the therapy room, leaving the door open so he could see. "How soft do you think the massage table is?"

"Soft enough, not that I think I'd mind the floor right now."

"Have I mentioned that you continually surprise me?"

"Do I?" She raised her eyebrows. "I think I like that I can do that. I hope it's in a good way."

"Oh, it certainly is that." He cupped her breast, lightly running his thumb back and forth across the nipple. "Your skin is soft, almost silky."

She unbuttoned his shirt and pushed it off his shoulders. "Are you sure you won't let me give you a massage?"

"Sweetheart, you can massage my body any time you want, but later. Right now I just want to make sweet love to you." He leaned his head down and took her into his mouth, rolling his tongue around her nipple. Damn, she was sweet.

She gasped, tugging his head closer. "Oh, damn, that feels good."

He moved to her other breast and gave it just as much attention.

"I'm not very experienced. Only what I've read in books and I've been with a couple of men. I'm not sure I know exactly what to do."

"So far I like the kind of books you read," he said as he looked at her and grinned. Her face turned a rosy shade. He noticed she blushed easily.

"They were really good books."

"Well, this is the real thing." He lifted her and set her down on the table. "Lie back." She did without question.

He started at her breasts, lightly caressing each one. She arched toward him, but he only moved down her body, over her abdomen, lightly grazing through the blond curls at the vee of her legs. "Don't we have some oil around here?"

She swallowed hard. "In the drawer there's lotion."

He lit the candle while he was turned around, then got out a jar. He twisted the lid off and raised it to his nose. "Vanilla. It's nice."

"Brian?"

He smiled. "I thought I would give you a massage." He scooped out some of the thick cream and put it on her stomach.

She sucked in her breath. "It's cold. You're supposed to rub it in your hands to warm it."

"Cold is sexier. Besides, it won't take long to warm." He started at her shoulders and began to massage. He knew the exact moment she started to relax. Then he slid his hands down to her breasts.

Celeste wasn't quite so relaxed as she had been. He tugged on her nipples, then circled the dark orbs, then massaged her breasts again.

"But I want to touch you," she said.

"You will," he promised.

"When?"

"Soon."

"At least take off your clothes. I feel strange being the only one completely naked."

He wiped his hands on a towel and tossed it to the side before removing the rest of his clothes. She stared at him the whole time. It was funny watching her reaction. She blushed, but she didn't look away.

"Is this better?" he asked.

She visibly swallowed. "Wow." She looked at his face. "I mean, yes, much better."

He grinned. It was nice knowing he rated a wow.

"You're laughing at me."

"I would never do that. You're wow, too."

"There's not much room on the table."

"We'll manage."

"I rather thought we would."

He again massaged lotion across her breasts, then slid his hands over her stomach and hips before moving to her thighs, then her calves. When he knew she was totally relaxed, he began to caress her sex. Light strokes at first, then with a little more pressure. She wiggled her bottom as he intensified his touch.

"You're making it hard for me to think."

"I don't want you to think; I only want you to feel."

"Then join me."

"Like you said, there's not much room on the table."

She moved to her side. "Now there is, and I want to touch you, too."

What could he do but join her. "If I fall, I'm taking you with me," he said.

"Would you?"

"Probably, but I'd let you land on top."

"Then maybe I wouldn't mind landing so much if I was on top of you." She reached between their bodies and stroked up his length, her touch just as feathery as his had been. He closed his eyes and sucked in a deep breath. "That feels nice."

"I bet I can make it feel better than nice," she whispered close to his ear so that her hot breath tickled his face. She encircled his penis with her hand and began to slide his foreskin down, then back up. "How's that?"

"Fantastic," he breathed.

"I think I know how we can do this. Move onto your back."

He didn't know what she had in mind, but right now he was agreeable to just about anything. He held on to her and eased to his back. Her lotion-slick body easily slid over him until she was situated on top.

"Better?" she asked.

"Your naked body is pressed against mine. I can feel your luscious breasts and your tight nipples are poking my chest. Your sex is nestled against my erection. What do you think?"

Her laughter filled the room. "I didn't know you could be funny."

"Sweetheart, I'm serious as hell." He grasped her ass and snuggled her in a little tighter to him. She gasped with pleasure.

"This is going to be so good." She wiggled against him and he thought he was going to come right then and there.

"I need to get a condom out of my pocket," he said.

"I'll get it," she quickly said, then was sliding off him and the table, and reaching for his pants. As soon as she had one she ripped it open, then looked at him. She didn't move, only stared. "Good Lord, you're beautiful."

"And horny."

She met his gaze. "Oh, right." She looked at the condom, then him. Finally she thrust it toward him.

He rolled it on. Before he could do much more than that she was back on the table snuggled on top of him, then positioning herself so that she was sliding onto him. He grasped her hips, holding her as he joined in the motion of her body.

His passion-glazed eyes stared up at her, watching the way her breasts bounced. She was beautiful, she was gorgeous, she was . . .

Celeste cried out, her body stiffening. She was fascinating to watch as she came. Then he didn't think anymore. He closed his eyes and let his release engulf him in the heat of the moment.

Her body collapsed on top of his, their ragged breathing filling the small room.

"I've never ever felt like this before," she whispered.

"I know. I feel the same way."

"This could get complicated."

"I won't let it. I promise."

She nodded.

And he meant what he said. He knew there was something between them. He'd sensed it the minute she'd stepped from her car and raised her face as if to worship the sun.

Chapter 24

"What do you mean you weren't always the good guy?" Nikki asked as she lay on her side across from Cal, the fire flickering between them, casting shadows over her naked body.

It was all he could do to stop staring at her luscious body and raise his gaze to her face. Great, now he had to look her in the eye and lie to her.

Dammit, she'd pissed him off when she kept probing for answers about Cynthia. And maybe he wanted to get a little back, and if he had to lie to do it, then so be it. It wasn't like she hadn't been lying to him since she'd called for reservations.

He'd tell her the truth before she left, but he wanted to see how fast she'd leave after she got what she came for. And maybe he just wanted to see if their time together had meant anything to her at all.

So he took a deep breath and gave her his most serious look. "Steroids."

That hadn't been so difficult. Easier than he thought. He'd been afraid he would feel guilty lying, but he didn't. On the contrary, he felt the total opposite. He inwardly smiled. Actually, this was kind of fun. How bad could he make his life?

She gasped. "You're doing steroids?"

"Not right now. I did in the past."

She relaxed again. "But that was in the past. She still shouldn't have broken the engagement for something you did in the past."

Damn, she looked good with the firelight flickering over her as the sun set behind her. But then she frowned.

"It is in the past, isn't it?"

"Oh, yeah. I haven't done steroids in a few years." He gazed off into the darkness. "The alcohol was a bit of a problem, though."

"You're not an alcoholic, too, are you?"

"It's not as bad as it used to be." His sigh was audible. "I pretty much have it under control now. That is, if I don't miss a meeting."

She moved to a sitting position and for a moment he couldn't think—hell, he could barely remember to breathe. Her breasts were right there in front of him, begging him to take them into his hands and massage them until she cried out for more.

"When did it all start?" she asked.

For half a second he thought she might really care, the way she was looking at him with concern. Hell, she was probably taking all this down in her head so she could write her tell-all article about his sordid past.

Ah, but wouldn't she be surprised to know that he was still a member of the Baptist church in Frog Hollow and that he gave to charities on a regular basis. But she only wanted all the dirt, so he'd give it to her in spades.

He picked up a stick, and rubbed his thumb across the rough surface. "It started when I was fifteen. I started running with a wild bunch from school."

She sat back, looking confused. "They have a wild crowd here? The town's not that big."

She had a point. The wildest thing that had ever happened here that he knew of was when Jamie Warren plowed up the front school yard on his daddy's new tractor. He was drunker than a skunk, but no one really blamed him since he was about to ship out overseas. Course, he was only going to

Germany, but the town figured overseas was overseas, so he didn't get into much trouble.

"What happened to all the values you said your grandparents taught you?" she asked, bringing him back to the present.

Damn, he'd forgotten about telling her that. It wasn't easy telling lies. "I really tried to stay on the straight and narrow, but the temptation was too great. I'm a sinner—what can I say?"

"Do you want to talk about it?"

Oh, now her asking him that was priceless. Of course she wanted him to talk about it. And that's exactly what he planned to do.

"You don't mind listening? There aren't a lot of people who would without taking advantage of what I tell them."

"Uh, what do you mean?"

"People love a scandal. They want to believe the worst about a person and especially someone who's in the spotlight, like I am." Now let her squirm a little.

"I would never use anything you told me. I mean, I write history books."

Yeah, sure. Well, two could play her game. "I knew you wouldn't. There's something good and kind about you." He took a deep breath. "When I was seventeen, I started running around with this wild bunch."

"I thought you said you were fifteen?"

"You're right. Sometimes I forget things. It's because of the alcohol." He had to keep his lies straight.

Her forehead wrinkled. "That's okay." She moved to her side again, head resting on her arm. "Go on, please."

How the hell could he keep anything straight when all he wanted to do was stare at her naked body?

He cleared his throat and tried to concentrate. "We made moonshine."

Not exactly a lie there. Hell, you could find moonshine in

just about any little backwoods country town—especially in Texas. He'd drunk some once. It had taken him a good two minutes to catch his breath. He never so much as got close to homemade brew again.

"We sold it out of the back of Timmy Collins's old Ford that had been souped up. We'd make runs late at night. The cops never caught us, but not because they didn't try."

Tim would kill him if he knew he was talking about him like this. Tim was the preacher at the Baptist church, and as far as Cal knew, he'd never taken a drink in his life.

"That's how you got hooked on alcohol?"

"That, and stealing it out of liquor stores when the revenuers would find our still and blow it up."

Her eyes narrowed. "You're a thief, too?"

Maybe he was laying it on a little too thick. "Only once. I didn't steal after that. It scared the hell out of me. I figured I was a lot of things but not a thief."

Nikki seemed to relax. "When did the use of steroids start?"

"College."

"They didn't do random drug testing?"

"Yeah, but you pay someone clean to pee in the cup. It's no big deal."

"So, why did you stop taking them?"

Crap, why would he stop taking them? He wasn't very good at lying.

"My heart," he blurted.

"You had a heart attack?" Her eyes widened.

He thought back to everything he'd seen or heard about the use of steroids. "No, my heart was beating too fast." That sounded plausible and she looked as though she bought his story.

"You dated a lot when you went pro," she said.

"I thought you didn't follow sports?" It was her turn to look nervous.

"I don't. I just assumed that since you're a nice-looking man that you would've dated a lot of women. At least, until you met your fiancée."

Good fix for her blunder. She'd impressed him. There'd been barely a hesitation between her slip and her recovery, but then, she had a lot more experience at this.

Cal sighed deeply. "They all wanted something from me." That was the truth. When he'd become popular with the media, he'd had women crawling all over him to get in the spotlight. "And then I met Cynthia."

"But she couldn't accept your past."

"That, and the affairs." He almost laughed out loud at the affronted expression on her face.

"Affairs?" She sat up. Nope, she didn't look happy.

"Well, yeah. I'm a star player. She should've known I couldn't be faithful to one woman."

"And why couldn't you . . . keep your pants zipped?"

"Well, hell, that should be easy to figure out. Talk about temptation. I mean, look at you."

Her frown deepened. "What about me?"

"Honey, you've been all over me ever since you got to the ranch. You just couldn't resist the Braxton charm."

"You know, it's getting a little chilly." She stood and went to the bag of things she'd brought with her.

He silently laughed until he saw her pulling on a pair of sweat pants and a sweatshirt. Well, hell, he should've realized his last lie would put her in a tiff. No woman wanted to think a man was a cheater. The bad part about it was that he'd never cheated on a woman in his life.

But apparently, as his lies had progressed, he'd gotten pretty good at it. Enough that Nikki bought every word, and the only way to undo it would be to tell her it was all a lie. He really doubted that would help matters. It was a lose-lose situation.

He had a feeling it was going to be a long, cold night. He

hadn't brought anything to sleep in. He hadn't thought he would need it.

He was wrong again.

Nikki watched Cal out of the corner of her eye as she yanked her shirt down. What she wanted to do was pick up the iron skillet and throw it at him.

She could forgive him for his wayward youth, even the steroids and the alcohol, but cheating on his fiancée? And because he thought he was some kind of macho football player?

Oh, that burned her up!

She grabbed the flashlight off the ground. "I'll be back." Mountain lions didn't scare her a bit right now. In fact, if she happened on one she'd feel sorry for the beast.

She couldn't believe Cal had even admitted to his wild youth, but then to add wood to the fire, he'd told her he would never be faithful—when he was sleeping with her!

Dumb jock.

But boy, did she have a story now. She'd probably get a raise out of this, along with a nice vacation. Cal would get exactly what he deserved: his career ruined, his life down the tube. That would suit her just fine. She could easily picture him as a broken man drowning his sorrows in drugs and alcohol.

Her heart skipped a beat.

Is that what she wanted? To ruin him? She looked toward camp and saw him laying out sleeping bags. He'd pulled on jeans but he wasn't wearing a shirt. Her mouth went dry. He had a magnificent body. Her heart broke at the thought of him wasting away.

Desolation filled her. Politicians were one thing, but Cal? She couldn't help remembering how gentle he'd been with her, how his touch had inflamed her.

And when they'd ridden to the pond, he'd been patient as he'd taught her how to ride Taffy. And even today, when he'd shown her how to fish.

She didn't want to ruin him. She wouldn't mind seeing him suffer a little, but not total ruination.

Her shoulders slumped. What was happening to her? Where was her edge that she'd honed over the years?

It hit her in one big whoosh.

Oh, Lord, she'd fallen for the guy. It wasn't just his body she lusted after. It was Cal. If she wanted a man with a buff body, she could get one, but she didn't. Not that it didn't help to have a buff body, though, which he did.

No, she wanted the one man who made her heart beat faster every time he glanced her way. She frowned. At least, she did until he'd opened up to her. Why did he have to ruin everything?

One thing for certain, she couldn't write a story that would destroy his life. She'd tell Marge there was nothing exciting about the breakup. Nikki would lie to her boss. She could do that. She was good at lying.

When she returned to camp, she made an excuse about wanting to turn in early, but it was hours before she fell asleep, and even then, she tossed and turned, which wasn't easy in a sleeping bag.

Cal already had coffee made the next morning when she dragged her eyelids open. It smelled great. She'd missed her coffee.

She sat up, rubbing the sleep out of her eyes, and stretching her back. Good Lord, she pitied the pioneers. Sleeping on the ground wasn't all it was cracked up to be. She longed for a real mattress.

"Morning," Cal said, looking entirely too cheerful.

She grunted.

Mornings weren't her favorite time of day, and she wasn't the best at communication this early. She glanced around. She kind of missed seeing the crazy rooster, though.

After mumbling something that she was pretty certain was unintelligible, she pulled on her boots and headed for the trees. There was another thing she hated about living off the land.

She finished and headed toward the river to wash. For a moment she could only stare at it. The water was so clear as it flowed over the rocks. There was something pure about being outside this early.

A fish jumped into the air, twisted and turned before it plopped back into the river. For just a second, she wished she had her fishing pole.

Oh God, she was going country. She needed to get back to the city as soon as possible.

Back at camp, Cal handed her a cup of coffee. She cupped it in both hands and blew across the steaming liquid before taking a sip.

Bleh!

"Is there cream or sugar?"

"We're pioneers, remember. They didn't have cream, and more often then not, they didn't have sugar. Nothing fancy here. They'd call this wake-up coffee."

It would certainly do that and then some. She squatted on the ground noticing that even though her back hurt from sleeping on the hard ground last night, her thighs weren't nearly as sore. She took another sip. The coffee was so strong it curled her toes.

"I take it you're not a morning person."

She raised her eyebrows. "I would've thought you'd have figured that out by now."

"The coffee will help."

She wasn't sure she wanted to get woke up. If she was awake, she'd have to think about everything Cal had told her last night and she wasn't sure she was ready to face the truth. Maybe it would be better if she left, went back to Fort Worth. That was the only way she would be able to get over Cal.

"I think I have enough for my story," she said. "I should probably leave so I can finish the book."

"I'd like to help you out, but Tornado picked up a stone and is favoring her leg. She should probably rest it today. We can head back in the morning."

But she didn't want to spend another day in his company. That would only make it harder for her to leave even knowing what she did about him.

It would seem she didn't have a choice in the matter. She looked up at him then and realized maybe she didn't want to leave. God, she was such a fool and that was one thing she'd never been, at least not over a man. She guessed there was a first time for everyone, but it didn't mean she had to like the situation!

Chapter 25

For just a moment, Celeste thought about sneaking back inside the therapy room when she saw Brian at the reception desk talking to Rhonda. Drat, she had to face him sooner or later. That knowledge didn't make her feel any better.

What had gotten into her yesterday? She couldn't believe she'd told him anything, let alone spilling her whole sordid family history. She never talked about her past to anyone.

But then to make love with him . . . no, there had been nothing wrong about what they'd shared. Maybe it was the most right thing that had happened in her life in a very long time, and she refused to feel regret.

A whole lot embarrassed, but she figured that was only natural. But, damn, he was the most handsome man she'd ever seen.

He turned from the reception desk and saw her at the door of the massage room. There was nothing for her to do but walk to the front desk. It wasn't as if she wouldn't run into him sooner or later.

"Hello," she said.

His gaze slowly swept over her. Tingles spread down her body in the wake of his heated gaze, but then, she knew he wanted her. That had been evident last night. There was definitely a mutual attraction going on here.

"Have lunch with me," he said.

She twined her fingers together and glanced at Rhonda. The receptionist quickly looked down at the desk and began to thumb through the pages of the appointment book.

Celeste could feel the heat rise up her face. "I can't," she blurted as she silently wished for him to go away. She needed time to think about what was going on between them. Things were happening way too fast for her.

"Actually," Rhonda said, "you don't have another appointment until two. You can take a nice long, leisurely lunch." She was smiling when she raised her head but apparently noted Celeste's not so pleased expression and downed her head again.

"Good. I'll drop by around noon and we can walk over together."

Brian didn't wait for her to protest. He strode to the door and left her to wonder how she was going to get out of having lunch with the boss.

"I think he likes you," Rhonda said.

"I think you need to mind your own business."

"Are you really mad at me?" Rhonda looked genuinely worried as she fiddled with the top button on her blouse.

"No, I guess not." She had to work with her and she was more mad at herself than she was at Rhonda.

Rhonda smiled brightly. "You like him, don't you?"

"He's the boss."

"And he's still a man."

Oh yeah, that he was, and she couldn't stop the thrill that swept over her as she remembered just how much of a man he was.

But she had a feeling no good would come out of their relationship. Her past experiences should be enough warning that nothing would work out between them.

Nikki glared at Cal's back as she sacrificed a worm on the sharp hook. What she wouldn't give to jab him in the butt with the barbed piece of metal. Cal had used her. Made love to her all the time he planned to dump her. No, not dump, just have other women. He probably expected her to make appointments for his time.

Not that she even remotely thought their relationship stood a chance, but did he have to be so blunt about not being able to stay true to just one woman?

It was a good thing she'd chosen to fish downstream from him or she'd be tempted to whack him over the head with her pole!

"I bet the town loves having their star football player back in town," she said sarcastically as she tossed the line out. It whistled through the air, and then the sinker plopped into the water, sending out ripples.

"They like making a big deal. I don't see the harm." He glanced over his shoulder and winked. "Especially the ladies. They trip all over themselves trying to get to me."

Anger coursed through her.

He suddenly frowned. "But I won't mess around while we're having so much fun. I'll wait until I start getting bored."

"How nice," she said between gritted teeth.

He was thoughtful for a minute. "I'll probably wait until you leave town."

"How generous."

"I'm really trying to do better." He turned back around, throwing out his line.

She glared at him. There was a tug on her line. She quickly reeled it in but there wasn't anything on the hook, including the damned worm.

"You missed that one," he told her, then went back to his own fishing.

Ohh, she'd like to . . . to . . . How could she ever have thought she might love him? She needed to have her head examined.

She threaded another worm on the hook and flung her line out, except it didn't go anywhere. She whipped it back and forth—still nothing.

His laughter filled the air. "You have to let some of your

line out—give it a little slack—and don't forget to push the button." He turned his back to her, but she could tell he was still laughing. He'd probably been laughing at her every time she came on to him.

She released some of her line.

"But I will say that I've never had such good sex as what I've had with you."

Oh, now he was comparing her to his other women! That was just great.

She whipped the fishing pole at the same time she released the line. It sailed through the air, but not toward the water.

"Ow!" Cal jumped, grabbing his butt.

"Oh, crap." She threw her pole down. He jumped again when the line tightened. "I'm sorry." She scooped the rod back up and ran toward him but stumbled and jerked the line tight again as she tried to catch her balance.

"Just walk, don't run," Cal said between gritted teeth.

Nikki immediately slowed. Dammit, she might have been thinking about jabbing her hook in his butt, but that was all she'd been doing—just thinking it. Oh, maybe she was telekinetic. Darn it, she hadn't meant to hook him. She stopped beside him, carefully laying the pole down.

"There's a knife in my pocket," he said. "Get it and cut the line."

"I'm so sorry. I would never . . ."

"Just cut the line."

"Okay, okay, you don't have to bite my head off." She stuck her hand in his pocket and dug around. Her fingers encountered two hard objects. A frown turned her lips downward. How could he get a hard-on with a hook in his ass? She had a feeling the knife was the smaller of the two.

She was right.

She quickly opened it and cut the line. "Now what? Do you want me to pull the hook out?"

"No!"

Sheesh! "I was just asking. How the hell do I know what you want me to do if you don't tell me?"

"Help me back to camp."

He put his arm around her shoulder, his hand landing on her breast. On purpose? Probably. She was not going to be the next girl in the Cal Braxton harem. She moved his hand to a safer place as they made their way back to camp.

"Hey, you're not mad at me because I can't be faithful, are you?"

"Why should that bother me?" she grumbled.

"You sound mad."

"I'm not mad." The sooner she returned to Fort Worth, the better. She would throw herself back into her work and she'd forget all about Cal—eventually.

Once back at camp, she helped him ease to his knees. Their bodies came into close contact, his chest pressing against hers. An ache began to build inside her, but she quickly thought about all he'd told her the night before.

It didn't work. She still wanted him. For a second, she closed her eyes, letting his body bathe her in heat. Her nipples hardened.

"The hook," he said. "I don't think I'm up for lovemaking right now, darlin'. Maybe later."

"Don't worry, I don't need servicing." God, you'd think she was one of the cows and he was a frigging bull!

Nikki moved out of the way a little too fast. He grunted in pain as his hands reached out and his palms landed on the hard ground. He lowered himself the rest of the way.

Okay, she felt bad, a little, that he'd landed so hard when she moved out of his way. "Now what do I do?"

"Cut an opening in my jeans where the hook is."

She knelt beside him. "I don't have any nursing experience. Not that I'll faint at the sight of blood or anything. I just wanted you to know that I really doubt I'll be able to perform surgery or anything."

She'd been at the emergency room a couple of times when a shooting victim was brought in, but that had been a long time ago and really early in her career. She'd decided the political arena was messy, but at least it wasn't quite as gross as a bullet wound and blood spilling out everywhere. A hook shouldn't pose any problems that she couldn't handle, though.

Until she'd cut away his jeans a little too much and exposed his butt. She normally wasn't a butt person but Cal had a really nice one. She liked that it was tanned. It took a supreme effort not to caress it.

"Now, baby, you have to stop ogling my ass. You'll have plenty of time to look at it after the hook is out."

She raised the knife, then closed her eyes and counted to ten. She would not plunge it into his back. They put people in jail for stuff like that. She had no intention of spending the next ten years locked up in a correctional institution. Even though her actions would be justified.

But the temptation was really strong.

Cal figured Nikki was about ready to kill him, and since she was holding the knife, he decided to quit pushing her. He'd hate like hell if she plunged it into his back. Besides, his ass hurt every time he moved a little.

"I wasn't staring at your ass," she spat out.

He grinned. She probably had been staring at it. Nikki was easily aroused. It hadn't taken him long to figure out that one look, one caress, and she was ready to make love. Well, that was until he'd pissed her off.

It should have made him feel better that she was furious with him. Now the shoe was on the other foot and maybe she was starting to feel used. But it didn't. All he could think of was what he'd be missing when she left. But it wasn't like they had anything going for them. She was a reporter. She and Cal together were like oil and water.

"Do you want me to cut the hook out?" she asked, sounding a little too pleased at the prospect of carving him up.

"Look in my saddlebag. There's a pair of wire cutters. Grab the bottle of whiskey, too."

"Do you really think this is a good time to start drinking?"

"It's to disinfect the wound."

"Oh."

She stood and went to the saddlebag. When she bent over to dig through it, he had a nice view of her ass. Damn, she had a nice ass. He couldn't help remembering how it had felt when he'd cupped her cheeks and brought her in closer to him. The way she moved perfectly to the rhythm of his body. An ache started to build inside him.

"Are these the wire cutters?" She held them up.

He jerked his thoughts back to the present. Thinking like that would get him into a lot of trouble. "Yeah. Did you find the whiskey?"

She straightened, the whiskey in one hand and the wire cutters in the other. "The bottle was under all the condoms," she said, one eyebrow quirked upward. She looked put out. "There were at least two dozen of them."

"There was a special on at the drugstore." He hadn't planned on ending their relationship until they got back. It had been dumb to tell her all those lies last night. "I'm a horny man. What can I say?"

He could almost see the flames shooting from her head. Cal had to remember he had a hook in his ass and she was the one who was going to remove it. He still wasn't positive she hadn't done it on purpose.

Nikki marched over and knelt beside him again.

"Cut the end of the hook that has the line attached to it. It's not going to be easy. Make sure you grip the wire cutters real tight."

She didn't do anything.

He suspected her bravado was slipping. "Hey, it's okay. This isn't the first time I've been hooked. Brian got me once. It might hurt, but I'll live."

"I'm not worried I can't do it. I was getting a drink."

She was getting a drink? He hadn't seen her pick up one of the canteens . . . "You're not supposed to drink the whiskey. I'd rather not have you drunk when you remove the hook."

"Then I'll make sure I'm only a little tipsy."

"Listen, it's not that big of a deal." He wasn't convinced she wasn't just nervous. "You can do this."

"Of course I can, but I really was thirsty. Don't worry, I saved enough to pour on your butt."

Okay, so maybe she wasn't nervous. She was a whole lot sarcastic, though. He didn't think he liked her attitude, either. Maybe he'd made too light of his injury?

He heard her take a deep breath, and then her knuckles brushed against the cheek of his ass as she gripped the hook. He bit down on his lip when the hook wiggled. A few seconds later there was a snap.

"The end is cut. Now what?"

"Grasp the curved end of the hook with the wire cutters and bring it out. Don't pull straight up. You'll want to curve it as you remove it."

"It looks pretty deep."

"Thanks for letting me know."

"Sorry. If it's any consolation, the hook is thin."

"I feel much better."

Silence.

"What are you doing?" he asked.

"Looking at it. If you'd been a fish, there's no way you would've gotten off. I hooked you pretty good."

"Do you mind?"

"I was just making an observation, Braxton. Okay, get ready."

He held his breath as she brought it out, but she brought it out fast without hurting him too much. He sucked in his breath for effect. Might as well make the most of the situation.

"It wasn't *that* bad," she said.

Had she run out of sympathy? "It hurt," he complained.

"It was a small hook."

"Well, pour some of the whiskey on it so it won't get infected. That is, if you haven't finished off the bottle."

"I'm laughing on the inside."

The liquid burned as it hit the wound. "Ow! You could've warned me before you poured it."

"I'm going to pour it," she said dryly.

"Funny."

"I'm sure it didn't burn that much."

"You pour eighty-proof whiskey on an open wound and see how it feels."

"I can't even see the injury. The hook was really small. I have a feeling you didn't want me to catch a big fish."

"You landed me, didn't you?"

"You have a point."

When he eased to his feet, she started laughing. He frowned. "Now what the hell is so damned funny?"

She covered her mouth. "You look as though a shark bit the ass out of your jeans."

No, just a barracuda, he thought to himself. And it might be a little wound but it still hurt like a son of a bitch. The bad thing about it was that he hadn't brought a change of clothes, so he had to go around with half his ass out of his jeans.

Nothing had gone right in his life since Nikki had come into it. Why the hell would he think it would get any better the longer she stayed?

Chapter 26

Brian was waiting to take Celeste to lunch as soon as she finished her last massage of the morning. As she walked toward him, his heart pounded so hard inside his chest he thought it might burst.

"People are going to talk," she said.

He grinned. "They already are. They've been talking ever since you showed up looking so pretty."

"Maybe they were talking about my car."

"Probably, but they stopped after they got a look at you." When she frowned, he laughed. She had a cute way of puckering her bottom lip. It was all he could do to keep from leaning over and kissing it, but he was afraid it would embarrass her.

"I'm going to trade it off the first chance I get."

"Good idea."

"You're not helping matters." But there was a twinkle in her eyes.

"Then I'll change the subject. I thought we'd eat on the patio. It's a beautiful day."

He thought that would please her, but her squared shoulders and the way she nervously fisted and unfisted her hands told a different story. Then he remembered they'd kissed the last time they were on the patio. Was she afraid that it would happen again? Or that it might lead to more? They hadn't talked about last night or the fact they'd made love.

"Just lunch," he said.

She glanced up at him and he marveled again how clear her gray-green eyes were. Her lightly tanned skin and delicate features only added to her ethereal beauty, but damn she filled out the pair of shorts and T-shirt she wore.

It was all he could do to concentrate when she looked at him. How could anyone look so damned innocent and hot at the same time? Every time he looked at her, he was amazed.

"If you'd rather eat with someone else, that's okay, too." He didn't want her to think he was forcing her to eat with him just because he was the boss. He hadn't realized just how complicated their relationship could get.

"I'm sorry," she said. "I'm still a little nervous about how much I talked yesterday. I don't usually unload my past on anyone." She took a deep breath. "I wasn't looking for sympathy or anything."

"I've already told you it's okay. Everyone needs to talk to someone, and I have a feeling you've been needing someone for a very long time."

"But you're not a therapist."

He smiled. "Would that help?"

"No. At least it didn't help me before. The state sent one to evaluate my mental status after the . . . the shooting, but I think the woman was more concerned with her own problems than mine."

"Her problems?"

"She'd just broken up with her boyfriend. His name was John and apparently he didn't believe in work. She was tired of supporting him."

They walked past the dining area. He opened the door, and she walked in front of him out to the patio.

"It doesn't sound as though she was qualified to help you."

Celeste shrugged. "They were short-staffed. Besides, I didn't really need her. There was nothing that she could do to bring my mother back. It wasn't as if she could put the pieces of my life back together again."

"But she should've been able to help you through a rough time."

"My foster mother helped."

"Except you wouldn't let her get close."

She studied him. "You're going to play therapist, aren't you? Believe me, I've put the past behind me." Her eyes pleaded with him to let it go.

"Good." He regarded her for a moment, then smiled. "I hope you like hamburgers," he said, waving a hand toward the table.

"It's my favorite food. How did you know?"

"I read minds on the side."

God, she hoped not. Even she was afraid to look too closely into her thoughts. No one had ever made her see her past quite like Brian had. She'd always thought if she ran fast enough, far enough, then she wouldn't have to examine anything too closely.

So she'd shut the door on her past, then locked it, tucking the key away in a pocket that she guarded well, but Brian had found it and made her open the door.

When she got her first paycheck she needed to hit the road and go far, far away from here, from him.

She sat in the chair he pulled out for her, her shoulders slumping. How many places had she already run away from? She really liked the ranch.

She glanced up as he took the chair across from her. And she really liked Brian. She didn't want to leave, but if she stayed what would happen? Would she get close to him? She had a feeling she would. Then what would happen?

A shudder swept through her. She'd never thought this much about her relationships. Maybe because she'd never gotten close enough to anyone that she could be hurt again.

"Did you want mayo rather than mustard? I can have them bring you another one."

She looked at Brian, then her burger. "No, this is fine. I love mustard." She picked up the burger and bit into it. It was all she could do to swallow, though, as she mentally made plans to leave. Why had she even thought she could stay?

"Don't think too hard about it," Brian spoke softly.

She set her burger back on the plate. "I don't know what you mean."

He covered her hand with his. She wanted to pull away, but his felt so warm and comforting.

"Our relationship. I want you to know I've never dated, let alone made love to, someone who works for me. There's something about you and I know you feel the same way about me, but it scares you. It scares the hell out of me, too, because I've never felt like this before. Please promise me that you won't run the first chance you get. That you'll give us a chance."

Celeste looked up and saw the sincerity in Brian's eyes. God, she was so tired of running. "I want to give us a chance," she finally said and knew she meant it. Maybe she'd finally found a place she could call home again.

"I said I was sorry. What else do you want me to do?" Nikki asked Cal.

He didn't look pleased that she wasn't making more out of his wound. It hadn't been that bad. The worst was over. At least it was almost over. They'd padded his saddle with one of the sleeping bags, but the longer they rode, the more irritable he became.

She felt sorry for him—really, she did. But when she rode behind him, she couldn't help smiling. He'd caught her smile once when he'd turned around and had been even more irritated.

Could she help it if one of the cheeks of his ass just happened to be exposed? Maybe she should tell him that it was a very nice ass cheek. Yeah, like she wanted to feed his ego any more than she already had. The sooner they got back to the cabin, the better. She wanted to pack and then she was out of there.

They topped a small rise and she was looking down on the cabin. Finally. The ride had seemed endless, with Cal in the mood he was in.

Her gaze swept the area. Everything looked the same as when she'd left. She could see the rooster in the barnyard with his two faithful chickens, and Bessie Two stood in her pen, the calf with her.

She would kind of miss it. *Kind of* being the operative phrase. She glanced at Cal. Even after he'd told her what he had, she knew she would miss him. There was no reforming a man like him, though. A shame, but it was better to make a clean break.

They stopped their horses in front of the cabin and she slid off hers. At least her legs weren't shaking as much.

"I think you'll understand that I won't be dismounting." Cal's words were clipped.

"I didn't expect you to." She handed him the reins, but then guilt attacked her again. "I'm sorry I hooked you."

He met her gaze, his expression grim. "Like I said, I'll live." He nodded, then started toward the ranch.

She sighed as she watched him ride off, ass cheek shining. It was still a really nice ass cheek.

She turned and started up the steps, but a noise at the side of the cabin drew her attention. A woman stepped from the shadows. Nikki grabbed the rail. The ghost! Oh, God, she was too young to die.

"I'm sorry if I frightened you," the woman spoke softly. She held up a bag. "I needed more mint."

Mint? Okay, not the ghost. She took a deep breath, then laughed. "I thought you were the . . . uh." If she mentioned the ghost the young woman would probably think she was crazy.

"I'm not the ghost if that's what you were about to say."

"I don't really believe in them."

"You should since there's one haunting the cabin."

And Nikki had been afraid this woman would think *she* was a nutcase. "Are you staying at the ranch?" It might be safer if she just changed the subject.

The young woman stepped closer. "I'm the new massage therapist." She frowned. "You're Nikki, aren't you?"

"Yes."

The woman's frown deepened. "Odd, Brian told me you were really ugly and you were some kind of . . . of shark reporter. No wait, he said they called you a barracuda." She laughed, her gaze scanning Nikki. "You're certainly not ugly and I can't see you going for the throat. I think his brother, Cal, must've been pulling the wool over his eyes."

Nikki's heart skipped a few beats. Cal knew she was a reporter? But how, who, when?

But she knew the answer. Cal knew who she was when he'd shown her the cabin on her first day at the ranch. She'd suspected a change in him but brushed away her imaginings.

Damn! The outhouse, the milking and gathering eggs, the cleaning, riding, making love—he'd known all along who she was. Fury swept over her as fast as a wildfire across the prairie.

He'd used her. Damn!

It didn't matter that she'd been using Cal, because she'd decided not to write her story. He'd been laughing at her the whole time.

"Do me a favor and don't mention that you told me what Cal said to his brother. I'd hate for Cal to be embarrassed."

"Of course. My name is Celeste, by the way. And I guess I'd better hurry back. I have an appointment in an hour."

"It was nice meeting you," Nikki said. Very nice.

She marched inside the cabin and straight to the bedroom. She grabbed her cases from under the bed and slapped them down on top of the mattress, fuming.

"It hasn't meant a thing to him. Making love has just been sex to Cal. He probably hoped I would fall off Taffy and break my neck." Damn!

She jerked the zipper closed on the case and filled the next one.

Something wet dropped on her hand. Oh, hell, she was crying—over a dumb jock.

"It's only because he got the best of me," she said. She didn't care anything about him. Not now, not since she knew she'd only been a big joke.

She flopped down on the bed, resting her head in her hands. Where was the barracuda who'd come to the ranch? Where was her fierce determination to get the story at all costs?

The barracuda was dead.

She lay back on the bed, closing her eyes. Never once in her life had she felt as broken as she did right now. She sniffed.

Music began to play, soothing her soul. She smiled. It was nice.

Wait, there was no electricity. Maybe someone was walking by. She frowned, opened her eyes. There was a blue mist in the corner. She could almost make out the face of a woman.

Very slowly, she sat up.

The mist grew denser. She slipped her hands through the handles of her suitcases and ran as fast as she could to the door, her cases banging her legs.

Cold washed over her. It clung like a heavy mist, seeping into the very pores of her skin. She body slammed the front door and jumped past the steps.

"Cock! Cock! Cock!" The rooster saw her and wildly flapped his wings as he flew out of a nearby tree and plopped on the ground, then took off toward the barn.

She flung her suitcases into the backseat and jumped inside her car. A cloud of dust like a small tornado whirled behind her as she zoomed away from the cabin. She looked in her rearview mirror and saw a woman at one of the windows.

Okay, she and her mother were going to have a long talk about ghosts.

When Nikki was a safe distance away from the cabin, she pulled to the side of the road and slowed her breathing. Had she really just encountered a ghost? Hell, she would believe just about anything right now.

As soon as she was calmer, she checked her appearance in the mirror. She was a mess. She didn't want to confront Cal looking like this, and confront him she would. As soon as he'd found out she was a reporter he should've thrown her off the property. But no, he'd played cat and mouse with her.

She got out of the car and found a pair of black pants and a red top, then went behind a tree and changed. The clothes hugged her body, showing off her curves. A splash of the finest French perfume money could buy, to get rid of the horse smell, and sexy red heels before she ran her hands through her short hair.

She was ready to face the dragon. Oh, yeah, he was going to regret screwing with her. She'd show him exactly what he'd toyed with.

The barracuda was back and Cal was about to face her wrath!

Chapter 27

Cal made it to his bedroom without being spotted. If a guest had caught him with half his bare ass showing Brian would've killed him. He eased into another pair of jeans. His butt was still sore. Nikki had hooked him good.

Nikki.

He shook his head. She'd probably have her bags packed and in her car. He didn't expect her to hang around long now that she had enough dirt on him to write a story.

What if he hadn't told her all the lies? Would she have stayed?

Yeah, right. The Barracuda had gone for his throat but ripped his heart out instead. He'd finally admitted it to himself. He liked Nikki more than he'd anticipated. But did she return his feelings?

He'd know soon enough. If she left today, then she was only after the story and everything she'd said and done was all a lie.

Cal left his room, walked down the long hallway and into the main sitting area. Just as he passed a window, he saw a familiar baby blue Jag pull up.

"Great," he muttered, then stilled when Nikki's convertible pulled up next to it. They climbed out at the same time, each giving the other the once-over.

His gaze moved to Nikki. She'd changed clothes. Damn,

she looked hot. He was really going to miss her. Then he looked at Cynthia. A bad taste formed in his mouth.

"Oh, hell." Cal looked from one to the other. The instant dislike was palpable. The claws were coming out. He hurried to the front door.

"Hey," Brian called.

"Talk to you later." Cal hurried past as Celeste joined his brother.

"Cal," Cynthia said as he came barreling through the front door. She pulled off her sunglasses and walked to the end of her car. Her blond hair trailed down her back in carefully arranged disarray.

He had to admit, she was a sexy woman, and today was no exception. She wore a tight-fitting black minidress that hugged every one of her curves. Her lips were painted a deep red, and at the moment, they were pouting.

Cynthia. In the flesh, and there was quite a bit of flesh showing. His gaze moved to Nikki. He had a feeling this wasn't going to be good.

"Hello, Cynthia," he finally said.

Cynthia's smile dropped as she turned to Nikki. "If you don't mind, this is a private conversation."

"I don't mind a bit." Nikki crossed her arms and leaned against her car door.

"What are you doing here, Cynthia?"

Cynthia's lips pouted even more, if that was possible. "I missed you. I thought by now you would've forgotten about our little disagreement. I know I should've waited for you to propose before I announced our engagement, but I misunderstood your intentions. We could start over, though."

He glanced toward Nikki. That little bit of news didn't look as though it sat well with her.

"I thought you broke off the engagement because he was running around with other women," Nikki said.

Cynthia raised her perfectly plucked eyebrows. "My Cal never even looked at another woman when we were dating.

He didn't have to because I was all the woman he needed." Her gaze slid over Nikki. Cynthia curled her lip. "Who are you?"

"She doesn't matter," Cal broke in.

"I didn't think she did, darling."

Nikki planted her hands on her hips. "Now I don't matter?"

"That's not what I meant." Hell, he didn't know what he meant anymore.

"I guess the wild youth, the drinking, the steroids were all a lie, too."

"Are you accusing Cal of taking steroids and drinking?" Cynthia asked. "He's never done drugs and he certainly isn't an alcoholic!"

"You lied about everything," Nikki accused.

"Yeah, I lied." Cal couldn't believe Nikki was pissed off. "I told you exactly what you wanted to hear." He glared at her. "And you accuse *me* of lying? What about you?"

"All you had to do was throw me off the property, but no, you had to make me pay. The milking, putting me on a horse when you knew damned well I'd never ridden one, gathering eggs, churning butter, that frigging rooster from hell." She threw her hands in the air. "Then you seduced me!"

"*I* seduced *you?*" He glared at her. "Lady, I think you have your facts wrong. You're the one who seduced me."

Cynthia's mouth dropped open as she looked from him to Nikki. "You . . . you slept with her?"

"No," Nikki's words dripped with sarcasm. "We only had sex. There was no sleeping involved."

"But you love me, Cal."

Cal ran a hand through his hair, grimacing when he looked at Cynthia. "No, I don't love you. I didn't ask you to marry me. We only went on four dates. I don't think I even like you."

"Oh! Oh!" Cynthia stomped her foot. "I'm telling Daddy. You'll be so sorry for treating me like this, Cal Braxton!" She marched to her car and climbed in. She was gone in a flash and a cloud of dust.

"Just print what you want because I don't give a damn," he told Nikki, fed up with all women. He turned and stomped back to the front door but stopped at the last second and faced her again. "Consider yourself thrown off this ranch, and I'd really appreciate it if you didn't come back."

"That's fine with me. I was leaving anyway."

"Of course you were. You thought you had all the dirt you needed."

She opened her mouth but snapped it shut at the last minute. He wondered what she'd been about to say but then figured it was probably another lie.

She jerked open the car door and climbed inside, following in the wake of Cynthia's dust.

"Good riddance!" He yelled, even though she wouldn't have heard him. He went inside, nearly tripping over Brian and Celeste. "What? Have you nothing better to do than eavesdrop?"

"It was kind of hard not to hear," Brian said while Celeste guiltily downed her head.

"Well, it's over."

"You should be happy. You've killed two birds with one stone." Brian laughed.

Cal had no idea what his brother found so amusing. He was certain Brian would explain.

"You slept with the reporter," Brian said.

Cal frowned. "Yeah, so what?"

Brian grinned. "You also said she reminded you of that old nag Grandpa had. The one with the buckteeth." He shook his head. "Either you need glasses or there was a spark of interest and you were afraid I might get in on the action."

"I wasn't interested," he growled.

"I think I have a massage or something," Celeste said, but before she could escape, Brian grabbed her hand.

"I'd say you didn't want me to go near her, so you lied

about her looks. Not getting territorial are you, brother?" Brian asked, looking smug.

"I could care less about her. Now, if the inquisition is over, I think I'll go to my room and lie down." He strode past Brian.

"You're limping. What happened? Tornado finally realize she could do better?"

He sighed and turned back around. "If you must know, I took Nikki fishing and she hooked me."

"I'd say she hooked you in more ways than one."

"Whatever."

His brother was losing his mind. Yeah, so he'd liked Nikki, but look where it had gotten him. He shook his head. No telling what she'd write about him, either. His short laugh held no humor. Whatever she wrote, he doubted it would be good. He hoped she was proud of herself.

He went inside his room and closed the door. Maybe he should've thrown her off the property when she'd first arrived and Jeff had told him who she was. His idea to teach her a lesson had backfired.

He lay down on the bed as exhaustion swept over him. But when he closed his eyes, all he saw was Nikki. Nikki milking the cow, even though he could tell she hated touching the animal, but then later, he'd caught her petting Bessie. He smiled. So she hadn't been as fierce as she'd pretended.

She hadn't backed down from anything, either. He liked that about her. Cynthia had been a damsel in distress. There was nothing shy and retiring about Nikki.

She hadn't been at all shy when they'd made love, either. A shudder of regret rippled over him as he remembered how she'd felt, how she'd tasted.

Cal jerked to a sitting position, wincing when the skin pulled taut around the area where he'd been hooked.

What the hell was he going to do now? His career would more than likely be over when Cynthia told her daddy that Cal had broken her heart. Her father spoiled her and Cal didn't really think the man would let anything slide when it concerned his little girl.

Yep, he was pretty much screwed. Add the article Nikki would write and he could see his career going down the tube.

Brian had once suggested they become partners in the ranch. His idea was starting to look like Cal's only choice between eating and starving. God, he really hated the country.

"What are you smiling about?" Celeste asked Brian. He still held her hand. She found she was reluctant to pull hers away. It was very comforting. That, and his touch, sent little tingles of pleasure up and down her arms.

"My brother's in love."

Her eyebrows shot up. "With whom?" Was there a third woman in the triangle? It all sounded very confusing to her.

"Nikki."

She shook her head. "I don't think so."

"Oh, yeah, he's in love."

She looked at her feet, then back at him, chewing her bottom lip. "I told Nikki that Cal knew she was a reporter, but only because I thought he must've been joking with you. I mean, she certainly didn't look like an old nag." She took a deep breath. "And that's what you'd told me. I'm sorry if I ruined it for him."

"You didn't ruin anything." He kissed her on top of her head. "My brother is a good judge of character. His gut instinct about people is always right on the mark. I think he sensed Nikki was a good person. I also think he likes her more than he wants to admit right now."

"But she's gone."

He looked down at her, his eyes filled with warmth. "If it's meant to be, it'll happen."

She could feel the color drain from her face. That's what her mother had always said.

His forehead wrinkled in worry. "Are you okay?"

"Yes, I'm fine. It's just that I remember my mother telling me that very same thing."

"You had a smart mother."

She smiled. "Yes, I did."

"When did you see Nikki?"

"I ran out of mint."

"You went to the cabin by yourself?"

She nodded. "I felt the presence of the spirit. She's so very sad. I wish we could help her."

He pulled her closer to him. "I don't want you going up there by yourself again."

She ignored him, wanting to know more. "What do you know about her?"

"My grandmother said a young girl had been murdered there. That's why Grandma's parents got the land so cheap. No one wanted the haunted house."

"Was she really murdered?"

"I never looked into the history of the place."

"I want to." She looked up at him. "If you don't mind?"

"Just don't go up there by yourself."

"I won't." But she did want to know what had happened. It was almost as if she'd felt a bonding with the spirit. It would be interesting to see what she could discover.

Chapter 28

Nikki stared at her reflection in the mirror. She looked like death warmed over. She'd barely slept since she'd returned to Fort Worth, and two weeks of tossing and turning was taking its toll.

"Whoever invented makeup, I thank you," she muttered before she sponged on liquid foundation and a little blush, then a dusting of face powder.

Better. Not great, but better. The dark circles under her eyes weren't quite as visible. She didn't want Marge questioning her any more than she already had.

Marge hadn't looked as though she'd believed Nikki's lies about the Cal and Cynthia story being totally worthless. An amicable breakup.

Not that Nikki cared. She wanted to forget her time at the ranch.

Her energy suddenly drained. She tossed her lipstick to the side and plopped down on the toilet seat.

Who was she kidding? She wanted to forget Cal. But it was kind of hard when her dreams were filled with him caressing her, his lips kissing hers, their bodies joining in passion. She closed her eyes and could almost feel . . . could almost . . .

She was so pathetic.

Enough! She stood, grabbed the tube of lipstick, and applied it in two quick, sweeping motions before she left the bathroom. She glanced around her tiny apartment to make sure she wasn't forgetting something, then grabbed her purse and went to the door.

But when she opened it, her gaze fixed on a broad chest. She tried to slam the door, her heart racing, but his foot blocked it.

"Nikki!" Cal said.

She looked up when she heard the familiar voice. "Cal?" Her pulse raced even faster. Had she wished him here? Maybe she was asleep and this was just another delicious dream and he was about to ravish her.

Could you actually ravish someone if they were willing? Who cared? *Please don't let me wake up if it is a dream,* she silently prayed.

"Can I come in?" He didn't wait for her to answer as he brushed past her.

"I didn't say yes."

Now that the initial shock was over, why was he here? Did he want to tell her again how despicable he thought she was? Well, she'd already beaten herself up plenty for not telling him the truth. She really doubted he could do more harm.

Dammit, she'd never had any guilt until she met Cal. She wasn't sure she liked the way he'd turned her life upside down.

"Nice place."

She glanced around at the clothes draping the sofa, the glass that she'd drank wine out of last night and hadn't bothered to take to the kitchen. She'd been depressed. She was almost certain somewhere there was a rule book that said you didn't have to clean house if you were depressed.

"It was the maid's day off," she replied, her words dripping sarcasm.

"So I see."

He turned around, facing her, then very slowly, as though

he was making sure he didn't miss an inch, his gaze roamed over her.

"What are you doing here?" She shut the door when a curious neighbor walked by, his steps slowing. Cal was no one's business besides her own and she wasn't about to air her dirty laundry in public.

"You didn't write the article," he said, his gaze moving back to her face.

"Yeah, well, you're not that interesting. I'm sorry to disappoint you."

"I would've thought you'd have been more worried about a lawsuit for libel. It's not as though you had any information you could actually use."

"That, too." There was a gleam in his eyes. She wasn't sure she trusted him. But Lord, she drank in the sight of him. It seemed like forever since she'd seen him, rather than only two weeks. Her body had already started to come alive, a familiar need racing through her.

"Something interesting happened." He leaned against the back of her sofa, then picked up a thong, fingering the black lace.

She marched over and yanked the undergarment out of his hands. He only grinned.

"What could have possibly happened that would drag you to my doorstep? We both know what you think of me." He was making her nervous. She didn't like feeling nervous.

"Cynthia told her daddy that I broke it off with her, but the strangest thing happened—he called me."

She hadn't thought it would get back to Cal. "So?" she hedged, then realized she was making knots out of her thong. She tossed the garment onto the end table.

"Her father said he didn't plan on raking me over the coals. He wanted to make that perfectly clear."

"I'm happy for you." She walked to the door. "I really need to get to work now. It was nice to see you again."

He didn't budge from his spot. "It seems two hotshot, badass lawyers called him and threatened to expose a few things about him if he didn't let the matter drop. He wanted me to call them off. I don't suppose you know who they might have been."

She shrugged. "No, why should I?" When he didn't say anything she gave up the fight. "I called my parents and asked for a favor. It was no biggie."

"I wanted to say thank you."

"You've said it, now good-bye."

He straightened, then slowly walked toward her. "Why did you ask them to do it?"

She shrugged again. "Cynthia was a bitch. I knew she would run to daddy."

"And?"

She frowned. "And I lied right from the very start. I wanted the story and that's all I cared about."

"And?"

Her palms began to sweat. "I don't know what you want me to say."

He rested his hands on her shoulders. "Don't you?"

Man, when he went for revenge, he went for it. He wanted to know the truth. Okay, she'd give it to him. "I care for you. There, are you happy?"

He quirked an eyebrow. "Just care? Is that all?"

When she looked up at him he lowered his head, his mouth taking hers. A shiver ran through her. God, it seemed like forever since she'd tasted him on her lips. She sighed, wrapping her arms around his neck.

But before the kiss could go very far, he broke it off. "Just care? Is that all you feel for me, Nikki?" He teased the back of her neck, lightly massaging.

"No, dammit, I love you," she whispered. "There, I've said it. Now are you satisfied?"

"Why the hell did you let me suffer the last two weeks?" He hugged her close.

"I didn't think you'd ever want to see me again. What I did was so wrong. It's one thing to alert the public to dirty politicians and businesses out to fleece the innocent, but it was different with you."

She pulled away and looked at him again as what he'd said finally sunk into her brain. "You said I made you suffer. How did I make you suffer?"

"Haven't you guessed?"

She shook her head.

"I fell in love with you the second I answered the phone."

Her smile was slow. "Was that before or after I told you I liked it rough?"

"Before, after, and during."

He pressed his mouth to hers again. Her body trembled with need. God, how she'd missed this man. He was her life, her soul. He was each breath she took or would ever take.

She held him close, resting her head against his chest when they both came up for air.

"Are you going to quit football?" she asked.

"Yes. I'm spending more time at the doctor's getting my injuries taken care of than I am playing football. You don't mind, do you?"

"Not at all, but after we get married will we have to live in the country?"

Cal leaned back and looked at her. "I thought you didn't believe in marriage."

"I changed my mind. Does that bother you?"

He grinned. "Not at all, but remember when I tell the kids you begged me to marry you, I'll be the one telling the truth."

She frowned. "But we aren't going to move to the country, are we?"

"Do you want to?"

"Good Lord, no."

"Me, neither. I'll take the city any day. I had an offer—sportscaster with one of the stations. I think I'm going to take them up on it. So, do we have everything settled?"

"I think so."

"Good, then call in sick, because I doubt we'll leave your bed for the next week."

Nikki caressed her hand across his face before sauntering toward her room. At the door, she turned back and looked at him.

"I'll call in later."

Damn, she liked the look of passion that flared in his eyes. She had a feeling she'd be seeing it for many years.

Chapter 29

"I'm not so sure about this," Nikki said as she looked around at the others. Celeste was clearly excited, Brian looked hesitant, and Cal, well, he just looked amused.

Cal grabbed her hand, bringing it to his lips and kissing it. He did that a lot—kissing her, holding her close. She rather liked it.

"We have to," Celeste pleaded. "Her name was Aggie. Aggie Watson. I don't know why anyone didn't try to find out something about her years ago. It wasn't like it was that difficult."

"So, tell us about this . . . ghost," Cal said, then grinned.

Nikki frowned at him and wondered why he was being so stubborn. "I saw the ghost and she's real."

"I thought you didn't believe in anything you couldn't touch, feel, or taste?" He ran the back of his knuckles across her cheek. She automatically leaned closer.

"Would y'all like a little privacy?" Brian asked.

"No, they wouldn't. They want to do the séance, too."

Brian shook his head. "I don't think they look that enthused."

"Nikki, help me out here. Don't you want to set Aggie's soul free?" Celeste said.

They were standing by the barn at the ranch. Nikki glanced

toward the cabin, although she couldn't see it because of the trees. A cold chill of foreboding clutched her in an icy grip. "How exactly did you say she died?"

"She was strangled by the man who wanted to marry her. She didn't want to marry him because she was in love with someone else. So that's why he killed her, and we just have to tell her to go toward the light. Please."

Nikki didn't want to go anywhere near the cabin, but how could she say no to Celeste when she pleaded so convincingly? "Then let's do it," she said, suddenly making up her mind.

Cal leaned close to her and whispered in her ear, "There are no such things as ghosts."

Boy, was he in for a big surprise.

Celeste turned to look at Brian, giving him the same look she'd used on Nikki. Brian didn't stand a chance. It was as plain as the nose on her face how much he loved Celeste.

"Okay, okay," he finally caved.

Celeste smiled brightly. "We have to do it tonight."

"Why tonight?" Cal asked as he casually draped his arm across Nikki's shoulders. "Is there a full moon?"

Everyone automatically looked up, searching the skies.

"As a matter of fact, there is," Nikki said.

"Even better," Celeste chimed in. "Let's go."

They all piled into the double-cab pickup. Cal drove. Nikki wished she'd gone to the bathroom before they'd left. She was not about to take a chance her stickups were still working.

"I hope the psycho rooster has bedded down somewhere far away for the night," Celeste muttered.

Nikki cringed. How could she still feel so damned guilty over a stupid bird?

After bumping over the dirt road they pulled up in front of the cabin. For some reason it looked really spooky in the light of the moon.

"Are you sure you want to do this?" Brian asked.

"Don't tell me you're scared, little brother."

"Damned right I am."

Cal chuckled, then got out of the pickup. The others followed. Once beside him, Nikki made sure she held tight to his hand.

"Do you have the flashlight?" she asked, just to be on the safe side.

He flipped it on and put it under his face. "I want to drink your blood."

She bopped him on the arm. "That was so not funny," she said as they trooped inside the house.

"Okay, where are we doing this?" Brian asked.

"The kitchen, so we can all sit at the table." Celeste raised her chin and marched right in without looking back to see if they followed.

Nikki had to give Celeste credit for determination. Nikki just wanted to get this over with and get the hell out of here.

They sat at the table.

"Now what?" Brian asked.

"I think we're supposed to call her forth. Then we'll tell her she's dead and needs to go toward the light. I've never done a séance, but how hard could it be?" Celeste looked at each one of them, her gaze stopping on Cal. "No laughing. A young woman is depending on us."

"No laughing, I swear." Cal crossed his heart.

"Hold hands." Celeste reached hers toward Cal's and Brian's.

They all clasped hands. Cal rubbed his thumb along the back of Nikki's. She dug her fingernail into his and he backed off. The man was incorrigible.

"Aggie Watson, we know you're here," Celeste said. "We know why you're here. That you were murdered long ago and we want to set your spirit free. Go, go toward the light."

A blue mist began to form. Nikki held her breath, squeezing Cal's hand. He grinned and glanced over his shoulder. When he looked back at her, his grin was gone.

"What the hell is that," he whispered.

"The ghost," Nikki said.

"It's okay, Aggie. Go toward the light," Celeste intoned.

The mist became a young woman. She was covering her face with her hands, weeping softly. Pity washed over Nikki. Slowly, the ghost lowered her hands. She was the most beautiful thing Nikki had ever seen.

"She's so pretty," Brian said.

The ghost looked at him. Her face changed from beautiful to grotesque. Her mouth opened and the scream that came from the spirit curled Nikki's hair.

As one they jumped up, chairs tipping over, and ran from the cabin.

"Cock-a-doodle-do!" the rooster yodeled as they ran outside.

Nikki stopped just off the porch and turned to look toward the barn. There was Romeo on the top fence rail with his chest puffed out as he pranced back and forth without a wobble, his adoring hens on the ground looking up at him so they could admire his fine form.

Okay, so maybe he didn't quite have his timing down right since technically it was the middle of the night, but she didn't think the hens cared.

"Look, the rooster is all better."

Cal turned and grabbed her hand. "Ghost, remember the ghost." He tugged her forward as they ran toward the pickup and all piled in. Brian was already taking off before they could get the doors slammed shut. They hung on to the seats rather than risk their lives reaching for the doors.

"No more séances," Brian said as they raced toward the ranch.

"Never again," Celeste said, shaking her head.

"I think we're all in agreement about that," Nikki said. "I was so scared I almost wet my pants."

"Me, too." Celeste's laugh was shaky.

Cal and Brian didn't say a word.

Be sure to catch WATCH OVER ME by Lucy Monroe,
available now from Brava . . .

"Dr. Ericson"

Lana adjusted the angle on the microscope. Yes. Right there. Perfect. "Amazing."

"Lana."

She reached out blindly for the stylus to her handheld. *Got it.* She stared taking notes on the screen without looking away from the microscope.

"Dr. Ericson!!!"

Lana jumped, bumping her cheekbone on the microscope's eyepiece before falling backward, hitting a wall that hadn't been there when she'd come into work that morning.

Strong hands set her firmly on her feet as she realized the wall was warm and made of flesh and muscle. Lots and lots of muscle.

Stumbling back a step, she looked up and then up some more. The dark-haired hottie in front of her was as tall as her colleague, Beau Ruston. Or close to it anyway. She fumbled with her glasses, sliding them on her nose. They didn't help. Reading glasses for the computer, they only served to make her feel more disoriented.

She squinted, then remembered and pulled the glasses off again, letting them dangle by their chain around her neck. "Um, hello? Did I know you were visiting my lab?"

She was fairly certain she hadn't. She forgot appointments

sometimes. Okay, often, but she always remembered eventually. And this man hadn't made an appointment with her. She was sure of it. He didn't look like a scientist either.

Not that all scientists were as unremarkable as she was in the looks department, but this man was another species entirely.

He looked dangerous and sexy. Enough so that he would definitely replace chemical formulas in her dreams at night. His black hair was a little too long and looked like he'd run his fingers through it, not a comb. That was just so bad boy. She had a secret weakness for bad boys.

Even bigger than the secret weakness she'd harbored for Beau Ruston before he'd met Elle.

She had posters of James Dean and Matt Dillon on the wall of her bedroom and had seen *Rebel Without a Cause* a whopping thirty-six times.

Unlike James Dean, this yummy bad boy even had pierced ears. Only instead of sedate studs or small hoops, he had tiny black plugs. Only a bit bigger than a pair of studs, the plugs were recessed in his lobes. They had the Chinese Kanji for strength etched on them in silver. Or pewter maybe. It wasn't shiny.

The earrings were hot. Just like him.

He looked like the kind of man who had a tattoo. Nothing colorful. Something black and meaningful. She wanted to see it. Too bad she couldn't just ask.

Interpersonal interaction had so many taboos. It wasn't like science where you dug for answers without apology.

"Lana?"

The stranger had a strong jaw too, squared and accented by a close-cropped beard that went under, not across his chin. No mustache. His lips were set in a straight line, but they still looked like they'd be Heaven to kiss.

Not that she'd kissed a lot of lips, but she was twenty-nine. Even a geeky scientist didn't make it to the shy side of thirty without a few kisses along the way. And other stuff.

Not that the other stuff was all that spectacular. She'd always wondered if that was her fault or the men she'd chosen to partner.

It didn't take a shrink to identify the fact that Lana had trust issues. With her background, who wouldn't?

Still, people had been known to betray family, love and country for sex. She wouldn't cross a busy street to get some. Or maybe she would, if this stranger was waiting on the other side.

The fact that she could measure the time since she'd last had sex in years rather than months, weeks or *days*—which would be a true miracle—wasn't something she enjoyed dwelling on. She blamed it on her work.

However, every feminine instinct that was usually sublimated by her passion for her job was on red alert now.

What's a lady to do when she finds herself
IN BED WITH A STRANGER?
Find out in Mary Wine's Brava debut, new this month . . .

Brodick reached out, stroking a finger over one of her cheeks. "Aye, I am pleased."

She shivered again, this time in some odd response to the way his tone had softened. He was no longer angry with her.

Anne turned quickly to hide the strange reaction from his keen stare. Her face was hot where he'd touched it, the skin oddly alive with sensation. There was a part of her that liked hearing that he approved of her. A man such as he was far above any that she might hope to have of her own.

"Face me, Mary."

Hearing her half-sister's name was like icy water being tossed onto her feet. She turned slowly, struggling to conceal her emotions before facing him once more. This man would not take being deceived very well. Now that her face veil was gone, she needed to be more attentive to concealing her feelings.

"I've no taste for timid women."

The gruff tone of his voice annoyed her once again. "You may always return me home." She looked at the ground, doing her best to look like a coward. For one brief moment hope flickered in her heart that he might reject her.

"You should take me to my father. He is returned to court."

A hard hand cupped her chin, raising it to lock stares with

him. "It's clear you've been at court. That place is ripe with schemes." His lips lost their hard line as he stepped up closer holding her jaw in a firm grip. "Do I really look like a man who would cry surrender so soon after greeting ye?" He chuckled, the sound sending a quiver through her belly. His warm scent filled her head with each breath as he tilted his head so that his breath teased her lips.

"You dinnae know very much about Scotsmen, Wife. We're nae intimidated by a few cold glances. In Scotland, we're more practiced in the arts of warming up our women."

He touched his mouth to hers and she jerked away from the contact. It burned clear through her, all the way to her toes. Her freedom was short-lived. With a twist of his larger body, he snaked an arm around her waist. He moved toward her in the same moment, surrounding her and pinning her against his hard body.

"Now that won't do." He pulled her flush against his frame, tight enough to feel his heart beating. His gaze settled onto her mouth as he slipped a hand up the back of her neck to hold her head. "It won't do at all. Kissing my new wife is something I'm nae in the mood to miss."

He touched his mouth to hers again, this time slowly. She twisted in his embrace, too many impulses shooting along her body to understand. The few kisses in her past had been stolen ones and brief. Brodick lingered over her mouth, gently tasting her lips before pressing her jaw to open for a deeper touch. His embrace imprisoned her but not painfully. He seemed to understand his strength perfectly, keeping her against him with exactly enough force, but stopping short of causing her pain.

She shivered as the tip of his tongued glided across her lower lip. Sensation rippled down her spine as she gasped in shock. Never once had she thought that a touch might be so intense. Her hands were flattened against his chest and her fingertips were alive with new desires. Touching him felt good. She opened her fingers wider, letting them smooth over the hard ridges of muscles that his open doublet had allowed her to see. Pleasure moved through her in a slow cloud that left a haze over her mind. Forming thoughts became slow and cumbersome as he teased her upper lip, tasting her.

"Much better."

No hero comes close to MIDNIGHT'S MASTER, the latest from Cynthia Eden, out next month from Brava . . .

"Throw her out, Niol. You want the vamps to keep comin', you *throw that bitch out.*"

The tapping stopped, and, because the vampire had raised his shrill-ass voice again, the nearby paranormals—because, generally, the folks who came in his bar were far, far from normal—stilled.

Niol shook his head slowly. "I think you're forgetting a few things, *vamp.*" He gathered the black swell of power that pulsed just beneath his skin. Felt the surge of dark magic and—

The vamp flew across the bar, slamming into the stage with a scream. The lead guitarist swore, then jumped back, cradling his guitar with both hands like the precious baby he thought it was.

The sudden silence was deafening.

Niol motioned toward the bar. "Get me another drink, Marc." He glanced at the slowly rising vampire. "Did I tell you to get up?" It barely took any effort to slam the bastard into the stage wall this time. Just a stray thought, really.

Ah, but power was a wonderful thing.

Sometimes, it was damn good to be a demon. And even better to be a level ten, and the baddest asshole in the room.

He stalked forward. Enjoyed for a moment the way the crowd jumped away from him.

The vampire began to shake. *Perfect.*

Niol stopped a foot before the fallen Andre. "First," he growled, "don't ever, *ever* fucking tell me what to do in *my* bar again."

A fast nod.

"Second . . ." His hands clenched into fists as he fought to rein in the magic blasting through him. The power . . . oh, but it was tempting. And so easy to use.

Too easy.

One more thought, just one, focused and hard, and he could have the vamp dead at his feet.

"Use too much, you'll lose yourself." An old warning. One that had come too late for him. He'd been twenty-five before he met another demon who even came close to him in power and that guy's warning—well it had been long overdue.

Niol knew he'd been one of the Lost for years.

The first time he'd killed, he'd been Lost.

"Second," he repeated, his voice cold, clear, and cutting like a knife in the quiet. "If you think I give a damn about the vampires coming to *my* place . . ." His mouth hitched into a half-grin, but Niol knew no amusement would show in the darkness of his eyes. "Then you're dead wrong, vampire."

"S-sorry, Niol, I—"

He laughed. Then turned his back on the cringing vampire. "Thomas." The guard he always kept close. "Throw that vamp's ass out."

When Thomas stepped forward, the squeal of a guitar ripped through the bar. And the dancing and the drinking and the mating games of the *Other* began with a fierce rumble of sound.

His eyes searched for his prey and he found Holly watching him. All eyes and red hair and lips that begged for his mouth. He strode toward her, conscious of covert eyes still on them. He could show no weakness. Never could.

I'm not weak.

He was the strongest demon in Atlanta. And he sure as

hell wasn't going to give the paranormals any cause to start doubting his power.

His kind turned on the weak.

When he stopped before her, the scent of lavender flooded his nostrils.

She looked up at him. The human was small, to him anyway, barely reaching his shoulders so that he towered over her.

She was the weak one. All of her kind were.

Humans. So easy to wound. To kill.

He lifted his hand. Stroked her cheek. Damn but she was soft. Leaning close, Niol told her, "Sweetheart, I warned you before about coming to my Paradise."

There was no doubt others overheard his words. With so many shifters skulking around the joint, a *whisper* would have been overheard. Shifters and their annoyingly superior senses.

"Wh-what do you mean?" The question came, husky and soft. Ah, but he liked her voice. And he could all too easily imagine that voice, whispering to him as they lay amid a tangle of sheets.

Or maybe screaming in his ear as she came.

He cupped her chin in his hand. A nice chin. Softly rounded. And those lips . . . the bottom was fuller than the top. Just a bit. So red. Her mouth was slightly parted, open.

Waiting.

She stepped back, shaking her head. "I don't know what you *think* you're doing, Niol—"

He stared down at her. "Yes, you do." He caught her arms, wrapping his fingers around her and jerking Holly against him. "I told you, the last time you came into *my* bar . . ."

Her eyes widened. "Niol . . ."

Oh, yeah, he liked the way she said his name. She breathed it, tasted it.

His lips lowered toward hers. "If you want to walk in

Paradise, baby, then you're gonna have to play with the devil."

"No, I—"

He kissed her. Hard. Deep. Niol drove his tongue right past those plump lips and took her mouth the way the beast inside of him demanded.